OPERATION
ETHAN

A Willow Bay Novel

by Laurie Ryan

www.laurieryanauthor.com

Copyright

QUALITY CONTROL: We strive to produce error-free books, but even with all the eyes that see the story during the production process, slips get by. So please, if you find a typo or any formatting issues, please let us know at laurie@laurieryanauthor.com so that we may correct it.
Thank you!

Dedication

To the firefighters who keep us safe.

CHAPTER ONE

"You've got to be kidding me," Joey blurted to the head of maintenance before she surveyed the upscale lobby of the Pacific Lodge to make sure no one had heard.

"Not kidding," John said. "Room 302 got completely flooded and won't be usable for at least two to three weeks. We can fix the one below that in a few days, but 402, where the leak came from, also needs quite a bit of work." John ran a hand through his short salt-and-pepper hair making it stand up even more than usual.

"The Beer and Chowder Festival is in ten days and we're booked solid. We cannot lose a single room."

"Then maybe you should convince your guests to stand inside the tub to shower, not outside."

Joey tucked her blonde hair behind an ear and rolled her eyes. She'd been called downstairs at midnight last night when guests complained of water dripping from the ceiling over their bed. Turns out, the couple in the room above came from a country where bathing was different. They'd filled the tub then stood on the bathroom floor pouring water over themselves.

The water had buckled the ceiling in the room below. Now ceiling, floors, walls, furniture—it all needed to be fixed or replaced.

"Thank God the couple below got out of bed before the sheetrock fell," John added.

"There is that." Joey sent a prayer skyward for the blessing and took another look around the lobby of the five-story lodge, decorated in mellow, pleasing tans accented with deep blue, sea green, and white—the colors of the ocean, the defining feature of Willow Bay. Guests often complimented her on the ambiance of the place. The serenity and beauty of the lobby filled her with pride every time she walked through the door.

But back to the problem at hand. Having to cancel one reservation wouldn't go over well with the owners. The loss of two would make them apoplectic, especially the bottom-line-focused Christian Reynolds. To picture his nearly all-white hair framing his red, puffy face as he sputtered his indignation brought the smile back to Joey's face. It faded quickly when she glanced at the entrance's revolving door.

Her worst nightmare had just walked in and stood looking around with his permanent frown firmly in place.

Joey turned back to John. "Get the top room working within two days. I don't care what you have to do, what laws you break, or what it costs. Get. It. Done. Now. Go."

She whirled around, pasted the smile on her face that had gotten her this job, and watched as Mr. Reynolds strode her way. Out of the corner of her eye, she saw Gladys, Willow Bay's resident street person, set her cart beside the door. *Not now, Gladys. Please, not now.*

Alas, Joey's pleas went unheard. Gladys, a sweet, old lady who seemed to wear every bit of clothing she owned, stepped lively through the revolving door and straight to a nearby settee where she liked to "rest her bones." Joey never minded. Gladys was a font of information about Willow Bay happenings and Joey enjoyed talking to her. Or would at any other time.

Facing the challenge head-on, Joey met her boss at the large round table in the center of the lobby, its large vase of cut flowers a reminder for folks that spring would return.

"Mr. Reynolds, it's lovely to see you again this week, though I can't imagine the rain made for a very nice drive."

"It didn't. And I'm none too pleased to be here instead of at my club, but this was an errand I wanted to do in person." He glanced beyond her toward what she knew was John's retreating backside. "Why were you talking to maintenance?"

"I check in with each department every day to stay on top of things." Joey crossed her fingers behind her back.

"Hmph. Good idea." The rare compliment was grumbled out like it wasn't easy for him to say. "Flowers?" he said, looking at the vase.

"From a local florist. They make folks smile and remember better weather."

"Hmph. And these brochures?" He picked up a stack and thumbed through them.

"Information about points of interest, tours, gift shops, etc., all around town."

He plucked out a Square Peg Pizza menu—her favorite restaurant—and held it up. "Don't we have a restaurant?"

"Well, yes, but— "

"Then we don't need to advertise other restaurants, do we?"

Heat flooded Joey's cheeks and she bit the inside of her mouth to keep from saying what was on her mind. "This is a small community." She'd learned that quickly from wandering around during her first week here. "We advertise for each other. Square Peg, for instance, has Pacific Lodge brochures out in the restaurant."

"But they're not a hotel, they're an eatery." He threw the brochures in the garbage can below the table. "I bought this place as an investment and I expect it to perform, not send guests to other venues."

"Customer satisfaction is the highest it has ever been, Mr. Reynolds. Things like these brochures help with that rating. I'm sure you understand how important reviews are to this business and ours have been great the last couple months. Even with winter upon us, we're three-quarters full or above at all times."

"Yes, well, let's try to bump that up. And while we're talking about this, I'll need one of the penthouse suites and two other rooms for the upcoming festival."

"The— " Joey froze. Her brain melted into a pile of seagull poop at her feet and she couldn't think of a damn thing to say.

Reynolds watched her closely. Was he waiting for her to fail? Trying to force that issue?

"Pacific Lodge is completely booked for the festival, including both penthouses. People made reservations months in advance."

As his scowl deepened, Joey raced to find a solution. "With that large a party, how about I search for a house rental?" That wouldn't be easy, either. "I'm sure it would be more relaxing to be all together."

"Absolutely not. I will stay in my hotel and nowhere else."

Joey switched gears. "You'll be giving up revenue by kicking people out of their rooms. And the negative publicity could have far-reaching effects."

"That's your problem, not mine. One penthouse

suite and two rooms for Friday through Monday. Or both penthouses. Either will work. I'll be back that Friday with my family." He grabbed up the rest of the brochures, handed them to Joey, and turned to leave.

Just when she thought she'd avoided an ugly reaction from Reynolds, Joey inwardly groaned. He'd zeroed in on Gladys then turned back to Joey.

"Street people in our lobby? Absolutely not. Get rid of that… woman. And no brochures unless they are touting what we have to offer." He left without another glance at anything but the door.

Joey stood there fuming, clutching the brochures until they bent. She wanted to stomp her feet like Baby on that bridge who couldn't get the dance moves right. She allowed herself one tiny stomp. Not enough, but it would have to do. She'd come here two months ago with a shiny new hotel management degree and a desperate need for a job. After three years of online classes, moving around, and looking over her shoulder, the peace of Willow Bay had settled her. In fact, already tired of living in the provided hotel room, Joey had been thinking about searching for a condo or small house to buy. Making a go of this job meant Willow Bay could be home. And she wanted that very much.

The town had welcomed her. Sam at the grocery store now stocked her favorite yogurt, having asked after he noticed her dawdling around the dairy aisle. The mayor had immediately enlisted her help with the Beer and Chowder Festival and she'd met a lot of the community through related meetings.

Rescuing the brochures from the garbage, she smoothed them all out and laid them back on the table, smiling with satisfaction.

Mr. Reynolds didn't understand what made Willow Bay so special. He didn't get the small-town feel that people came here to experience. And he sure as heck didn't understand reservations and what breaking them meant.

With one more defiant little stomp, Joey walked over to see Gladys. No way would she kick this nice, down-on-her-luck woman out. Joey would quit first. Stopping short, her heart rate spiked. She couldn't quit. She needed this job.

Rock and a hard place. That phrase had a whole new meaning these days.

~~~

Gladys Hawthorne sat and watched the goings on, her ears perked in the direction of her nice friend. Joey stiffened as the older gentleman, presumably the lodge owner, tossed papers in the trash.

"Street people in our lobby? Absolutely not. Get rid of that... woman."

Pompous ass. Gladys glared at the man as he strode out. This was exactly why she'd left New York. She'd become fed up with that kind of holier-than-thou attitude from her husband's cronies. Men and women who'd called her their friend right up until she'd taken things in a direction that didn't suit them. More pompous asses. This one went through the revolving door so fast, it almost hit him in said ass. Gladys smiled. Too bad it didn't actually happen.

Her smile widened when the cute manager plucked the papers out of the garbage and smoothed them out on the table. Joey had guts and Gladys liked that in a woman.

"How are you doing today?" Joey asked as Gladys patted the seat beside her and Joey sat down.

"Much better now that I've seen your smile. You light up a room, young lady."

Joey grinned. "Why, thank you. You always know how to brighten my day."

"I guess that makes us both happy people."

The young woman's lilting laugh settled like a warm blanket around Gladys's heart.

"Your husband is lucky to have you," Gladys said. No ring didn't necessarily mean unmarried and Gladys decided it was an important matter to clarify.

"No husband. Not yet anyhow."

"Not even a boyfriend?" Gladys's eyes gleamed.

A brief shadow touched Joey's face. So brief, Gladys almost missed it. She knew about regrets and hoped this young woman didn't have the same type she herself carried.

"No. I'm pretty married to this lodge at the moment."

"But you still find time to get out and enjoy life, don't you?" Joey wouldn't have that air of perennial joy if her life wasn't balanced."

"Oh, yes. I think it's important to include both work and fun in my life."

Gladys patted her arm. "Good attitude. That'll keep you young."

"Like it has you," Joey said as she covered Gladys's hand with hers and looked her over. "You doing okay? Do you need anything? A place to rest? Some lunch?"

"What? You're not kicking me out like that stuffy boss of yours said to?"

"Never. You're welcome here anytime. You're part of what makes Willow Bay so special and I look forward to our visits."

She said it like she meant it, too. Gladys had been watching Joey for a while. The girl generally took people at face value and tried to be uplifting. She also wore her emotions on her face including a wariness at the edges, as if something haunted her. She needed someone to help her break through that final doorway and come fully into herself.

"I don't need anything to eat, but thank you for

offering." Gladys stood. "I've had my rest and now I can get on with my day."

"You can stay longer, you know."

"I know, and I appreciate it. No need, though. I've stayed the perfect amount of time to regenerate." Gladys patted Joey's cheek. "You keep on being you, being happy. The rest will sort itself out in time."

A confused look furrowed Joey's brow for a moment. She said her goodbyes and walked back behind the front desk to talk to the red-headed woman working there. All that sunshine and fun-loving was wasted here, Gladys thought. The girl needed a project that fed her soul.

Gladys knew exactly what—or rather who—fit the bill. With a secret smile, she stopped at the red fire alarm box. Her grin widened as she yanked the lever down and slipped out of the building, walking off as the alarm blared behind her.

And feeling very, very pleased with herself.

CHAPTER TWO

"I don't get it."

Ethan Walker frowned at the confused young man and resisted the urge to rake his hand through hair already showing touches of gray. Working with the fire academy trainees meant a lot to him. Being able to teach them why the rules and regulations were there— to keep people safe, the mantra of anyone who worked for a fire department. Standing in the truck bay at the fire station always filled Ethan with pride. But right now, he was more frustrated than anything. He needed to rein that in.

"All right," he said in his most patient voice. "Let me explain it again."

"Woo-hee," voiced Ethan's second-in-command from where he leaned against the wall. "You're in for it now, Matt. Don't let that voice of his fool you. That's our illustrious chief's 'I'm losing patience' tone."

"Shut up, Riley," Ethan ground out.

"Look," Matt said, holding the hose like it didn't weigh a thing when everyone knew it did. "I understand what you're saying. I just don't get why it's necessary."

Riley sent Ethan's mood spiraling even further into

the crapper when he hooted again. "Don't you have something better to do?" he asked, glaring at his friend.

"Nope." Riley's grin widened.

When Riley was that amused there was no changing his direction, so Ethan gave up and focused again on his trainee.

"Every station— "

"It takes too much time," Matt insisted. "There are quicker ways to store the hoses."

Ethan crossed his arms over his chest and stood every inch of his six-foot-four frame, waiting.

Matt threw up his hands. "Fine. Explain it again."

"Thank you. As I tried to say, every fire station in this county does things exactly the same way. If you want to change protocols, you'll have to talk to someone higher up than me. As things stand now, all firefighters expect a hose to be a certain way. That knowledge saves time in a fire. They know it's put away correctly. There will be no kinks, nothing to slow them down when they need to save lives. So, until you manage to get the entire district to change protocols," Ethan jabbed a finger at him, "you will put those hoses away per the training doctrine, as you've been taught. Now, shall we try again?"

"Fine," Matt grumbled.

Riley laughed and finally, mercifully, walked off as Ethan watched Matt work. The kid had ambition and lots of ideas. He'd either be fire chief by forty or run hell-bent into a fire and not see thirty. Ethan worked very hard with all the recruits to make sure they had a shot at the first option and did not fall to the second. Safety first, then speed. Rule number one.

The kid wasn't going to be happy when Ethan yanked down all that nicely stowed hose and made him do it again. Each firefighter needed to do this by rote, by muscle memory. If they didn't have to think about this, they could focus on the important thing: saving lives. He'd keep at the kid until he got it right.

The claxon's blare changed Ethan's plans. "Stow this and the other three hoses on the racks. I'll check them when I get back." Without a backward glance, Ethan raced for his gear, stepped into his turnout pants, yanked on the jacket, and was through the passenger door before Riley slipped into the driver's seat.

"You're late."

"You were right next to the truck. No one could have beat you here."

"No excuses."

Tapping his device as he waited the few seconds until everyone made it on the truck, Ethan wondered if there was a way to shave some time off their go protocols.

"All on," Riley said, tapping the siren. "Where?"

"Pacific Lodge."

"Shit." He pulled out and sped up.

"Yeah." He ran some quick figures as they roared their way down the street. Five floors. Lobby, restaurant, and spa on the main. Bar on the top. Rooms in between. Maybe twenty rooms per floor, so eighty rooms minimum Figuring winter capacity at fifty percent and two per room, that could be 80 to 100 people with staff The lodge was mostly a wood structure with large beams capable of burning for hours. This could turn into a disaster. He went over the priorities in his head. Safe evacuations, verify the extent, path, and drift of the fire, design the containment plan, implement plan, put fire out, mop up, and report.

As Riley pulled into the parking lot, Ethan was relieved to see no plume of smoke and evacuations well underway. The sole annoyance was the people milling around, blocking their way.

"Tap the horn."

That got people moving. Once they'd parked, Ethan leaped out, knowing his team would be right behind him and would tackle their individual jobs with safety and speed. He'd trained them to be a cohesive unit.

"Who's in charge?" he asked, raising his voice to be heard over the chaos.

"I am."

A petite blonde woman with the bluest eyes he'd ever seen strode his way. Ethan's gut did a couple of three-sixties as he watched her hips sway. He'd have to think that one through later. Right now, they had a fire to put down.

"Hi, I'm Joey Sanderson, manager of Pacific Lodge." She held out her hand which Ethan ignored until she dropped it.

"Where's the fire?" he asked, with more gruffness than usual.

Lines creased her forehead, then disappeared. "I'm sorry for all this ruckus. I think it's a false alarm."

"Why?" Ethan scanned the building.

"We can't find a fire anywhere."

"You have a main system to track your alarms, right?"

"Yes, and it says the lobby alarm was triggered manually. We neither see nor smell fire or smoke." She stopped there, biting her lower lip as if holding something back.

Ethan's gaze dipped to those lips and he struggled to remember what they were talking about. "False alarms are punishable by law."

The cute manager put both hands on her hips. "I know that. I didn't trip my own alarm."

"We still need to check it out. Get these people moved to the side so they won't inhibit us." Without waiting to make sure she did as told, Ethan walked back to Riley and the rest of the team. "Manager thinks it's a false alarm. Says the lobby alarm was pulled. Riley, take someone and check out the main panel. Tom, you and Mike do a floor walk-through."

Mike groaned and Ethan bit back a smile. The man, recovering from his first-ever marathon last weekend, wouldn't love five flights of stairs. "Sorry, Mike. You want to trade?"

"No. I can do my job," he answered, stiffening.

Good man. "Mary, you and Zeke walk the exterior." He glanced at each one of them. "You guys know the protocols. Get to it."

"We're not all guys, remember, boss?" Riley said.

The only reason Mary didn't deck Riley—and she could—was because they were in the field. "I keep telling you, Ri. I'm one of the guys."

Ethan smiled inwardly. Mary had a husband and two kids but hated being singled out as a woman. "Get to it," he said again.

The team dispersed. As far as Ethan was concerned, he had the best team on the West Coast. They knew their jobs, did them efficiently, and did them right. He'd trust any one of them with his life. Had, in fact. Multiple times.

He turned back to the manager. Joey. The name fit her. She looked effervescent and full of sunshine, making the dreary February day brighter just by her presence. Geesh, where the hell had that mush come from? He glanced around, realizing that not a single one of the people milling around had moved. Gnashing his jaw to the point of pain, he strode over to the manager as his firefighters entered the lobby.

"Miss Sanderson, I told you to move these people."

"Exactly." She crossed her arms over her chest, drawing Ethan's gaze downward before he could stop himself.

"Why— " He cleared his throat. "Didn't you?"

She leaned in, close enough for him to smell the floral freshness of her hair.

"Because you didn't ask nice. And please, call me Joey."

Ethan took a step back to get some distance and regain his fucking masculinity. Did she not understand how dangerous this could be? "When I give an order, I expect it to be followed."

"I don't work for you, so I don't follow your orders, especially with a false alarm. This is my lodge."

Riley waved to him from the entrance to the lodge, giving the all-clear sign. It really had been a false alarm. Not quite ready to let go of his stress, he glared at the uncooperative woman. Her lodge. Technically, she was the manager, not the owner, but Ethan knew better than to argue that point. In fact, he admired her proprietary interest in the place. But disobeying him might have been a life-or-death choice.

"As fire chief, when we are on-site, I am the primary authority. By law, you have to do what I say." Ethan hated it when people flaunted rules. They existed for a reason, damn it. He stepped closer. She couldn't be much more than five-foot-three. She only came up to his shoulder. What a spitfire. "We got off lucky today with this false alarm. What if it isn't false the next time. What if it's real?"

"Then I will follow your orders to the letter, sir."

"Don't call me sir." God, he hated that. Made him feel old at thirty-four. Hell, standing next to her, he felt old enough as it was. She couldn't be more than twenty-five.

"What am I supposed to call you, then? You never gave me your name." She held his gaze, a smile tugging up the corners of one very delectable mouth.

Ethan gulped. The woman had an answer for everything. Any other time, he might enjoy sparring with her, but fire was serious business. He knew that firsthand and would not tolerate someone making light of any situation that could turn deadly.

"Chief Ethan Walker. I run your fire station."

"Ah, that explains why you're used to giving orders." That half-smile turned up a notch.

"And used to having them followed. Life and death, Miss Sanderson. One missed order could mean the latter."

"I get that. As I said, if this had been serious, I'd have done what you so nicely ordered me to." The innocent look on her face barely concealed the amusement in her eyes.

"Why did you think this wasn't serious?"

Her blush surprised him. It was also the cutest thing he'd ever seen. How he'd managed to turn into some fucking romantic in the past few minutes, Ethan had no idea. However, for the first time since he'd started this conversation, he had the upper hand.

"Who pulled the alarm, Miss Sanderson?"

"I, um, actually didn't see anyone pull the alarm."

"But you suspect someone."

God, even her frowns were cute. What the hell was happening to him? Had there been estrogen loaded into his breakfast eggs? It would take a lot of beer to exorcise this sunny disposition from his psyche. He didn't do sunny.

"I might have an idea who, but not why."

"Who, then?"

Joey shook her head. "Uh uh. This all ended fine. I'm not going to get someone in trouble based on a suspicion I can't confirm."

"If someone pulled that alarm as a prank, or for any other reason, they need to be held accountable."

"I think we can chalk this up to chicanery and move on, Chief. No harm done."

It was his turn to cross his arms over his chest and stand tall. When Joey laughed, Ethan knew he'd lost the fight.

"That blustering usually get you anywhere, Ethan?"

She'd switched to his given name and Ethan liked how it rolled off her lips. Too much. He had neither the time nor the desire to get tangled up with some woman who believed not all rules needed following.

"My trainees fall in line when I bluster, as you put it."

"Well, then, I'm glad I'm not your trainee."

The idea of her hefting a hose and holding it steady with full-force water behind it, made Ethan chuckle.

Joey waggled her finger at him. "Don't judge me by the cover. I'm mighty, and I could do the work."

"I'd like to see that," he said, realizing he meant it.

She stepped back, cocking her head as she eyed him. "Would you like to go out to dinner sometime?"

Shock rumbled through Ethan at the left-field request. "Umm." He glanced toward the lodge. Riley leaned against a pillar watching them and was close enough to hear their conversation judging by the grin on his face. Time to put a cap on this hose.

"I'm sorry. I don't date clients." Okay, that sounded lame even to him.

"I'm not a client. I'm a damsel in distress. Or would have been if this fire was real." She stepped into his personal space and smiled up at him, her dimples deepening.

Riley's guffaw echoed around Ethan's head. He glared at the man. This was going from bad to worse and he had to stop it. Right now. "No. Sorry. No dating." He dragged the words out of the sludge filling his lungs. Then Ethan did something very uncharacteristic. The man who always met problems head-on retreated. Quickly.

"I need to see to my team." Without waiting for a response, he turned on his heel and joined his group beside the truck.

"Everyone accounted for?"

"Yes," Riley said with that damned grin still on his face.

"Any injuries?"

"No."

"Great. Let's get out of here." The sooner, the better.

Riley, quiet on the drive back to the firehouse, waited until they'd cleaned and restocked the truck before wiping the smirk off his face long enough to speak. "So, the cute woman asked you out, huh?"

"My conversation with the manager of Pacific Lodge is none of your business." Ethan ground his teeth, knowing that wouldn't be the end of it.

"It is when everyone within a twenty-foot radius heard, including your team."

"Everyone?" Ethan raked a hand through his hair.

Riley shrugged. "Those that didn't hear have heard it from someone else by now, I'm sure."

Great. His conversation with Joey would be all over Willow Bay by dinner. Grinding his teeth some more, Ethan headed for his office and the mountain of paperwork the false alarm meant for him. Virtual paperwork, now that most forms were digital. He'd been a proponent of the change. Paper was fuel. The less of it laying around, the better.

Riley followed him, to Ethan's consternation.

"How come you didn't take her up on it?"

"On what?" Ethan stalled.

"You know exactly what. She's cute. Why didn't you say you'd go out with her?"

"I don't have time to date."

"Bullshit."

"Beyond that, it's none of your fucking business." Ethan turned to his computer, pounding the keyboard to wake it up. He could feel Riley standing there, eyes boring into his head.

"Well, if you're not interested, maybe I'll take a stab at her. She's adorable." With a laugh, he walked away.

Riley didn't see Ethan stiffen as he pictured Joey and Riley together. He clenched his teeth again. Ethan didn't make friends easily and Riley was about the closest thing to a friend Ethan had ever had. But to see him with Joey? The image grated on Ethan. He didn't do touchy-feely talks and so wasn't about to tell Riley that Joey had affected him.

And Riley was wrong. Joey Sanderson wasn't cute, she was drop-dead gorgeous. Those dimples, those blue eyes, and that body—they called to him. She was the quintessential girl next door. And her mind? That wit of hers made him want conversations.

What would it be like to let his guard down? To relax, hand the reins of responsibility over to someone else and just be himself, spending time with someone he liked. Just for a little while. Sometimes, Ethan yearned for more, and that was dangerous. Given enough time, Joey could make him forget just about anything, and Ethan refused to let that happen. Relationships were distractions. He would never allow himself to get distracted like that again.

Better to cut his losses than take that chance. Ethan pounded down the jealousy bug. If Riley wanted to date Joey, so be it. Decision made, Ethan shoved his demons back in the closet and opened a blank report to fill in as one last thought grabbed a hold of him.

Riley better not fucking cause her one bit of angst,

or he and Ethan would be having it out.

~~~

"It was a false alarm, Mr. Reynolds. Nothing to worry about." Joey walked outside, staying beneath the overhang so the rain wouldn't soak her. She stared into the growing twilight as she clutched her phone. Once she got past this conversation, she might get to some of the pile of work on her desk. How in the hell had the owner found out?

"Anything that disturbs my guests is a worry, Miss Sanderson. See that it doesn't happen again."

Joey shoved the phone into her back pocket and grimaced. This day had gone from bad to worse. It was mid-afternoon and she'd been fielding questions and soothing guests' concerns for hours, all while handing out free cocoa to calm frayed nerves. Joey hadn't seen anyone pull the alarm, but she had a very good idea who'd been around it just before it went off. She planned to have a talk with that person at the first opportunity.

Why would Gladys do something like that? Sure, she'd mentioned she didn't like Joey's boss, but she'd never caused an ounce of trouble before. At least, not that Joey knew of. So why now? And why this?

Only a conversation with the woman would answer those questions. Shaking her head, Joey went back inside and joined Rose behind the front desk. "You okay out here?"

"Sure. The questions and concerns are trickling down. All those planning to leave today are gone and our reservations are close to complete, too. Should be a quiet night."

Joey laughed. "Don't jinx us like that. I'll be in my office if you need anything." Joey pushed a panel in the wall behind them to open her office door. She sank into her comfy desk chair and kicked off her shoes, twirling to look out the window at the gloom. Three p.m. and she was beat. If anything else happened today— No. She wouldn't finish that thought. Knocking on her wooden desk three times to offset the jinx, she threaded her fingers behind her head and gave in to a long, soothing stretch.

Her boss seemed determined to make life as difficult for her as possible, and Joey had no idea why. For him to need the penthouse and two other rooms— with very little notice—on a weekend booked to the rafters was unconscionable. He wanted more and more profit, yet also wanted this kind of availability? How would she possibly work this out?

Mentally, Joey went down her still-too-short list of contacts in the area. She doubted she'd find anything available for festival weekend, but she had to try, and solving puzzles was her specialty. Reaching for her phone, she made her first call.

Two hours and eight calls later, she had a good start on a solution.

"Are you serious?" the woman on the other end of the line asked.

"I'm quite serious, Mrs. Jones. We apologize for the inconvenience of having to move you."

"And your apology is to move us to a rental house bigger than the penthouse, with a view of the ocean, and comp us all meals at your lodge?"

"Yes, ma'am. It's our fault the room is no longer available."

"Oh, miss, you've made my day." The woman's voice caught. "You see, my husband has stage four cancer. This is a family vacation and we splurged money we shouldn't have to make it extra special. I can't tell you how much it means that we have a wonderful place to stay and now our costs are so much less. You've made my day. Heck, my year!"

Oh, wow. Tears filled Joey's eyes. "Ma'am, if you have any trouble coming to the lodge for meals, we'll deliver." Joey gave the woman her cell number and the rest of the details. Afterward, she sat there grinning. This was the perfect thing to turn a bad day good. Joey lived for this kind of thing. Sure, it would cost Pacific Lodge an arm and a leg, but she didn't mind one bit. She'd seen the numbers. The lodge could handle the financial ding and they'd made a suffering family happy, at least for a time.

Yep, making lemonade out of lemons felt pretty darn good. Thanks to her more than heroic efforts and a few issued IOUs, Mr. Reynolds had his penthouse and she'd given the Jones's a gift that would last them a lifetime, memory-wise. Now to deal with the rest of the reservation overages.

Staring out past the dunes at the churning winter waves, Joey let the joy wash over her. Until now, the day had been an unmitigated disaster. From her boss's ultimatum to Chief

Ethan turning her down, her mantra to always end the day happy and in love with life had seemed doomed. Now, though, she felt like celebrating, even after that stinging rejection.

Ethan Walker. No, that wasn't right. Chief Ethan Walker. Had to have the title. The man was altogether too *chiefy*. Too rigid. He needed loosening up, but those coffee-colored eyes that saw everything intrigued her. That clean-shaven jaw was strong and masculine. A total package. Joey had felt drawn to him and her instinct to fix things, human or not, had reared up big time. She wanted to get to know the chief.

Sighing, she turned away from the window. Getting mixed up with Ethan probably wasn't a good idea. She'd only been here a couple months and still didn't know many people, though the idea of getting a place of her own had been growing in her heart and mind. She wanted to stay, to make a life in Willow Bay, even if that wasn't very smart. If her past caught up to her, she'd have to leave with only a moment's notice. Could she commit to a house? Probably not, but looking might be a fun way to spend her days off.

She also shouldn't pursue any sort of relationship, not right now. And something told her that Ethan wasn't a fling kind of guy. In the long run, Chief Ethan's rejection was a blessing. She'd be better off forgetting the man and staying focused on her own goals. She'd go out tonight, get a drink, listen to some music, and relax. Some harmless flirting, maybe even some dancing to help her forget all her problems, if only for a little while.

Decision made, Joey closed up shop, wished the evening front desk operator a quiet night, and headed to her room to change. She was more than ready to have some fun.

CHAPTER THREE

Done with his shifts for a few days, Ethan stopped at the Grog and Vine Pub for his "days off" beer. Unlike most firehouses, Willow Bay ran on twelve-hour shifts instead of the usual twenty-four. Twelve on, twelve off for four days one week, and three days the next. He'd requested it because research shows firefighters can better maintain maximum readiness if they get to sleep in their own beds at night. The three-month trial was almost over and his guys loved it. In a couple weeks, he'd find out if the county loved it. If not, he would have a battle on his hands, and he wasn't looking forward to it. Twelve-hour shifts meant four crews instead of three, which didn't sit well with the folks who oversaw the budget.

A glass of amber liquid with a thin froth on top showed up in front of him.

"Thanks, Gene," Ethan told the bartender.

"Just the one, right?"

"Yep. Then coffee." His usual. Relaxed, but ready. That was his mantra. Ethan rarely relaxed completely. He scrubbed a hand down his face then sipped his beer, appreciating the tangy hops. Twirling the glass in a perfect circle within the water ring it made on the bar, he tried to process his day.

What a day, too—between the guys ribbing him about the cute manager who they swore was flirting with him, to one problem piling up after another. He'd been more than happy to hand the mess off to Jeff, the assistant chief who, for some ungodly reason, had fallen in love with the night shift.

Ethan should've gone home and fallen into his bed. He was dog-tired. But habits were a tough thing for him to break, so here he was, sitting at the bar, having a beer to celebrate another week of shifts without serious incident.

He glanced in the mirror behind the bar and ran a hand along his stubble. He needed to shave. Firefighting aged a person and Ethan was the poster child for that rule. He looked old. Worn down. Sometimes, the job hit him like that. Or maybe not the job so much as the pressure to keep everyone safe. It would be nice to lay down that mantle and just be. Except, people got hurt when he did that. And worse.

No. This was his charge. His duty. Protect the people, at least from fire. Ethan closed his eyes, reminding himself why he'd chosen this path. He let the pain wash over him for a moment before pushing it back to the recesses of his mind.

Hands covered his eyes. "Guess who?"

Poised to defend himself, the voice sunk into him like the smooth burn of a good whiskey. He opened his eyes. The mirror behind the bar reflected the sparkling blue eyes of the manager of Pacific Lodge.

"You are looking way too serious, Chief," she said as she settled on the bar stool next to him. "Like the woes of the world have settled on your shoulders."

She could read him that well? Ethan almost closed his eyes again at this reminder of his day. He tried to look away, look down, look anywhere, and couldn't. Those eyes of hers held so much life. So much joy, laughter, and happiness. Mesmerized, he couldn't pull away and barely checked the impulse to jump into her well of happiness and drown himself in the bliss of a life without care.

"Ethan?"

He shook his head to dispel the bullshit taking over his brain.

Joey leaned in, her expressive eyes filled with concern. "Are you all right?"

Oh, hell no. This woman was not going to try to make him feel "better." Clearing the last of the fog from his brain, Ethan straightened, shrugging her hand off in the process. "Fine." His voice croaked. It fucking croaked. He cleared it, trying to decide if he should leave. Sure, it would be rude. Better rude than distracted, right? If he spent much more time around Joey Sanderson, his instincts said he'd be way more than just distracted.

"Just heading home," he said, standing up.

"Without your coffee?" the bartender asked, setting a steaming, dark cup in front of him.

"Uh, yeah, it's getting late and I've got some things to do."

With one elbow on the bar and her head in her palm, Joey turned on one thousand watts of danger with her smile. "Stay. Just for a few more minutes. Drink your coffee."

Against his better judgment, Ethan sank back onto the stool, the plea in her eyes too hard to resist. Joey's smile amped up a notch as she ordered a glass of Prosecco.

"Bubbly? Are you celebrating something?"

"Well, I happen to think I'm worth bubbly and that life should be celebrated every single day.

However— " She held up the glass the bartender set in front of her. "Today, I'm celebrating meeting you."

Tipping her glass in his direction, she waited until he picked up his coffee and tapped. He watched her sip. Red lipstick. He'd always loved red lipstick on women. She swallowed, arching her delicate throat as she did so. His body reacted.

"Mmn, that's good."

Ethan's jeans grew tighter. He took a swig of the coffee he still held. "Hot! Ouch!" The cup hit the counter with a thud, splashing hot coffee on his hands. "Ouch, ouch, ouch."

Jumping up, Joey handed him his beer, which he guzzled to cool the burn. He took a long swig while she got a wet rag and some ice from the bartender and wrapped it around Ethan's burned hand.

As his pain receded and his cheeks warmed with embarrassment, Joey kept hold of the towel around his hand, keeping the cold where it needed to be, her kind ministrations drilling their way right through the wall around his heart.

"Where'd you learn to triage like that?" he asked, his voice low and husky.

Joey shivered. Was she cold? Ethan tried to give her his jacket until she tightened her hold on his hand.

"Knowing First Aid is one of the first tenets of a good hotel manager."

Her breath tickled his ear, she was so close. If he turned, they'd damn near be lip-to-lip. He wanted that. His dick wanted that. Damn it.

Ethan pulled his hand out from the towel, breaking the magic of the moment.

With a fleeting touch of sadness in her smile, Joey sat back. She gave him space to breathe, one shaky breath at a time. Until she raised a manicured finger and tapped his throat lightly, when all the breath left him again.

"How's the throat?"

"Better, thanks to the beer."

She picked up his hand, inspecting damage that wasn't there. The coffee hadn't been so hot it left burns. "And this?" She ran her hand over the top of his lightly, just like he wanted her to run her hands over— Nope. Not going there.

"Fine." Ethan pulled his hand free.

Joey took another sip of her bubby, then leaned back against the bar as she watched him. "So, Chief, what brings you here tonight?" Bright eyes and a steady gaze told him she was interested in his answer, not just making conversation.

"Routine."

"Routine?"

"Post-shift week routine."

"Ahhh, so you're off for a few days now?"

"Something like that." No way was he giving Miss Sunshine a better idea of his schedule. Something told Ethan she'd use that to her advantage, whatever her reasons for chatting with him.

"Do you live in the fire station or have a place of your own?"

"I rent an apartment here in town."

Her eyes lit up. "I bet you live alone. Somehow, I can't picture you with a bunch of testosterone-loaded firefighters lounging around your place."

"I'm the chief, so no firefighters even if I wanted roommates, which I don't need."

"Hmmm. Do you like renting?"

"Haven't really thought much about it."

"I'm thinking of looking around for a place, maybe buy a condo or a small house."

"I've thought about that. Just haven't gotten around to it."

"I know what we should do." She slapped the bar. "We should house hunt together."

"No." Hell no.

"Oh, come on. It'll be fun. We could meet for breakfast, pour over the listings, hit the open houses. Maybe we'll each find a place to fall in love with."

Ethan gulped. "Sorry, I don't have time to do that right now."

"You're off for a few days, right?"

"Off, maybe. But still busy."

"With what?"

Crossing his arms over his chest, Ethan chose not to answer that question, mostly because he didn't have a damn thing going on over the next couple days.

"All right. I can see you've dug in your heels. Maybe another time," Joey said, mercifully letting him off the hook.

He didn't share his private life, whether searching for a place to live or answering personal questions. He kept the book of his life closed for a reason and he refused to look back. Or forward. He was a realist. Only the here and now mattered.

"Talking makes you uncomfortable, doesn't it?" she asked him.

"Sometimes." He gnashed his jaw.

"I can see that getting to know you won't be easy." She laughed, a lilting, happy sound. Despite himself, Ethan wanted to hear more. Joey ran the ever-so-soft back of her hand over his chin, then pulled it back so quickly he wanted to grab it, hold on to the warmth, the softness against his skin. "I like the stubble."

"Shaving when I get home."

Joey sat back, taking another sip of her Prosecco. "I accept the challenge."

"What challenge?" What the hell was she talking about?

"The challenge of learning all there is to know about Chief Ethan Walker."

No. No. No. They were not going there. Ethan did not do relationships or friendships. No lovey-dovey sharing shit. None of it. Standing, he pulled out his wallet and threw bills on the counter to cover his beer and her wine. "Not going to happen."

"Too late."

"No. It. Is. Not." He needed out of there before he gave into her cockamamie idea. He mumbled a good night, waved to Gene, and tried to walk out of the Grog and Vine without breaking into a jog or a cold sweat. His throat tightened. He needed fresh air.

The last thing he heard as he pushed open the door into the chilly winter air was her laughter. It followed him to his truck. He climbed in and slammed the door shut, but somehow, the echo of her laughter stayed with him. Leaning his head on the steering wheel, he wondered why Joey Sanderson had set her eyes on him. And how he could turn them in another direction.

Worse, he didn't know if he wanted her to turn away. A part of him, one he'd worked hard to suppress, didn't want that at all.

He was in so much trouble.

~~~

Joey watched him leave, her laughter dying after he disappeared through the door. What had gotten into her, challenging him like that? He seemed so down when she'd first seen him tonight, she'd wanted to cheer him up. Somewhere in the course of the conversation, things had changed. She really did want to know more about him. Which was crazy because he was authoritative, a trait that hit way too close to home. Joey shuddered. No way would she ever go back to that kind of life.

Glancing around the darker interior of the pub, Joey saw locals who were fast becoming her friends. Along with Bernie and Paul Gibson's Square Peg Pizza—her favorite place to eat—the Grog and Vine had quickly become one of her haunts thanks to its mostly local clientele. She dealt with tourists all day and that was enough. In the evening, her goal was to finish her day on a positive note and have some fun.

She'd heard winters were quiet months here, meant for hibernating and getting ready for the spring and summer. But right now, Willow Bay seemed restless. Soon, hoards would descend for the first annual Beer and Chowder Festival and most of the locals could hardly wait. Tourists provided a welcome income stream and she knew firsthand how full the town would be that weekend.

Betty and Mike Johnson sat in a corner booth close together. Joey had met the hardware store owners and their four-year-old twin boys, both still in their terrible twos. Must be date night. Joey smiled at how close they cuddled. As hard as they worked, they still made time for romance. Good for them.

When was the last time she'd had honest-to-God romance in her life? Joey stared at herself in the bar mirror. Not since Robert, handpicked by her parents and just as bent on the severe, perfectly formed life they'd planned for her. She'd rebelled against that life as a teenager and had paid the price.

Nope. She did not want that. Didn't need to be under someone's thumb. Certainly not the thumb of another strict rule-follower. Joey had thrown that off when she walked out of her parents' home, and she would never return to that lifestyle. It choked her, smothering all the living out of life.

Ethan seemed all about rules. Worse, he believed wholeheartedly in following them. Yet the stalwart man intrigued her. Pain lingered in those searching, dark eyes of his, plus a wealth of emotion he probably didn't think he showed. Joey lived for pet projects and had spoken before her brain could catch up with her vocal cords. Every time she got close to the man, she stopped thinking, her heart jolted awake, and her pulse ran marathons.

Not to mention, she couldn't stop touching him. After living in a family that discouraged touch, she craved it. Sometimes, that put people off, but Joey intended to live her best life. She imagined her hands caressing biceps even more pronounced without his work gear on, her fingers trailing through hair not always perfect, like he allowed himself this one flaw to feel human.

Walk away, Sanderson, her mind reasoned, but her heart faltered. Joey should renege on her promise to learn everything about him. Let the handsome fireman live life his own way, just like she wanted to live hers. Could she, though? The sadness in those eyes of his tugged at her.

Damn. She needed to exorcise this morose mood. Maybe she should hang it up and go home. Joey glanced again at the door Ethan had used to make his exit. Going back to her empty room didn't sound like much fun.

"Screw it." Joey downed the rest of her drink and flagged the bartender for another one. Heading for the jukebox, she picked a fast, upbeat song, dancing solo around the small floor, oblivious of the few folks who watched. Though she did glimpse a smile on Betty's face. The woman understood the need to let loose once in a while. Thankfully, Joey had become adept at making her own fun.

"Hey, beautiful."

When Joey whipped around at the unfamiliar

voice, she found two men standing there, eyeing her like predators eye prey. They even had their hunters' special camo t-shirts on. Joey had been ogled before—a lot—but the taint of something dirty churned bile in her stomach.

"Sorry, guys. Not looking for any company."

"No way a woman as gorgeous as you should be dancing alone," the blond one said, swaying his hips as he moved closer.

All of a sudden, Mike Johnson stood beside her. "The lady said she doesn't want company."

Both men glared at Mike. By the time they turned back to Joey, they'd plastered smiles on their faces. Very fake smiles. Blondie held up his hands. "No problem. Might have been fun, but we get the message. See you around." Without hesitation, they strode out of the pub.

Joey let out a long breath. She'd handled worse than these two before and would have been fine, but was comforted by Mike's aid, an unfamiliar feeling. "Thanks, Mike."

"We take care of our own here in Willow Bay."

Wow. She'd only been there a couple months and these folks treated her like a local, like family. Joey had never known that kind of acceptance. It stunned her.

"Yes, we do take care of our own," Betty said, slipping an arm into Mike's. "You okay?"

"It would take bigger cojones than theirs to scare me, so yes. I'm fine."

"Let me know when you're leaving. I'll walk you to your car," Mike said.

The jukebox song died away and Joey knew her night was over. No way would she ruin date night for them. "That's all right. I can get home okay. Thanks for everything."

"You sure?"

Joey nodded. "Just a quick pop out to my car and I'll be safe as a joey in Mama Kangaroo's pouch. I'll have Gene keep an eye out through the bar window." She gave Betty and Mike a hug and, with a wave at the bartender, headed out. Soon, she was scolding herself for parking her car where no lights shone on it. She hadn't been thinking.

"Hey again, beautiful."

That voice. She turned slowly around and stepped away from her car so she had a clear path if she needed to run.

"Really? You didn't get the idea inside that I didn't want to hang with you?"

The blond one shrugged. "We thought we'd try to change your mind."

His shorter, dark-haired cohort snickered.

"You won't. Please leave." Joey snuck her hand into the large bag she always carried, and her fingers closed around the comforting handle of her Taser. She flipped the switch just like she'd practiced.

The taller man looked at the other one. "I don't think she means it."

"Trust me," Joey said, pulling the ready-to-go Taser from her bag. "I mean it."

Blondie took a step back, then grinned. "You don't want to tase me. I saw you dancing in there. You're looking for a good time and we're it."

Like idiots, they stepped toward her instead of turning on their heels.

Looks like it's lesson time.

Joey raised her arm, aiming.

"The lady asked you to leave."

The deep-voiced warning came too late for Joey, who'd already depressed the switch of her Taser. A shadow stepped between her and the men just in time for the barbed electrodes to embed themselves in his shoulder.

"Gene!" Joey cried. He must have seen and come out to help her.

After a frozen moment that lasted a nanosecond but felt like hours, the man crumpled to the ground, his jerking muscles no longer able to hold him. And still, he flopped around like a fish dumped on a pier.

The men who'd tried to harass her ran off as the pub door opened. Gene and Mike raced her way. "Gene?" She looked down at the man on the ground, her heart now pounding. Gene turned him over.

"Ethan! Oh, God, Ethan. I'm so sorry!" Joey sank to the ground beside him. "Are you all right?"

What had she done? He no longer twitched, but why wouldn't he wake up? Joey ran her hands over his chest, grateful he was breathing. His heartbeats raced beneath her fingers.

He didn't answer.

A crowd formed around them. Tears threatened in Joey's eyes as Betty pushed through to the front. "He won't answer me," Joey said. "He won't open his eyes."

"I've had some first aid training." Betty kneeled on the other side of Ethan who was way too still for Joey's peace of mind.

Joey knew first aid, too, but everything she'd learned flew out the window as she stared helplessly at her victim.

"I've called 9-1-1," Mike said.

Betty leaned over Ethan's face. "He's breathing nice and strong." She placed a hand at his throat. "Heart rate is rapid but steady."

Trying to be at least somewhat helpful, Joey leaned in and raised an eyelid.

"Stop manhandling me, woman," Ethan growled, opening his eyes.

"Oh, thank God." Joey hugged him tight, too

relieved to maintain any sense of decorum.

"If you'd stop squeezing the air out of me, I'd be better." The growl remained firmly in place.

"Oh, gosh, I'm so sorry." Joey sat back, grabbing his hand and holding it tight. She couldn't let go completely, not until she knew he was truly okay.

~~~

Ethan lay there with his eyes closed, fighting dizziness and nausea. Had he hit his head? Did he have a concussion? His whole body still zinged from the Taser. He'd stared down some dangerous situations in his life, but never once had this happened. Until now, and he never wanted to endure it again. Losing control of his body like that—shit, had he wet himself? Ethan slid a hand over the front of his jeans. Dry. Thank God for small favors.

When he opened his eyes again, they looked directly into the round, concerned eyes of the one person he'd been trying to escape. Right now, he wasn't sure if he wanted to throttle her or kiss her. Damn it. The crowd behind her came into focus and a rush of embarrassment overlaid the tingling.

Ethan tried to sit up. Both Betty and Joey pressed him back down.

"Let's wait for the paramedics. And give you time to get your wits about you again," Betty said.

"Never had wits before. Why should he have them now?" Mike joked.

Betty's hand stayed firmly clamped on Ethan's uninjured shoulder. "You might have a concussion from the fall. What year is it?"

"2022. Biden is our President and I live in Washington State. Willow Bay, to be exact. I'm on the very gravelly ground outside the Grog and Vine Pub." Pebbles that felt like boulders at the moment. "Does that satisfy you that I'm oriented to time and place?"

"That, and your signature growl," Betty said with a laugh.

Ethan could hear the sirens. The night shift guys would be there any minute and he'd *never* hear the end of this. All he needed now was for the rain to return.

Why a fucking drop of rain chose that moment to hit his cheek would be a mystery he'd never solve. Ethan ignored it.

"Really, I'm fine. You can call off the paramedics. Seriously. Please?" Ah, damn. Flashing lights entered the parking lot. No stopping the carnage now. "At least let me sit up. These are my guys."

"You promise you're not dizzy?" Betty asked.

"Not one bit," he lied.

Joey helped him to a sitting position while Betty stood, shaking her head. "First rule: don't move the patient unless he's in harm's way."

"Trust me. If I'm lying on the ground, I *will* be in harm's way. I'll never hear the end of it from my guys."

The dizziness he'd denied hit him and he clutched his head, trying to stabilize his world. And failing. Joey moved with him, unwilling to let go of his hand.

"I need my hand back," he grumbled.

Joey let go like it burned. And damn it, he missed her touch. This night was going from bad to worse.

"Stand back, folks. Stand back." Jeff plowed through the group, which had gotten smaller but not small enough for Ethan's liking. Too many had already witnessed his humiliation.

"Yeah, move on, folks. Nothing to see here."

Jeff squatted down next to Ethan, grinning. Figured the night chief would come in person.

"You don't look too worse for wear," he said, signaling the two with him to start their checks. "Got tased, huh?"

Ethan glared at him, not easy to do with a

flashlight shining in his eyes as Jeff checked his reflexes. "I'm fine," he ground out.

"He should be checked out," Joey said. "He hit his head pretty hard." Ethan tried to turn the evil eye on her but another wave of dizziness grabbed him. "Ugh."

His grin disappearing, Jeff became all business. Ethan realized he might actually *have* a concussion, so he let the man do his thing.

"No issues from the Taser and just a couple small scratches from the electrodes," Jeff said. "I think you've got a concussion, though. That's one hell of a knot on the back of your head. You should go to the ER, let them check you out."

"No."

"Ethan," Joey said.

"No," he said more forcefully.

Jeff stood up, hands on hips. "I have to file a report on this. Battalion Chief isn't going to let you back on the job without a release."

Damn. Jeff was right. Man, you try to do the right thing and this is what happens. He did not want to endure a ride to the nearest hospital which was forty miles away. And no way would they get him in an ambulance.

"How about if I call the clinic and see if they'll take a look? They're open a couple more hours and I've heard they do triage work," Joey said.

More grateful than he could show at the moment, Ethan jumped on her idea. "Yes, I'll go to the clinic. Hell, I already feel less dizzy."

"Hmmm." Jeff scratched his chin. "I guess that will work. We'll get you there in the ambulance."

"No way in hell," Ethan said.

"I'll take him," Joey said right behind him. "That is, if you can help me get him into my car."

As a unit, all heads turned to her Mini Cooper,

then back to Ethan.

"Can you drive a truck?" Ethan asked Joey.

"Of course."

He dug out his keys and tapped the fob so she'd know which one. Without a word, Joey grabbed the keys, went over, and climbed in. Within seconds she'd pulled up beside him. Jeff and the two paramedics helped him stand. Surprisingly, he wasn't as dizzy.

Once in the car, Jeff leaned in. "No going home. You get to the clinic. I'm calling ahead to let them know."

Ethan gave him a one-finger salute. Jeff laughed as he closed the door. That was all it took for Joey to light out of the parking lot.

"Can you slow down, please? You're going to get us killed the way you're driving."

"Oh, gosh, sure." At which point she slowed to a fucking crawl.

"Not that slow."

By then, they'd arrived at the clinic. A man in scrubs, one in a leather jacket, and a woman in a white medical coat waited near the front door.

"Jesus, they've got a welcoming committee."

Joey pulled up beside them. "Yes, and we'd better get inside before the heavens open up."

Sure enough, the windshield grew wetter with each passing second. Ethan jumped when his door opened, then clutched his pounding head.

"Hey, Chief."

"Cade. Hi." Cade Huntington was the resident digital game designer and cable guy who'd snagged the town's newest doctor, Grace Benson.

"Came to take my lady to dinner and heard you were stopping by. Thought I'd stick around to make sure you're okay."

"Appreciate it." Ethan stepped out of the truck

and the woozies hit him again. "Might need a little help."

"We got you, big guy," Cade said, taking hold of his arm.

Joey's door slammed and bam! She was around the truck and at his side. Ethan had never needed help in his life. Right now, gratitude filled him as Cade took one side and Joey the other. He'd probably be flat on the fucking ground if he had to walk on his own.

Once inside, the scrubs guy took over for Cade, but Joey refused to let go of Ethan's hand. Truth be told, he was okay with that. Her touch grounded him.

Oh, man, if he weren't already hurting, he'd head-slap himself. *You don't do relationships, remember, bud?*

"Hi, Ethan," Dr. Benson said, pulling her white medical coat on and winding her blonde hair into a bun as she entered the room. "Feeling a little rough?"

"Yep," Joey answered.

"Not really. Just dizzy and my head hurts."

"He hasn't thrown up and didn't indicate he was nauseous before we got here," Joey said.

Dr. Benson's eyes traveled between Joey and Ethan. "Are you two related?"

"No," Ethan said.

"Sort of," Joey said at the same time.

"That clarifies things so well. I need to be sure, Ethan. Are you all right with Ms. Sanderson being in here?"

A little too late now. Ethan looked down at his hand, intertwined with Joey's. When had that happened? And why did he like it so much? He should pull his hand away, reset things right now. Instead, he gripped hers tighter. "I'm okay with it."

Joey's smile filled the whole room with sunshine and flowers. Geesh, he was getting it bad.

"All right then. Let's see what we've got going on."

Dr. Benson pulled on exam gloves.

Ethan endured the poking and prodding, barely. He didn't do patient. He was the one who helped others, not vice versa.

"We've got a CT scanner here or I'd be sending you to the hospital. I think you have a minor concussion. We'll scan and go from there."

"Okay, doc."

"We'll get you out of here as soon as we can. I'd imagine at this point you just want to go home."

"Definitely."

Dr. Benson chuckled as she left.

Once they were alone, the silence stretched out between Ethan and Joey for an entire two seconds before she wrapped her arms around him, hugging him tight.

"I'm so sorry, Ethan. I can't believe this happened," she whispered, her breath teasing his ear, warming him through and sending signals southward that he worked very hard to cut off at the pass. He did not do relationships and he really needed to get things back on track.

"If you hadn't tased me, it wouldn't have."

Joey pulled back and straightened. Fire entered her eyes, a fire that fueled him more than warm breath. "If you hadn't tried to be a knight in shining armor, you wouldn't have gotten hurt."

"You should never have walked out there alone. Those men did not have nice things planned," he said, his voice getting stronger.

"I had it under control," she raised her voice to match his.

"Bullshit. You were about to tase them." Ethan held his pounding head.

"Exactly."

Ethan opened his mouth, closed it, and opened it

again, but nothing came out. Did she actually believe she could defend herself against two horny men? Did she not understand how dangerous a situation that was?

"Don't you care about your own safety?"

"Sure, I do. But I can take care of myself. I don't need some strong-willed, authoritarian guy trying to save me."

"Uh, guys?" Cade opened the door a crack. "We can hear you down the hall."

Damn it. The gossip mill would be going nuts tomorrow with this story. Ethan glared at Joey, which hurt almost as much as yelling did. "Let's just agree to disagree, all right?"

"Fine," Joey said, stomping to a chair and plopping down.

An hour later, with the CT showing no signs of a bleed or any other issue, Dr. Benson came to discharge Ethan. "Who's at home who can keep an eye on you tonight?"

Ethan froze and, out of the corner of his eye, saw Joey sit up straight.

"I can take care of— "

"I'll make sure he survives the night," Joey said, moving to stand by the bed, her eyes bright with defiance.

Hell no. "I don't need a babysitter."

He'd heard the local doctor had a "don't mess with me" look. Cade had even mentioned something about it at one point. Dr. Benson's face turned to implacable stone as she stared him down. She was good at this. Scary good.

"She can take me to the station," he offered. "The guys will keep an eye on me."

"That works for me."

"Not for me," Joey said. "I'm the reason he got hurt. I should watch him." The fire dimmed in her eyes and true worry replaced it.

Ethan didn't want to think about how good it felt to have a woman so concerned for his welfare. No way was he spending the night in his apartment alone with her. Headache be damned, Ethan didn't know if he could keep his hands off her. Time to nip this in the bud.

"A couple of the guys are paramedics and they all have extensive first aid training. How will you be better at watching me than them?"

The hurt on her face almost made him flinch. She stiffened, then nodded her head.

"At least give me your phone number so I can check on you."

Fighting the urge to roll his eyes, which would probably hurt anyway, Ethan reeled off his cell number. Within ten minutes, they were on their way to the station. The rain had returned in earnest. Ethan stared at the rivulets coursing down the passenger window of his truck during the silent ride.

Joey pulled into the station, parked, then handed Ethan the keys. She reached for her door handle.

"I can make it in by myself," He said.

Her lips a thin line, Joey looked his way. "This is your truck. Either I'm taking it home or one of your guys is going to have to take me back to my car."

His head was rattled worse than he thought if he'd forgotten that. "'Kay."

Ethan got out before she could get around the truck. Walking into the firehouse with his head pounding wasn't easy, but he'd be damned if he'd lean on a woman.

"How you feeling, Chief?" Jeff asked, emerging from his office as they walked in.

"Like bombs are going off in my head, but otherwise okay."

Joey handed Jeff the note from Dr. Benson releasing Ethan *if* he laid low for a couple days.

"He walked in under his own power," She said. "The doctor verified it's only a mild concussion. He needs to be checked every couple hours overnight, then he can go home."

"We can follow the concussion protocols no problem." Jeff's said with a big admiring smile. "With a nurse like you, he should have asked you to take him home. I would have."

"Not him," Joey said. "He's stubborn."

"He is that."

"I'm right here, guys. I can talk for myself."

Jeff leaned against the doorjamb, eyeing Joey in a way Ethan didn't much care for. "You are looking lovely for all you've been through tonight."

Lovely? What *she's* been through? Ethan shook his head in disgust, which set off another round of fifty-pound weights ping-ponging in his brain.

"Why, thank you, Jeff. It has been a trying night." She smiled.

"You're married," Ethan said to Jeff. "And I'm going to bed." Halfway to the stairs, he turned back. "Can someone give Miss Sanderson a ride to her car?"

Joey's eyes widened at the formal use of her name.

Jeff laughed heartily. "We'll get your damsel home. No worries. You—to the bunk room, Mister." He shooed him with his hands.

Ethan went, but not happily. What the hell was the man doing? He had a wife he was crazy about and two adorable kids. And he flirted with Joey?

Ethan made it to his bunk, clutching his head. Even thinking hurt. He laid down, hoping for a nice, long sleep to get rid of all the toxic pain and emotions he had racing around inside him. This was not how he lived his life. He was always in control. Well, until they woke him in two hours to check on him, he would be.

CHAPTER FOUR

By morning, Ethan's headache had subsided to a dull throb. He had the paramedic on duty check him out and got the all-clear to drive home. Letting himself into his apartment, he looked around the spartan place. He'd bought furniture because he needed furniture, not because he particularly liked it. Couches were couches so the Ikea sofa worked fine, even if it wasn't that comfortable. The end tables didn't match, having been picked up at a couple different garage sales. The only chair that really mattered was his recliner and he'd splurged on the soft, deep brown leather. The window blinds were usually shut, giving a dungeon-like feel to the place.

He didn't care. It was a place to sleep, not his work. And his bed was the most comfortable part of this place. He headed there now.

His phone pinged. He sank down onto the mattress and looked at the text. Joey.

You make it through the night?

Ethan couldn't help but chuckle.

Yep.

Need a lift home?

No.

Though his phone showed no reply, he stared at the screen. Joey wasn't one to let things go when she grabbed hold of them. Already, Ethan knew that about her. Sure enough, after about thirty seconds.

You're already home, aren't you?

Yep.

How's the headache?

Down to a dull roar and the paramedic cleared me to drive.

Good. I'm glad you let them check you out.

Again, that feeling of being cocooned by someone else's caring surrounded him. And felt nice. Too nice.

I really am sorry I tazed you.

Last night's events rammed against the front of his brain. *No harm, no foul. But you need to stop walking out to your car alone at night.*

The pause was longer this time. Good. She was thinking about his words.

Gene watched me from the window and I can defend myself, as you saw.

Yet still, you got into trouble, and something much worse could have happened. Have someone walk you out and don't unlock your car until you're beside it. Basic safety protocols.

A full minute passed before Ethan set his phone down. He yanked off his clothes and climbed into bed. He was almost asleep when he heard the ping.

I do not put myself in danger, but I will not kneel to some protocol designed to save those who can't save themselves. I. Can. Take. Care. Of. Myself. Again, I'm sorry you got tazed. Have a good sleep.

How in the hell did she know he was in bed? The thought brought Ethan out of bed to look out his window. No red Mini in the parking lot, so she must be guessing. Of course, she was. He really needed to get her out of his head. Except she'd put herself in danger last night and he couldn't stop thinking about that. Joey wasn't invincible. No one was. She'd been in a bad spot because of stubborn pride and he didn't know what to do about it.

Not that he could do anything. He lay back down and tried to go to sleep, unable to expel his lingering worry.

Several hours later, groggy and in need of strong coffee, Ethan started a pot and took a shower. Tylenol had almost killed the remnants of his headache and he wasn't a bit dizzy, thank goodness. His stomach grumbled while he sipped his coffee and watched the midday news. He looked in his barren fridge and realized he desperately needed groceries.

Grabbing his keys, he headed for the local market to stock up. In the middle of selecting tomatoes, he glanced up to see Joey, in the same aisle, watching him. Ethan almost groaned. He simply could not get away from her. Here she was again, looking fresh and sunshiny on a dreary, rainy day. What was with that?

"Hey," she said, tucking a strand of hair behind her ear.

"Hey," he answered.

"You look none the worse for the wear."

He held his arms out to the sides. "All better. Like I said, no harm, no foul." He picked another tomato up and bagged it, fully aware that she'd moved closer to him.

"I want you to know, I take my safety seriously. I know how to defend myself. But I'm not going to let a couple assholes decide how I live my life. Those boys were all bluster and I was ready for them."

"You can't be sure of that. There were two of them and they were stronger than you."

She smiled. "I know Krav Maga."

"Doesn't mean they couldn't get the upper hand." Ethan set the bag of tomatoes in his cart. "At least consider being more careful. Instead of Gene watching you, maybe you could have taken Mike up on his offer to walk you out."

"How did you know that?"

"Mike called this morning to see how I was doing. And, well, small town, remember?"

Joey chuckled and Ethan felt his gut easing its tight hold. "All right. I'll concede that point." She glanced down at his cart and her chuckle turned into a laugh. "Why, Chief, do you have a secret you haven't told me about?"

What the hell was she talking about? Ethan glanced down and saw the woman's cream. He'd meant to grab antibiotic ointment. The heated blush, something he'd never been able to control well, went straight to the roots of his hair.

"Needed antibiotic cream. Grabbed this by accident." His voice was gruff as he picked up the offending item and set it on the shelf next to the tomatoes.

"What? Not putting it back where you got it? Doesn't that bend your rules a little bit?"

It did, but he wouldn't give her the satisfaction of knowing that. He remained stoic and still, waiting her out.

She balked first, stepping back and uncharacteristically shuffling her feet as she stood there, evidently deciding on something.

"The town bonfire is Saturday. Would you like to go? Not as my bodyguard, mind you. Just, um, friends attending a town event?"

Yes. He wanted to, more than anything. Pleasure at her question surged through him until he remembered his vow to stay away from her. "Sorry, I can't. I'll be on duty."

"So soon after the concussion?"

A little bit of sunshine disappeared from her eyes and that vulnerability tugged at Ethan. Too much, damn it. He scowled. "I'm cleared to work."

"You can't work and hang out with someone at the same time?"

"No. Sorry."

Joey flashed a smile that could calm the savage beast and leaned close enough for him to smell the spicy scent of her hair. A different shampoo? This surprised him. He'd expected a floral scent, not something straight out of the far east. The woman had layers, and the part of Ethan that wanted to peel them away struggled for release.

"You do know that saying about all work and no play, right? You should work to live, not the other way around."

Except when he did that, bad things happened. Ethan stiffened as the memories rushed in. "Not that I need to explain myself to you, but work is my life and I'm fine with that." Better she understand now that there could be nothing between them.

Her smile disappeared and the word "bastard" felt branded on Ethan's forehead. If Joey's smile was a catalyst for Ethan's libido, her pout was ten times worse. That bottom lip jutting out... Ethan reacted, as any man would.

She searched his face for a moment or two, then gave a short, clipped nod. "I get the message. You're married to your job. Mark my words, Chief. One of these days, you're going to want to play, and I might not be available."

Then, shocking the shit out of him, she stepped forward and kissed him, a light peck that stole every bit of his strength and shook him to his core. How could lips be so soft? So pliable? So perfect?

"Ta ta for now, Chief. I'm sure I'll see you around.

By the way, I dare you to leave that cream right where you set it. I bet you can't do it."

"Easy peasy," he said without thinking. No way would this ball of energy get the best of him.

Joey pushed her cart down the aisle and disappeared around a corner. Ethan's heart gave an extra thump as he thought about going after her but stayed frozen in place. It was better this way. Joey could never be a fling to him and he could not get involved. He learned the hard way that duty was meant to be front and center in his life. Always.

"Tsk. Tsk."

Ethan turned to find Gladys, hands on her hips, looking decidedly disgusted.

"Good morning, Gladys. How are you?"

"Better than you, young man."

What the hell was she talking about? Ethan frowned. "I'm not sure— "

Gladys poked him in the chest. "You that happy with your life that you let someone as nice as Joey go without a thought? You, Chief, are an idiot. That pretty young woman asked you out on a date and you turned her down flat." She shook her head. "I'm disgusted with you, Ethan Walker."

With an exaggerated huff, Gladys pushed her store cart off in the direction Joey had gone, leaving Ethan with his lower lip tapping the floor in surprise. Was the whole world ganging up on him?

Women were batshit crazy. Who would take him to task next? Ethan peeked around the corner. Neither Joey nor Gladys were at the check-out stands, so he beat feet out of the store in record time. He stowed his groceries in the backseat of his truck, then remembered he'd left that cream where he'd set it. That wasn't right but Joey had dared him. He couldn't go back in there. Not with her words echoing in his brain. Ethan kicked his tires, did a couple standing pushups against his truck, then climbed in.

He couldn't bring himself to start the motor, though. "Hell." Ethan slapped the steering wheel, headed back to the store, picked up the cream, put it back where it belonged, and walked—as fast as he dared—back to his truck.

Only to find Joey's Mini parked right next to him. Joey stood next to her car with a wide grin on her face.

"Couldn't leave it there, could you?"

Ethan knew his face was bright red. He could feel the heat. Disgusted, he ignored Joey, climbed in, and gunned his truck, leaving the parking lot at a higher speed than he should have. A couple blocks away, he pulled over, working hard to get his heart rate down. He sat there for a long time, wondering what was wrong with him. A beautiful woman had asked him to hang with her for a while and he'd retreated like a puppy, tail between his legs.

That woman enticed him to break all the rules, and he could not—would not—let that happen.

Never again.

~~~

The laughter died on Joey's face as she watched Ethan peel out, unsure why she couldn't resist aggravating the man. No, she had to admit that wasn't right. She wanted to rattle his cage because she liked him. A little too much. The man's serious stare heated her through and through. And when he smiled, though it was seldom, she melted completely. Sure, that protective bent of his was a little too cavemanish. Except with him, she didn't feel intimidated. But what really got to her was the blush. It was the sweetest, cutest thing she'd ever seen, and she wanted more of it. A lot more.

After climbing into her beloved car, Joey drove

back to the lodge. She sat in the parking lot, staring at the place she both lived and worked.

Chief Ethan wasn't the only one focused on a goal. Joey loved managing Pacific Lodge. A small inheritance from her grandmother had been a godsend when she'd decided to leave a bad situation. For three years, she'd roamed, looking over her shoulder at each new stop.

Somehow, over the two months she'd lived in Willow Bay, Joey had stopped looking back. Well, mostly. The town, with its welcoming community, had been a wonderful surprise and she wanted to stay. But jobs like hers were hard to come by, especially around there, so keeping the owners happy had to be one of her top priorities—not an easy one to accomplish. She needed to stay focused on that.

Joey had negotiated room and board into her contract for the first six months only because she'd never planned to stay in town that long. Carrying her groceries inside in a discreet Bloomingdale's bag—it wouldn't do to let the patrons know the manager lived in the hotel—Joey stopped at the front desk.

"Hi, Rose. How's it going today?"

"Good so far. Isn't this your day off?"

She chuckled. "Yes, but is there really ever a day off for management?"

Rose laughed. "No, I guess not. By the way, John got one of the two rooms fixed and ready for the festival."

"That's the best news I've heard today." Not quite as good as watching Ethan do the walk of shame back into the store, but close. "If I give up my room, that means I only need to figure out what to do with two reservations."

"Where will you sleep?"

"I'll find someone's couch to flop on. Can't be too hard just for a weekend, right?"

"That's kind of above and beyond, isn't it?" Rose leaned on the counter. "I was thinking about taking some hotel management courses, but seeing how hard you work, I'm not so sure now."

"The job has its rewards. You should look into it. I think you'd make a great manager." Joey meant it. Rose had backed her up so many times, she considered her an assistant. Now, if Joey could just talk the owner into the title and pay raise to go with it.

"Well, math and numbers aren't my strong point."

"Some courses relate to the business end of things, but honestly, I think you could do it. At least think about it."

"'kay. You hanging around?"

"I'll be in my room for a while, then I'm going to try to get a run in if the rain holds off. Feel free to call me if you have any issues."

"Will do, boss. Hopefully, I won't have to. You work too hard and deserve some downtime."

"Downtime? What's that?" Joey laughed and punched the elevator button. Once in her room, she set the groceries down on the desk. This room had worked for her, mostly because she'd spruced it up to her liking. The bed sported her own light, airy quilt and the bright throw over the dull brown sofa added color to the place. A small bookshelf next to the desk held her favorite stories and her college books. To keep from having to look at the standard hotel pictures, she'd covered them with cheerful fabrics to give the place a joyful, happy look. She'd done everything she could to make it homey, but in the end, it was still a hotel room. The timing seemed right to look for more permanent digs in Willow Bay. Find a place of her own. She had just enough money left to cover a down payment, and it would be nice to feel settled.

A glance out the window verified it wasn't raining

yet, so Joey changed into her running gear and headed for the beach and a long run next to the surf.

Clouds boiled over the water and further out, they were dark with rain. If she was lucky, she'd get back before they came ashore. The cold didn't bother her as she'd warm up quickly while running. Having lived inland her entire life, Joey found she loved the salt air and sea breezes. Even the winter storms didn't diminish how much she'd come to care for this town. Today's breeze, though, was creeping into the small craft advisory range and kept trying to nudge her away from the water and closer to the dunes.

Halfway through her run, she turned back and saw she wasn't the only crazy person on the beach this afternoon. Willow Bay's mayor jogged in her direction. Joey waved at Josh Morgan and he stopped near her, hands on knees as he caught his breath.

"Hey, Mayor," Joey said.

"Josh, please. I don't stand on ceremony. No one does around here."

"But you're due the respect. Especially with this festival that I hear was your brainchild."

He nodded. "Yep. It's going to be the death of me, too."

"Uh oh. Problems?"

"Just last-minute fires to put out."

"Managing fires is my specialty. Need any help?"

"Over and above the flyers you designed, along with the table banners for each vendor?"

Joey shrugged. "I like graphic arts and helping out."

"We're grateful. How's the lodge? Ready for festival weekend?"

"Not quite. We will be by then, though." She crossed her fingers, praying she was right. "We're jam-packed that weekend."

"Everyone is."

"Great news for the town."

Josh straightened, the pride on his face both earned and deserved. "Yes, it is."

A raindrop plopped on Joey's hat. "Downpour coming. We'd better get back."

They jogged in companionable silence to the main road onto the beach from town.

"Heading to your wife's shop?" Joey asked. Dana Morgan owned Tangerine Treasures, the town's biggest gift store.

"Yes," he said. "Dana's working half-time these days, so I'm taking her home."

"How's she doing?"

"Getting uncomfortable, but man, pregnancy looks amazing on her."

"Yes. I noticed the last time I was in the shop. Well, remember my offer. If you need any help, holler. You've got my cell number."

"I will." With a wave, Josh headed inland to the shop.

More drops plunked down around Joey and she sped up, sliding inside the back door of the lodge just as the heavens broke loose. Her attempt to sneak to her room so no one would see her sweaty and rain-soaked face failed when Rose called out to her.

"Problem, boss."

So much for that day off. Joey slipped behind the desk and sank into a chair hidden in an alcove. "What's up?"

"You know that room I said was ready to go?"

"It isn't?"

The look on Rose's face answered Joey's question. Damn.

"The floor beneath the tiles is mushy. John thinks water got under there before this last incident. He pulled up a few tiles and the wood underneath is rotten. The whole floor needs replacing."

Mr. Reynolds wasn't going to like this. Joey had to coax money from him for anything more than basic repairs. She needed that room because the lodge was already fully booked. That festival, and its advertising, had really brought people to the winter coast.

"Okay, let me think on it. We've still got a week. If anyone cancels, don't tap that waiting list until we find space for the three we have to relocate. I'll be in my room if you need me."

"Will do."

Joey made it to her room unseen, pulled off the wet clothes, and hopped in the shower, all the while thinking through solutions. Even if she gave up her own room, she'd still be three rooms shy. Damn. She'd just have to put the word out and ask the other places in town to give her first shot at any cancellations. Looked like she'd be making calls that afternoon.

After making herself a turkey, cream cheese, and cranberry sandwich—her favorite—she sat down at her computer to play with pictures. Graphic arts had always interested her and she'd almost chosen that direction in college. Right up until her parents pulled the plug and enrolled her in hotel management courses. She'd go back for that graphic arts degree one of these days. For now, she was proud of her job and Pacific Lodge. She'd been working on a new logo she wanted to pitch to Reynolds. With the rain outside, it was the perfect task to clear her mind. Then, she'd make those calls.

Hours later, Joey stood and stretched. The logo redesign was coming along and even though she hadn't found the three rooms she needed, she'd put the word out. Not hungry, and with worry over the rooms making her stomach churn, Joey crawled into bed and turned out the lights. Maybe tomorrow would offer better insights.

At this point, all she could do was hope and pray.

~ ~ ~

Gladys contemplated the heavy rain from her comfortable chair in the parlor of her house. There would be no strolling around town today. She was getting too old to be out in this foul weather, forecast to last overnight and into tomorrow.

The weekend weather didn't look good either. Rain, rain, and more rain. Thank goodness the festival was next weekend. That little brainstorm of the mayor's was turning into quite a boon for local businesses. Gladys knew she'd made the right choice when she'd pushed for Josh Morgan to step up and run Willow Bay. Of course, all of that pushing had been in the background. A word here, a nudge there. Never giving anyone the chance to figure out who really ran her town.

Because that's how she thought of Willow Bay, as her town. She'd never felt at home anywhere until she'd come there. No one knew who she was beyond her persona, and that was fine by her. If they knew, they'd treat her differently. Gladys was quite happy with all the friends she'd made here and had no plans to change anything anytime soon.

She'd helped this town thrive, both through nudges and donations. And she'd helped it grow. At least two of the couples she'd brought together would soon have babies.

Gladys gave herself a happy hug. She loved babies. She'd never been able to have one of her own, so she'd adopted this town. Unbeknownst to them, of course. Yes, everything was fine just the way it was.

Her phone rang and she picked it up, uttering a carefully modulated hello until she knew who was on the other end. She'd never been one for that caller identification stuff. It made life too dull. She liked surprises.

"Hello, Gladys."

"Henry, how nice to hear from you. How are you?"

"I'm doing as well as I can be. You?"

"As spry as ever. Though the rain is putting a damper on my travels today."

"I still don't understand your need for subterfuge. Willow Bay should know who's helped them all these years."

"You don't have to understand. You just have to manage my money."

There was a silence on the other end of the line.

"Is everything okay, Henry?"

"Yes and no. I'd like to come talk to you in person. There are some things we need to discuss."

To have Henry, her oldest and dearest friend, see her in this frumpy state? Well, that was *not* going to happen. "If you have something to say to me, you can say it right here on the phone."

"It's been ages since we last dined together."

"We dined together just last week."

"Over the phone, in our separated abodes. You've never even told me where you live. I have to send your mail to a post office box."

A post office box that Luke, Willow Bay's handyman and the only one who knew she had a home, checked for her.

"Henry, what is this all about? You've never minced words with me before, yet I feel like you're holding something back."

"George is dead."

The stab to Gladys's heart surprised her. She'd left her husband years ago, unwilling to put up with the choices he'd made.

"Gladys?"

"I'm here. Just… digesting."

"You're officially a widow."

"I haven't been part of George's life for a long, long time, Henry. You know that."

"I also know you never actually divorced the man."

She almost dropped the phone. "How the hell could you know that?"

"Because I was George's friend, too, and he confided in me."

Damn that man. Always sticking his nose in her business, even from beyond the grave.

"How come you never divorced him, Gladys? I've never known why."

Because if she divorced her husband, she'd have to think about the feelings she had for someone else and how she could act on them. And she couldn't act on them. She couldn't take the chance.

"George and I had an agreement and it worked for us. Just because we didn't see eye-to-eye didn't mean we lacked affection for one another." An affection that made her chest ache with this news.

"I think there's more to the story than you're telling me, my dear."

My dear. He'd used that term with her for years. If only he meant it.

"I know it wasn't easy for you to tell me about George. Thank you."

"There's more, but I'd rather discuss the rest in person."

"Sorry, but that's out of the question. What else is there to talk about?"

"Well, for starters, other than some charity bequeaths and a small inheritance for me, George left the bulk of his estate to you."

"That rat bastard."

Henry laughed—loudly—on the other end of the phone.

"It's not funny. I don't need his money. And I don't want it. Just don't let anyone know about it. I'll sign any papers to gift it to charities. You pick them. Keep my name out of it."

"That's going to be a little hard to do."

The shoe was about to fall. Gladys could feel it like arthritis in her bones on a cold, rainy day. "What have you done, Henry?"

"Nothing, except to follow the instructions in George's will to the letter."

Gladys huffed at how long it was taking Henry to get to the point. "Spit it out. This isn't like you."

"I know. I just wanted to enjoy the moment. I sent a copy of George's will by courier, which you should get some time today. The will requires a press announcement."

The doorbell rang. "Hold on," Gladys said. "The courier's here."

She answered the door, completely forgetting that she never answered her door. That hardly anyone knew she lived there, including Henry.

Frowning, she kept her head down, signed for the package, and closed the door. She went back to her phone.

"How did you know where to send this?"

"George had given your address to a mail company and left me explicit instructions. Open the manilla envelope, Gladys."

When she did, her face blanched. "How could he do this to me?" she whispered.

Henry's voice softened. "He thought he was doing what was best for you."

"Oh, this is bad. This is very bad."

"Give me your address, Gladys. Let me come out

there. Let's talk about this. Everything will be fine."

"No. It won't. George has ruined everything. I need to think. I'll talk to you later." Gladys hung up the phone and stared at the press release. Two pictures, one of their wedding day and one taken the day she'd left. Along with a heartfelt plea to the world to forgive her. That he'd love her forever. That he forgave her. And that she should now follow her heart as he had followed his in staying married to her.

Silent tears dotted Gladys's cheeks as she finished reading. That damn fool had put their life out there for the whole world to know. A life she very much wanted to keep private, especially when it came to the people of Willow Bay.

Only one person in the town knew who she was. Gentle Luke, whose PTSD had gotten so much better since Gladys had paired him up with Jasmin. She was good for him, as he was for her. When Jasmin had come home to care for her ailing parents, he'd been there for her. Together, they'd cleared some major hurdles. Luke was a good man, and Gladys felt some guilt over making him keep her secret, even with Jasmin.

Now, it would all change. Everything she'd worked so hard for would be destroyed because of one lovesick fool. Damn it all to hell.

Gladys sat there well into the dark of night, grief slowly overtaking anger as she said goodbye to one of the nicest and most frustrating men she'd ever met.

CHAPTER FIVE

Saturday dawned overcast, but the chance of rain was minimal. It had rained overnight, which pleased Ethan because that ill-advised beach bonfire had less of a chance to catch something serious on fire, like the dune grass.

After spending Thursday and Friday resting and recovering, he was back at work without having to take any sick leave. Granted, he hadn't gotten half of what he usually liked to get done on his days off, and had, under orders, gone nowhere near the gym. He'd get back to that next time. Today, he'd come to work so Riley and Jeff could have the night off to enjoy the bonfire.

Sitting at his standard-issue metal desk, Ethan went over the personnel schedules for the next weekend. Festival weekend. The whole town was buzzing about this damn thing. He just wanted it over with, with no dire happenings. Most of his guys wanted the weekend off to enjoy the festival, so they'd opted for a skeleton crew with everyone at the ready if a large-scale fire event happened.

Ethan would work all three days and take an extra

day or two off this week to accommodate that. No way he could stay away from the station during the festival, even if he wanted to.

"Hey, Chief. Got a minute?" Riley poked his head into the office.

"Sure."

Riley pushed the door open and turned one of the two chairs around, straddling it with his arms resting on what was now the front of the chair, his usual stance when he had a problem to solve.

Pushing back from his desk, Ethan crossed his arms and allowed Riley to say what he needed to say.

"You know the Chief's exam is coming up, right?" Riley said.

Of course, Ethan knew. He nodded. He'd put Riley up for a promotion and all that stood between the man and the title was this exam.

"Well, the test is a week from Tuesday."

"I know that."

"I, umm, don't have the best record with tests. I don't know what it is about them, but I sit and stare at the paper and my brain goes blank."

"Test anxiety is a real thing, buddy. Have you looked at ways to get past it?"

"Yeah. This is too important not to. There's the usual—plenty of sleep, healthy diet, things like that. They also say to study in an environment similar to where you'll be testing, to make the surroundings normal for you."

"The test will be administered in Olympia, so I'm not sure how that is possible."

"It's not, but I wondered if I could take over our conference room for the next week and a half. Use it for studying."

"We've got nothing scheduled. The room is yours."

"Would you help me study?"

"Anytime." Ethan meant it. Riley was his friend. He was also very good at his job and had earned this promotion. "If you'd like, I can grab one of the older tests and proctor a mock exam."

"That would be awesome. How about the Monday before the test?"

Ethan consulted his schedule. "I'm off, so that works well. We can meet here, run through the test, then maybe grab some lunch?"

"Perfect. You're a lifesaver, Ethan. Thanks."

"Anytime."

Riley put the chair back in place and left Ethan's office with a wave. As Ethan watched him go, he swore he'd do whatever he could to get Riley through that exam. The man deserved it.

Hours later, Ethan shut down his computer and sat back in his chair to stretch. Budgets sure meant a lot of paperwork. A glance at the darkness outside reminded him he was on duty tonight. Pushing up from the desk, he grabbed his coat, gloves, and hat and headed out. He'd prefer to have a fire truck near the bonfire, but after a conversation with Josh, Ethan caved and took his command vehicle instead. Better for public relations. Plus, it was only three minutes from the station to the beach site where the fire was set up.

Ethan would be a visible reminder to be careful, and he'd guard against anything that might go wrong. That was his job.

That was his life.

~~~

Joey walked down the beach in the dark. The clouds had disappeared. The moon was full and light glinted off the ocean waves, so seeing wasn't difficult. She left her flashlight in her pocket, preferring the ambiance of the crisp evening. Not much wind blew, unusual for any time at the beach, winter or summer. Still, the chill air bit, and she was glad she had a winter cap to keep her ears warm. Otherwise, she'd be tempted to go back to the lodge and hug a mug of hot cocoa. The hotel had a station set up in the lobby. Free cocoa on bonfire night. It was the small-town thing to do, even if her boss had refused when she suggested it. What he didn't know wouldn't hurt her, right?

Now, after dealing with issues all day, some minor, some not, and helping the front desk—even playing bellhop a couple of times—Joey was more than ready to relax for the evening. She had her phone on max volume so she'd hear if anyone called. Right now, a bonfire beckoned.

As she got closer, it appeared to her the whole town had turned out for this event. And doubled in size which meant tourists were here to enjoy the camaraderie too. That boded well for next weekend. She'd heard how financially depressed the town had been last year, when the winter rains wouldn't stop. The Beer and Chowder Festival had been born from that circumstance and next weekend's event would be the first annual celebration. Seeing the crowd here tonight, a full week before the festival, was encouraging.

"Hi," Josh Morgan said, walking up to Joey with his arm around his wife.

"Hi, Mayor. Dana. Looks like the bonfire's a huge success."

Josh laughed. "Who knew people would brave the cold for this? I thought it was a cockamamie idea— "

Dana socked him in the shoulder. "Hey, this was my idea."

"Like I said, cockamamie, but it worked." He hugged his wife close and she nestled into him.

"Next year, we're going to do it the night before the festival," Dana said.

"We wanted to see if it would be a go or a bust before tying the two together." He smiled at his wife who looked up at him, communicating on some nonverbal level that made Joey put a hand over her chest to ease the ache. What would it be like, to share warmth and communication on that level? She'd never had that.

"I think that's a great idea," Joey said. "I'm glad everyone's happy with the kickoff event."

"Not everyone," Dana said. "The fire chief is stomping around like a grinch."

Joey searched the area, well-lit by the fire. Her gaze landed on the tall, scowling man, arms crossed over his chest, watching the events. Not participating, but a stalwart watchdog, committed to keeping everyone safe.

"Think you can get him to relax, maybe turn that frown into a smile?" Josh asked.

"Me? Why me?"

"Well, he did get tased trying to keep you safe."

"I was perfectly fine on my own," she huffed, then chewed her bottom lip. "Is that story all over town?"

"Pretty much."

"Oh, God."

"Don't worry." Dana waved in dismissal. "Gossip only lasts around here until the next juicy bit comes along. It'll be forgotten. Eventually."

"Well, trust me, there's nothing between the chief and me. That night was both the beginning and the end, so I'm not the person you should ask to make him smile." Joey was beginning to think no one could accomplish that.

Dana stepped closer and hugged Joey, whispering in her ear. "Give him time. Let him wrap his head around the possibilities and he'll come around. Our men always do."

"You sharing some secret formula for getting a

man to grovel at your feet, wife?"

"As a matter of fact, yes." She moved back into her husband's arms, a hand covering her protruding belly beneath her coat. "Look at how well it works."

Josh laughed. "Come on. We must circulate and remind folks why Willow Bay is the best place in the world to visit."

"Yes, husband." They waved goodbye and headed into the throng of people around the bonfire.

Joey watched them as melancholy settled over her like fog on the water. Maybe someday, she'd have that. A real relationship, not a dictatorial one like her parents and Robert had planned for her. Someday. She'd hold onto that hope.

Shaking herself, she marched over to Square Peg's beer and pretzel cart. Like the donation cup next to the cocoa station at the hotel, the proceeds from sales would be donated to the women's shelter that had just been enlarged and was too full already.

"I need a beer," she said to Bernie, the redheaded owner of the pizza parlor.

"So do I," Bernie answered, then grinned and placed a hand on her growing belly. "Have one for me, okay?" She handed Joey an IPA.

"Gladly. How've you been feeling?"

"Bloated and tired. Beyond that, amazing. Who knew pregnancy could feel so good?"

"Enjoy it while you can. I believe sleep loss is in your future."

Her husband, Paul, wrapped his arms around Bernie from behind. "We're already sleep deprived. This baby likes to kick at night. A lot."

"Yes," Bernie said, smiling. "He or she does."

"Whatever comes along, we'll handle it together, eh?" Paul said.

"Definitely. You get the middle of the night

feedings, I'll take nap times."

They all laughed and Joey wandered closer to the bonfire, grabbing a spot on a log as the melancholy tried to settle in again. Why was she wishing she had a special someone in her life? She'd never wanted it before. Robert had cured her of that. So why now? Joey glanced in Ethan's direction and found him staring at her. Raising her chin, she stared back defiantly.

"Is this seat taken?"

Joey looked up into the greenest eyes she'd ever seen and a ready smile on a face that looked like it smiled often.

"It's not. You're welcome to it."

"Awesome. I always try to sit next to the prettiest lady at a party."

"Just so you know," Joey said with a laugh, "flattery will not get you, well, anything."

He clutched his chest with the hand not holding a can of beer. "I'm mortally wounded. That, my lady, was a well-deserved compliment."

"Then I thank you, sir. But how can you even tell? I'm bundled from head to toe."

"Because I've seen you before, sweet lady."

Wow. This guy really laid it on thick. Right now, Joey needed this kind of harmless fun. She loved it. "Where have you seen me, kind sir? I don't remember meeting you."

The hand on his chest made a twisting motion. "And the knife goes further in. I saw you the day of your supposed fire."

Joey replayed the day in her head. She didn't remember him among the guests. That meant— "You're a firefighter."

He pulled the imaginary dagger from his heart. "So, you do remember me."

She scrunched up her face. "Well…"

"Alas, beautiful woman, your eyes were reserved for another."

Like that had done her any good. "He was giving me crap for not following the rules."

They both glanced at the deepening scowl on the face of the man in question.

"Ah yes," he said. "The man is a stickler for rules. And regulations. He really doesn't differentiate."

"Ever?"

Cute guy shrugged. "Not that I've seen. I'm Riley, by the way. And you are the breath of fresh air I've been looking for."

Joey's smile widened. She'd forgotten how good for the psyche it could be to flirt with someone. "Hi, Riley. I'm Joey."

Riley picked up her gloved hand, removed the glove one finger at a time, and kissed the top of her hand like a knight stating his intention to woo her. Then he put the glove back on. One finger at a time.

"Uh oh."

"What?"

"Don't look now," Riley said, "but the wicked warlock is on his way over."

Of course, Joey looked. How could she not? Ethan was bearing down on them like a grizzly who'd just had his dinner stolen.

While Riley stood, Joey kept her seat. She'd be damned if she'd bend to the glare of a man who wasn't interested.

Ethan stopped in front of Riley, legs spread for balance, arms crossed over his chest. "Riley? What are you doing?"

"Having a nice chat with the prettiest woman here. What are you doing, boss?"

His jaw gnashing, Ethan looked at Joey, then back at Riley. "Came to say that if you want to finish tonight's shift for me, you can. As chief."

Riley's eyes widened, then turned to slits. This must be way outside the norm. Joey watched the two of them, her interest piqued.

"I can't work now and you know it," Riley said, holding up his beer. "You should have asked me earlier." Riley stared daggers at Ethan for a long minute, then turned to Joey, breathing deep, visibly trying to get a hold of himself. "Sorry. I'm suddenly not feeling like good company, but I'd love to finish this conversation another day. Okay if I reach out to you?"

From the edge of her vision, Joey saw Ethan's stern jaw moving side to side again. What was this about? Riley seemed pissed about being offered the work when he couldn't take it on. Did all firefighters love their work this much or was there something else going on? This couldn't be about her, could it?

Putting on her widest smile for Riley's sake, Joey nodded. "Reach out to me at the lodge. I'd love to continue our conversation. It was very nice to meet you, Riley."

"You," Riley said to Ethan. "Low blow, man."

"I know it was," Ethan gritted out under his breath. "Let's talk tomorrow."

"Good idea." With an imaginary tip of his hat toward Joey, Riley stalked off.

By the time Ethan turned back to Joey, she was fed up. She stood and stepped right in front of him. "I'm not sure what all that was about, but it's pretty obvious you just pissed off one of your men."

"That's between Riley and me."

"Not when it's done to cut my conversation with the man short." Joey poked a finger in his chest. "Why did you do that, Ethan?"

He remained mute, which ticked her off even more. "Why are you here?" she asked.

"Keeping an eye on the bonfire," Ethan said with a quick glance behind him.

She poked him again. "That's not what I meant and you know it. You inserted yourself into my conversation with Riley. I asked you if you wanted to go to the bonfire. You. Said. No. Not even no thank you. Just no. So, what was that with Riley just now?"

Ethan grimaced. Discomfort, confusion, and a bit of his usual pissed-offedness rolled off him in waves. Apparently, even talking to her went against his better judgment. Despite her own anger, it stung, big time. Damn.

"I honestly don't know," he said.

"Huh?" Joey rubbed her chest, so stuck on that sting that she didn't hear him.

"I don't know what that was with Riley." At least now, he showed a touch of remorse. Still—

Joey poked him again. "You said you didn't want to date me."

"I didn't say I didn't want to date you. I said you were a distraction I couldn't afford."

"Same thing, in my book." She stepped back so she could look him square in the eye. "You don't get a say in who I do or do not associate with. Either you adapt or get the hell out of my life."

Time to go before things went from bad to worse. Or, God forbid, the tears gathering behind her eyes let loose. Angrier than she'd been in a long time, Joey picked up her beer. She was done with the bonfire. Intent on tossing the can in the trash and walking home, Joey almost missed Ethan's statement.

"Have dinner with me."

Joey froze mid-step. Had she heard him correctly? The bonfire crackled behind them and kids raced across the sand, even in the dark, screams and laughter abounding. She got all that, so her hearing was fine.

She turned to stare at Ethan, somewhat mollified by his unease, and walked back to stand in front of him, crossing her arms over her chest just like his pose.

"Did you just ask me out, Chief?"

"You know I did." The intensity of his gaze, lit by the blazing fire, burned through her.

"Why?"

Ethan's nostrils flared. "Accepting the dare you tossed me?"

Her ire fading, Joey laughed. The upward lilt of Ethan's last word made it a question, not a statement. The man wasn't ready to think through why he'd really asked her out. There was an attraction between them. A strong one. One that he wasn't ready to acknowledge. He would, though. He just didn't know it yet. But Joey did.

Stepping back, she canted her head to the side and gazed up at him. "Well, Chief, I believe I'll take that dare. When and where?"

"Monday night?" Ethan suggested.

"Works for me."

"Monday it is. I'll pick you up at the lodge at seven."

"Deal."

With a sharp nod, Ethan stomped off. Joey watched him with mixed emotions. What had she gotten herself into? The bigger question, maybe, was what Ethan had just taken on.

Joey grinned, tossing her beer in the trash, and headed down the beach toward the lodge. Oh, this was going to be fun.

CHAPTER SIX

Even though he'd taken the day off, Ethan stopped by the station. He had some fences to mend. One fence, anyhow. He stepped into his office staring at his already occupied chair.

"Good morning, Riley. Enjoying the chair?"

Riley twirled a full 360 degrees. "Yes, I am. Hoping to sit here after my promotion." He leaned on the desk. "I think you owe me an apology first."

Ethan nodded. "I do."

Once they'd switched positions and Ethan sat in his chair, he put his arms on his desk, threading his fingers together. "I shouldn't have done that to you last night and I'm sorry."

"Well, damn. I didn't think you'd start off with sincere."

"What did you expect?"

"Blustering."

"Then you don't know me as well as you think. You were right last night. It was a low blow. I shouldn't have done that." He'd hit Riley right where it hurt as he was studying for his promotion test. Not fair. Not at all.

Riley sat back in the chair he'd taken on the far

side of Ethan's desk. "Wow. You've really got it bad for this woman."

Ethan stifled the scowl that edged onto his face. "Not going to talk about it."

"You'd better talk to someone one of these days or you're going to blow. You're a powder keg."

Right now, he was. "You accepting my apology?"

"Definitely. Thank you, Ethan. I appreciate you coming in, not waiting."

Looking out the window at the winter gray, Ethan was pleased to find the pavement still dry. In fact, it wasn't supposed to rain for a couple days. "Thought I might go house-hunting."

"You? Put down roots?"

"I've been staying in that apartment too long."

"You mean that minimalistic, barely humanized apartment?"

Squinting at the man, Ethan nodded. "I'm planning to stick around so it might be time."

"Wow. That's a big leap. Good for you, man."

Shrugging, Ethan grinned at Riley. "Open houses don't generally start until the afternoon. I've got some time. Want to go work through some study materials?"

"You bet I do."

"Until you get a call out, of course."

"Of course."

They managed two hours of hard work before the claxons blared. Ethan jumped up.

"Not your duty, Chief."

"Yes, but— "

"We've got this. Go. Find a house."

Riley raced to the truck bay. Ethan followed, watching the fire truck exit, sirens blaring. Not able to bring himself to leave, he paced, but it wasn't long before his phone sounded.

Looks like a minor accident out past the cranberry bogs.

He appreciated Riley texting him. More than once, Ethan had joined a situation on his day off. Hard to stay away when lives were in danger.

Back in his truck, he pulled up one of the local realtor sites on his phone to check the open houses that day. The first one, which he was most interested in, wasn't too far and had just started.

In a few minutes—the place was nice and close to the firehouse—Ethan pulled up to the modern-looking, gray and black bungalow. Three bedrooms, two baths, an off-center slant to the roof. Ethan liked the style and loved the location. Walking in, he saw more that he liked. Reminiscent of a mid-century modern, it was open concept with dark granite in the kitchen and polished concrete floors. A couple wandered around, chatting about aspects of the house.

"Chief Walker," a voice said behind him.

Ethan turned. "Hi, Becca. Is this your listing?" Becca Strong owned her own realty company. Ethan had done the walk-through inspection of her new offices.

"Sure is." She brushed her blonde highlighted hair back, a thoughtful smile curving her mouth. "You finally looking to settle down?"

"Just looking to see what's out there at the moment."

"Well," Becca said, twining her arm in his. "Let me show you this little gem."

Someone exited what must be the bedroom hallway. Someone who also had blonde hair, coupled with the bluest of blue eyes that had invaded his dreams. Joey was there?

She grinned, but her smile faded when she saw the lock Becca had on his arm.

"Umm, I can look around on my own," he said, trying to disentangle himself.

"Nonsense. This is what I do. And, if you don't like this place, it will give me a chance to get to know you better. To help you find the perfect place, of course."

Becca pulled him toward the kitchen. When he glanced back, Joey was watching them, curiosity in her large, blue eyes. Then she disappeared out the front door. He wanted to go after her, which was impossible with the realtor latched onto his arm.

" —all new appliances. And black accents. Very masculine, don't you think?"

He still watched the door.

"Ethan?"

"Sorry. What did you say?"

"I said these accents are very manly, aren't they?" She ran her hand slowly over the elongated faucet.

"Umm, yes."

She grabbed his hand. "Let's check out the bedroom."

His thoughts still on Joey, Ethan let Becca tug him down the hall. So, Joey had been serious about house hunting, which meant she planned to stick around. Deep inside, in places he didn't know he could feel things, Ethan liked that idea.

Several minutes passed before he could wrangle free of Becca's interest, and he'd had to give her his phone number so she could let him know about new listings. Or so she claimed. Ethan walked outside, taking a long breath as he turned to stare at the house. Becca was close to him in age, only a couple years younger. She'd made motions that she'd like to be more than acquaintances. Ethan had never taken her up on her not-so-subtle offers. First, because he didn't date. Second, Becca sparked nothing in him. She was pretty in a perfectly made-up kind of way, but he just didn't feel it. Not like with Joey.

Heading for his truck, he found the subject of his thoughts leaning against it.

"Hey," Joey said.

"Hey," he answered, giving in to the grin his mouth wouldn't deny.

"You like the house?"

"It's nice, but the first one I've looked at. You?"

"This is the first place I've looked at, too."

"What did you think of it?"

Joey glanced past him to the house. "Well appointed, but a bit too modern for my tastes."

Ethan looked back. Becca watched them from the window.

"I kind of liked the house. Orderly."

"Sterile," countered Joey.

He chuckled. "We might have different tastes in houses."

"You know what? We really should look for houses together. Are you working tomorrow?"

"Well, no, but I don't think— "

"Come on. If we like different things, we won't be competing. And it'll be more fun together."

Joey's eyes sparkled with excitement and Ethan was powerless to say no. "Where are you living now?" he asked.

"A room in the lodge. That gets old after a while, no matter how much I personalize it."

"How do you personalize a hotel room?" He took a step closer to her.

"Oh, with my own things." Her voice had gone breathless. "My quilt, throw blankets, colorful rugs." Her eyes seemed to be focused on his lips. "Oh, and I covered the hotel pictures with bold cloth."

He took another step closer. "I can't picture that."

"You'll have to come see it sometime."

They both froze at her words. The image of being

with Joey in a room where the biggest piece of furniture was a bed sent instant heat through Ethan's veins. Heat that sped up his breathing and made the outside world disappear, leaving only him and Joey, there, in that moment.

When her tongue slipped out to lick her lips, he almost groaned.

"You are the most distracting woman I've ever met." Ethan reached for the collar of her coat and snugged it tighter against the winter cold. "I think you could distract me from a blizzard, Joey Sanderson."

The sparkle in those wide, expressive eyes kindled a flame that held him captive. There was nowhere he wanted to be more than right there, with Joey.

"Someday… " she whispered.

"Someday what?" Her knit hat, complete with pom-pom, didn't keep him from smelling the freshness of her shampoo. She was back to the flowery scent.

"Someday… oh, who cares." Joey grabbed Ethan's jacket and pulled him down. Lips locked with lips, intense and exhilarating. He deepened the kiss, nudging her lips open. Soft and yielding, she answered his request with a welcoming caress of her tongue.

As with life, Joey threw herself into the kiss and took everything Ethan gave her. Her hands moved up his arms, over his shoulders, her fingers twining together against the back of his neck.

His hands snuck beneath her coat, wrapping around her, moving up and down her back, pulling her in tighter. To him. To his staggering need.

She groaned against his lips, a sound that vibrated through his body. His lips crushed hers and still, she begged him for more. And more. He was drowning in her essence, her truth. He wanted her as much as she wanted him. Ethan vibrated with need.

Wait. The vibration wasn't him. It was his pocket.

Ethan broke the kiss, leaving them both gasping for air, and dug his phone out.

"Shit."

"What?"

Her breathless voice tugged at his raging hard-on. "I can't. I'm sorry. I've been called in." Three times they'd reached out and he hadn't noticed any of them. Damn it. "This is why I don't do relationships, Joey. I lose focus. I'm sorry, but this just can't happen."

Without waiting for a reply, Ethan gently moved her back from his truck, jumped in, and sped off. A fire had broken out near the hospital in Aberdeen. A big one. He'd lost time not hearing his phone. Damn it all to hell. How had he gotten so distracted?

Ethan flew down the road, vowing again to never let distraction stop him from his duty. He buried his regret deep, but not deep enough to quell the ache in his heart. That would probably take a long, long time.

~~~

Joey walked to her car and leaned against it on unsteady feet, not feeling the chilly day. Fingers against her lips, she still felt Ethan's touch. Correction, his possession. Or hers. Hell, she didn't even know who took lead on that kiss. As soon as their lips touched, she forgot everything except him. Nothing else mattered but getting closer to him.

And then he disappeared. Granted, he had a good reason. That didn't make her feel any better. Not only did he desert her after the best kiss she'd ever had, he'd said it wouldn't happen again. Damn. That couldn't be the only time she'd ever feel that way. The only close moment with Ethan. Her brain already wanted to get to know him better. Now her body wanted that too. Kisses, time together, more kisses. Was dinner tomorrow off or on?

Her phone chimed and Joey answered it without

looking as she climbed into her car and started it up.

"Hey, boss," Rose said. "I've got some news you're going to like."

With her heart still beating wildly and her head wrapped in the fog of Ethan's kiss, Joey couldn't figure out what Rose was saying. "What?"

"I think your room woes are solved for this weekend. Or close to."

Room woes. Oh! "The overbooking? Did we get a couple cancellations?" *Please*, she prayed.

"One."

"That still leaves two."

"Yes, but John called in a few favors and will have one of the waterlogged rooms ready to go by Friday."

"That's awesome!" Joey thumped on her dash and let out a few hoots of joy. "I'm going to owe him big time."

"Oh, he says you'll be paying. Subcontractors, though. He's just doing his job."

"I owe them all. So, we're down to one room short."

"Weeeelllll, the Water Lily just called. They have a cancellation and offered it to us."

"Oh, my God. Take it. Take it."

"I already did. It's going to cost."

"I don't care. Wow, that means we're covered. Rose, I'm going to fight to get you promoted to assistant manager as soon as this festival is over. You've made my day."

"That would be so cool. Do you think it's possible?"

Joey hadn't planned to mention anything until she had a conversation with the notoriously stingy Mr. Reynolds, but she'd gotten caught up in the moment. "I honestly don't know, but I've been thinking about this for a while and you deserve it, so I'm going to fight for you."

"Thanks, boss. That means a lot."

When the call ended, Joey tossed her phone on the passenger seat and leaned her head against the headrest. What a rollercoaster day. The boss had his rooms without the lodge having to cancel a reservation. No one was upset.

Well, Mr. Reynolds probably would be when he saw the financials for this fix. Joey didn't care. They'd done it, and made the weekend much nicer for a family in dire need of some happiness.

A tap on her window startled Joey. The realtor, Becca, stood bundled up outside. Joey lowered the window.

"Are you all right?" Becca asked.

"Yes. I'm fine."

"You were in your car for quite a while without pulling out. Then I heard you screaming."

Joey laughed. "Happy screams. I was on the phone and found out a work problem has been solved. But wow, thank you for checking on me. That's very kind."

"That's the Willow Bay way." Becca chewed her lower lip. She looked like she had more to say but the silence rolled on.

"Well, thank you. I'd better be going," Joey said.

"Are you seeing Ethan Walker?" Becca blurted out the words in a rush.

So, Joey was right. The woman *had* been flirting with Ethan. How should she answer this? A simple yes might get Becca off Ethan's trail, but Joey didn't work like that. Fair was fair, so she chose honesty. "Not really." Oh, that was way too honest. "Sorry. With Ethan, it's complicated. I'd have to say, right now, that we're friends." Okay, that was a stretch.

"With benefits? I saw you kissing."

"Honestly, I don't know what we are." Joey looked

at Becca. Her cheeks were flushed by more than the cold sea air. "You're interested in him."

The woman's eyes gained a touch of fire. "Have been since he first came to town."

A twinge of hurt snuck past Joey's rib cage and lodged in her heart. Ethan may not want her, but imagining him with someone else filled her with dread. "Well, he doesn't seem very interested in me, so I'll just wish you luck and get on my way."

As her window rolled up and Becca stepped back, Joey tightened her hands on the wheel and pulled away from the curb. She could have warned Becca that Ethan wasn't interested in dating anyone. Instead, she'd kept that information to herself and that didn't sit right. Hanging with Ethan, or trying to, turned Joey into someone she didn't recognize. She did not manipulate people. That's what her parents did. What Robert did. That wasn't her way.

Against her better judgment, she turned around and drove back down the street, catching Becca before she went inside.

"Becca?" Joey called as the window rolled down. "Just so you know, Ethan says he isn't interested in dating period. That he's married to his job."

Coming closer to the car, Becca asked, "Are you trying to scare me off him?"

"No. Not at all. That's not how I do things. I just wanted you to have the same information I have. Even playing field. For your sake. And for Ethan's." *For mine.*

"Thanks. I think."

Mission accomplished, Joey headed out, not stopping until she got to the lodge. No more house-hunting today. Time to curl up with some mindless television and forget that Ethan Walker even existed. In her room, she decided it was five o'clock somewhere and pulled a beer out of the fridge. Toasting the gods to keep Ethan and the crews safe at the fire, she threw her pillows against the wall and sank back against them, pulling the blankets up to ward off the chill.

An hour later, with the TV still dark and no more than a sip gone from the beer, Joey sat up. She did not give in this easily. She'd taught herself to fight for what she wanted, so why was she laying there feeling sorry for herself?

Joey had to convince Ethan that he was wrong. That they were worth a chance. He needed that balance between work and life or he'd become a shell of the person she knew he could be. With a new resolve, she picked up her phone. No. It would be too easy for him to say no to a text. This should be in person. Grabbing her coat and keys, she ran out, fighting off the logic in her head all the way to the fire station.

Inside, a woman sat at the desk, her shoulder-length bob swaying in time to the country music playing from her phone.

The music ended. "Hi, can I help you?"

"I'm looking for Ethan—Chief Ethan Walker."

"He's out on a call. Can I help you or give him a message?"

Her name tag said Mary, and Joey remembered the pranked fire alarm at the lodge. She'd seen a female firefighter pull her hat off just as they left. "You're part of his crew, aren't you?"

The woman smiled. "Yes. I'm Mary." She put a bandaged foot up on the desk. "Stuck here with an ankle sprain."

"I'm sorry. Bet that hurts."

"Not as much as being here and not there."

"They're still out on that fire?"

"Yes. Will be for hours, though the tides changed and they're getting the upper hand."

"No injuries?"

"None that I know of." Mary eyed Joey up and down. "You're the lodge owner that gave the chief a hard time."

Joey grinned. "Guilty as charged."

Expecting Mary to toss her out on her ass, Joey couldn't believe it when the woman started howling with laughter.

"One of the best moments of the year. We're still talking about it."

"Um, you don't like Ethan?"

"Love him, at least as a boss. He's got our backs. We all know that. We just wish he'd take the thorns out of his ass and relax once in a while."

It was Joey's turn to hoot with laughter.

While they bonded over a shared desire to get Chief Ethan Walker to chill out, Joey asked for paper and pen.

"If I write a note for the chief, can you give it to him?" Joey asked.

"I'd be happy to. I'll even give you an envelope so you can seal it." She rooted through the drawers as Joey wrote.

Ethan,

I want more. Of you. I think we'd be good together and not too distracting. At the very least, we'd have some fun. Meet me at the C&C Café tomorrow at 11. We'll have a late brunch, then go house hunting together. We've already got dinner on the calendar, so let's make a day of it.

She signed her name and handed the note to Mary.

"I'll put it on his desk so he should see it as soon as he gets back. He'll have reports to write up."

"Thanks, Mary."

Having done all she could, Joey headed back to the lodge, this time choosing the dining room for dinner, along with some wine to quell her nerves while she waited.

She'd barely dug into her beef stew and homemade rolls when her phone pinged with a text.

No.

Ethan. One stubborn, pig-headed, pain-in-the-ass. Joey set her phone down with exaggerated care, pushing it across the table until it was almost out of reach. She picked up her wine glass and took a sip, then a gulp. She set it down and dug back into her stew. All the actions of a normal person, not a woman planning revenge on the man who'd just shut her out. Completely. And revenge she would have. One way or the other, Ethan was going to get to know her, and vice versa. If he decided at that point he didn't want to date her, so be it. Using his job as an excuse wasn't an answer Joey planned to accept.

Done eating, she pushed the plate back and finished the last sip of her very good wine. Then, she reached for her phone and sent a one-word response to Mr. No.

Chicken.

CHAPTER SEVEN

Joey got to the café early on Monday, grateful she had the day off. Hell, she'd hardly slept. She could have been there when it opened at five a.m. Being a Monday, she'd gone down to her office and worked, or tried to, for a few hours.

Now there she sat, her finger thumbing the file folder she'd set on the table, waiting to see if Ethan took the bait. If he didn't, she planned to hunt him down and make him tell her to her face that he didn't want anything to do with her. Not that she'd believe it after that kiss. Her lips still tingled. No way he wasn't affected by that. By them. No way he hadn't lost the same sleep she had, thinking about that kiss.

She glanced at her faint reflection in the window, hoping the makeup covered the circles under her eyes. This had never happened to her before, being so consumed by a man who didn't want anything to do with her.

Eleven o'clock came and went and Joey figured she had her answer. Five minutes past the hour, after she'd ordered breakfast for one, a big truck with a fire department emblem in the window backed into the space right outside her window.

Resisting the urge to scream halleluiah, Joey couldn't quite tame the wide grin on her face as Ethan walked into the restaurant and glanced around until he found her. He settled across from her in the booth.

"Hi, Chief," said Connie, the matronly owner of the C&C Café. "Coffee?" She held up the carafe in her hand.

"Yes, please." Ethan turned over the mug on the table and waited while Connie poured, never taking his eyes off Joey.

"Your lady has already ordered."

With a deep scowl, Ethan told Connie he'd have his usual, then continued to stare at Joey, who continued to grin until Connie had walked beyond hearing distance. Although, with Connie's eavesdropping skills, who could tell if there was such a thing? She was legendary for knowing all sorts of clandestine Willow Bay facts.

Joey really, really wanted to mention the "your lady" comment, but judging by Ethan's scowl, she'd thought she'd better not push it.

"I don't take dares," Ethan said.

"And yet, you're here."

He clutched his coffee and looked out the window. "And yet, I'm here."

The man looked serious. And sad. She could see shadows under his eyes that hadn't been there before. *What is it, Ethan Walker? What's holding you back?*

When he looked back at her, the briefest hint of longing flashed like fire in his eyes, then disappeared. "I can't date you."

"Why not?"

"Because I need to remain focused. You distract me unlike anyone else ever has."

"There's got to be a middle ground, Ethan. All

work and no play makes Ethan a dull boy."

"Better dull than dead."

"What happened to you that you refuse to even try to find balance in your life?"

"Things I'd rather not talk about."

"Ever?"

"Probably."

Their food arrived. After Connie left, they both stared at their plates.

"Spend the day with me," Joey said.

"You're not listening to me."

"Yes, I am. Just the day, Ethan. We'll have breakfast, house hunt, maybe take a walk on the beach if the rain holds off, then have that dinner you promised me."

"Another dare."

"It seems to work with you."

"What's a day going to do? I'm telling you right now we can't go any further. I can't."

"The day, that's all. If, at the end of it, you can still say you don't want to see me again, I'll honor it. Take time to get to know me. Let me get to know you, and we'll go from there."

He sprinkled salt and pepper on his eggs and hashbrowns.

Joey did the same, giving him all the space he needed to think things through.

"All right," he finally said.

She wanted to whoop-whoop, but held herself in check. Barely. Her fists clenched in happiness beneath the table.

"By the end of dinner tonight, I *will* tell you that this can go no further. Understood?"

"Understood," she said, though nothing could diminish her happiness at this moment. She had an entire day to convince Ethan to give them a chance. An entire day! Joey dug into her plate with a zeal she hadn't felt until now.

After watching her for a few moments, Ethan picked up his fork and ate, too, a scowl still furrowing his brow.

~~~

A rare winter sunshine broke free of the clouds as they left the diner. Joey took that as a good sign. She glanced at her Mini, bright and tiny beside his truck. "I'm happy to drive."

Ethan eyed the vehicle. "I'll drive." There was no give in his voice.

Joey stepped back and surveyed Ethan from tip to toe. The man looked better than a man should. Even bundled in a rugged work jacket, he looked built and trim. His eyes, hooded by the WBFD cap he wore, watched her with guarded interest. Joey wanted to pull him down for the kiss she so badly wanted to repeat, but Ethan would put the kibosh on the day if she did. So instead, she let him open his truck door for her.

"Need a boost?"

Say yes. Say yes. With her eyes on the prize—getting Ethan to relax and enjoy their day together—Joey jumped into the truck without assistance, gratified to see a hint of regret in his dark eyes. He didn't say anything, just shut the door and went to the driver's side.

Opening her file folder, Joey pulled out her printed list of potential houses.

"You're organized," Ethan said.

She side-eyed him. "Don't sound so surprised."

"Sorry, but you strike me as more of a fly-by-the-seat-of-her-pants kind of woman."

His eyes dipped to said pants for a moment, warming Joey more than any mug of cocoa.

"I think spontaneity is important. It keeps life

interesting. However, I do try for the right mix between that and organization."

"Hmmm. Well, what have you got?"

"Since you tend toward modern and I tend eclectic, I pulled a few options that cover both. I took the liberty of setting up appointments."

He turned in his seat, his arm resting on the top of the steering wheel. "What would you have done about the modern ones if I hadn't shown up?"

"I'd have gone." She shrugged. "You never know. I might surprise you and fall in love with a modern house."

Nodding, he straightened and started the truck. "I expect just about anything from you."

"Good. Don't forget that."

"All right. Where to first, boss."

Joey preened at his deference to her lead. She gave him an address and he headed in the right direction without her pulling it up on her mapping. Joey almost smacked herself in the forehead as she realized the fire chief must know his way around Willow Bay better than most anyone else.

They arrived at house number one about ten minutes ahead of their appointment. Though there were only a couple realtors' offices in town, Joey had made a point of scheduling this appointment with someone other than Becca. Not because of the competition angle, she told herself, but because it would be uncomfortable for Ethan and she wanted him to enjoy this day. If he chose, down the road, to date Becca, so be it.

As they sat in the car waiting for the realtor, they examined the two-bedroom house. Off-setting slants to the roof, one higher than the other, screamed modern.

"This one's for me, I take it?" Ethan asked.

"I thought it was a good place to start. What do

you think of the outside?"

"I like the contrast of light and dark. The brick will probably mean less maintenance."

"Ocean air can be rough on exteriors."

"All in all, I like the ambiance," he said. "Looks like the realtor's here." He got out and came around the truck.

When Becca Strong got out of the car in front of them, Joey's file folder slipped out of her hands and her papers dropped to the floor of the truck.

Ethan scowled as he opened her door.

"I swear I set the appointment up with one of the other realtors, Ethan."

"Becca is nice."

Joey bristled. "I get that she's nice. But when two women are interested in the same man, throwing them together with said man is not conducive to relaxing."

The first grin of the day touched Ethan's face as he leaned in. "Hmm. Guess that means you're interested in me."

"You already know that. Now move. I don't want to make this any more uncomfortable—for any of us—than it already is."

"Ethan," Becca said, walking toward the truck. She faltered when Joey climbed out to stand beside him, though not too closely.

"Oh, it's you."

"Good morning, Becca," Joey said, smiling. "Ethan and I are house hunting."

When Becca's face turned pale, Joey realized what she'd said. "Separately. I mean, we're looking together, but for different houses. Oh, darn, I'm just not saying this right." She turned to Ethan, who'd leaned against the truck and crossed his arms, completely at ease with her discomfort.

"Well, then," Becca said, her eyebrows lowering

back to a normal level. "I can see you picked this one out, Ethan. It's totally your style. When I saw this appointment on the calendar, I switched with Scott. I thought you'd prefer a more personal experience. Shall we go see the inside?"

"Sure," Ethan and Joey said at the same time. Both of them grinned while Becca's perfect smile dropped a touch.

"Okay, follow me." Becca led the way and leaned over the lockbox for what seemed to Joey to be an extra-long time, wriggling as she undid the lock and opened the door. "Welcome to your new home."

"Maybe," Ethan said.

Joey saw his reluctant interest as he looked around the room. He liked the place. Joey had to admit she liked it better on the inside than she thought she would. They'd staged it with comfortable furniture, not 70s retro. It gave the open expanse a homey feel, and the two ceiling heights weren't as noticeable inside as they were outside.

"Check out this kitchen. It's been completely remodeled to match the mid-century outside. You'll love it, I know."

The homey feel disappeared in the kitchen. Gray and white made the stainless-steel appliances blend well, but Joey was afraid to touch the stark white granite on the island. The same granite covered the rest of the counters. It was so pristine, she backed out of the room. Messy was more her style.

"Look at this," Becca said, grabbing Ethan's hand and waving it under the faucet. "No touch faucet. Great for when your hands are all dirty from seasoning steaks for the BBQ."

Pulling his hand back from the running water, Ethan looked around for a nonexistent cloth, then wiped it on his jeans.

"The biggest bedroom is next. You'll love it," Becca said, putting her arm through Ethan's. "Vaulted ceilings, lots of room, and a fireplace for those cozy nights at home in bed."

The hunger in Becca's eyes as she turned them into the bedroom was downright embarrassing.

"I'll, umm, wait outside." No way was Joey going into a bedroom with Ethan and Becca. No menages for her, even mentally. When she was with a man, she wanted to be his sole focus.

Ethan frowned over Becca's head, as if saying this was twice now Joey had left him at Becca's mercy. As she tugged him into the room, Joey beat feet for the front door. A light mist had begun to fall, so she sat in a chair on the porch berating herself for leaving them alone. What were they doing that took so long? Was Becca making her case with Ethan? Coming on to him harder than she already had?

Not once in her life had Joey been bitten by the green bug, not even with Robert, who'd enjoyed looking at other women even when they were out together. She didn't like how it stole her joy.

So she sat there, stewing and not liking herself much for feeling that way, for another ten minutes before Ethan and Becca came back outside.

Becca grinned up at Ethan, ignoring Joey. "I knew you'd like that yard. The perfect size for small parties."

"As I mentioned, I'm not big on parties."

"Well, but maybe your wife will be. You know, when you pick one." She patted his arm.

Joey rolled her eyes. She'd had about enough. "We're going to be late for our next appointment."

That got Becca's attention. "You're looking at more than this place today?"

Ethan extracted his arm from beneath her hand and moved to the front of the porch. "Yes. As Joey said, we're both looking for houses."

"I'd be happy to show them to you."

"We've already made appointments," Joey said.

"I can come along as your realtor." She stepped closer to Ethan. "This is my business. I know the positives and the pitfalls."

"That's very generous of you," Ethan said, smiling. "But we're good on our own for now."

Becca's pout lasted about two seconds before she plastered the smile back on her face. "Well then Ethan, if you have any questions or need any advice, please call me at any time. You have my card, right?"

Joey wondered if she could also call Becca with questions.

"I have your card," Ethan acknowledged.

"Great. My personal cell is listed there. Really, call anytime."

Back in the truck, Ethan pulled away from the curb as Becca waved to him. "If you ever," he said, low and tight, "leave me alone with that woman again, I'll throttle you."

The green bug flew away and Joey's joy returned. She should feel bad for Becca, but right now, basking in being Ethan's preferred company felt too good.

~ ~ ~

"Where to next?" Ethan said. His smile was genuine. He was enjoying himself, and would probably pay for that later. Right now, the pleasure of Joey's company was all he wanted to think about. The ramifications would have to wait. He hadn't even checked in at the station, which he usually did on his days off. At the next house, he texted his counterpart, relieved to find out all was quiet.

Together, Ethan and Joey looked at two more houses, one right on the beach. The owners had taken the beach theme to extremes and they'd both giggled like kids as they wandered through. A badly painted mural of the beach and ocean covered one wall in the bedroom.

"It looks more like a nightmare than a peaceful beach."

"Oh, come on. It's not that bad," Joey said. "The sawgrass looks really well done."

Ethan leaned in closer. "Sharp as knives, that sawgrass. How could they sleep at night next to it?"

"This place was a rental for years," Scott, the realtor, mentioned. "The renters did that and didn't paint it over when they moved out. It would be easy to paint over."

"Yes, but this house would require a lot of work to get in shape," Ethan said, looking around at the belongings left behind, the old furniture, the '60s paneling. And popcorn ceilings, which very well might have asbestos.

"Which is why you can get beach property at this price," Scott said. "Look at that view."

He and Joey did, standing side by side, arms touching.

"I could live with this view every day," she whispered. Turning to Ethan, she shrugged. "But not enough to take on this kind of project."

Thanking Scott, they headed to one last showing before dinner.

"Do you feel like any of those houses are possibilities?" Ethan asked.

"Every house we've looked at has something I love but none of them have felt like home. You?"

"The one Becca showed us was nice."

"Kind of sterile."

Ethan nodded. She was right.

"I guess you can accent to take some of the sterile out," Joey said.

"Hmmm. Decorating. Not my thing."

"Well, if you decide to buy that one, I'm sure Becca would be happy to help you decorate it."

"Stop," he said, huffing out a laugh. "You know, I feel bad. Even if I were open to dating, I don't feel any spark with her, and I don't want to take advantage."

She turned to him. "Isn't this a date?"

Stepped right into that one, didn't I? "This is two compatible people searching for homes together." The interesting part was that he didn't care anymore if this was a date or not.

Joey smiled. "Yeah, right."

When they pulled up to the final house, Joey gasped in pleasure, sending thrills coursing through Ethan. Even he had to admit the house looked perfect. From the outside. New construction made it seem modern but bits of craftsman styling and two dormers, along with slate blue siding accented by white trim, also gave it a traditional feel.

They got out and Joey walked with slow reverence up the steps. She reached for one of the posts supporting the porch roof, pausing before she touched it. When she did, the slow bloom of a sated smile took Ethan's breath away. Without her saying a word or going inside, he knew she'd found her home.

"I love this house already," she said, giddy with happiness.

"Don't let the realtor know that or you'll never be able to bargain the price down."

"I don't care. I'd pay anything for this house."

With a chuckle, Ethan grabbed her hand and tugged her toward the door. He knocked. "Let's see the inside first. Do me a favor and keep your thoughts to yourself until we are away from here. Just ask questions. It'll be easier for you if you decide to buy the place."

Joey looked up at Ethan with bedazzled eyes. "If?"

Ethan shook his head. The woman was a goner.

The door opened and Becca Strong stood there, her eyes dipping to their entwined hands and her smile disappearing for a long moment before she pulled herself back into realtor mode. "You saved the best for last, Ethan."

"This house is on Joey's list."

"Oh, well then, why don't you have a look around, Joey? I can keep Ethan company while you do that."

Without a word, Joey went to the front window and looked out.

"Nice hardwoods," Ethan said.

"Yes, and they go throughout the two-story house. You should consider this place, Ethan."

And start a bidding war with Joey? No way. He hedged. "It's not really my style."

The empty house had a touch of echo to it as they spoke. Joey had made it to the kitchen. She looked out that window. "I can see the ocean!"

"There's a peekaboo view from here," Becca said. "You're two rows back from the beach, so it's not a bad walk to get to the water."

"I never thought I'd have a chance of a view."

Not a single star had left her eyes. Joey was in love, and it made Ethan wonder what it would be like to have that kind of love turned toward him.

"The counters are quartz, right?" Joey asked.

"Yes," Becca said as she and Ethan joined Joey in the kitchen.

The room was a bit eclectic for Ethan's tastes. Though brand new, the island and countertops were two different colors of quartz, one white with gray veining and one a medium gray. The island was painted a dark gray, the cupboards and drawers a light gray. It struck him that these were the same colors as in the first house, but here, it didn't look like a hospital. It looked… homey.

Joey ran her hands along the counter, turned the faucet on and off, and gazed out the window again. Ethan moved behind her and looked over her head.

"That's a pretty nice peekaboo view."

She whirled, so close, she brushed him in all the wrong places. "Isn't it?"

Ethan realized it didn't matter if she gushed or not. The look on her face said it all. She wanted this house.

"Go see the rest of the house, Joey," he said quietly, trying to reign in the urge to kiss her right there in front of her view. And Becca, whose eyes Ethan could feel boring holes in the back of his head.

He stepped away and Joey headed up the stairs to the bedrooms.

"There are two bedrooms and a shared bathroom upstairs."

"But there's a large walk-in closet," Joey hollered down. "Ethan, you *have* to see this. The view is even better from here."

Becca sighed and waved toward the stairs. "Go look. I'll wait here."

Ready to take the stairs two at a time, Ethan forced himself to keep a measured pace until he turned the corner at the top. He found Joey in a roomy bedroom, once again staring out the window.

She turned to Ethan, her eyes bright with happiness. "Look!"

Joining her at the window, he stood behind her and stared out at the expanse of waves. It was the most natural thing in the world for him to wrap his arms around her. When she leaned back against his chest, something inside him broke open. This felt right. Hell, it felt fucking perfect.

"It's the ocean, Ethan. I can see the ocean from my bedroom."

He should tell her it wasn't her bedroom yet, but Ethan didn't have the heart to break the magic of the moment. They stood there for a time indeterminate, staring out at the view. The emotions that washed over and through Ethan threatened to overwhelm him. He'd never known this feeling before and right now, he didn't want to dissect it. He'd do that later. For now, he rested his chin lightly on her head, inhaling everything Joey, loving the moment.

"Did you two get lost up there?"

Becca's voice, from downstairs, broke them apart instantly and Ethan regretted the change.

"We're fine," Joey called. "Be down in a moment."

Remembering he was supposed to play devil's advocate, Ethan looked around. "It's a nice size, but won't you miss having a bathroom attached to your bedroom?"

"For just me? No."

"What about down the road? You might marry, have a couple kids."

Joey stumbled and grabbed hold of the door jamb as she turned back to Ethan, the imp inside her suddenly shining forth. "Why, Ethan, are you offering?"

"What? That's not what I said. No. Sorry, but no." Panic stole his breath, right up until Joey hooted with laughter.

"Gotcha," she said, skipping across the hall for a quick check of the bathroom and the other bedroom.

Ethan followed more slowly, still trying to get his heartbeat under control. The funny thing, though, was that he wasn't sure what panicked him more, the idea of marrying her or of not marrying her. How would he feel if someone else lived in that house with Joey, making those kids?

He shook his head. He didn't plan to think about it. Ever. He and Joey were oil and vinegar and he was more than married to his job. It was his vocation and Ethan would not turn his back on it for Joey or anyone.

"I'm, umm, going outside to check in at the station."

"All right," Joey said, peeking around the corner from the bathroom. "Tell Becca I'll be down in a moment."

"Will do." Once again, though he wanted to race down the stairs, Ethan measured his pace. Outside, he called the station. Riley answered.

"You're working?"

"Yeah. Carlos's wife went into labor, so I'm covering."

"Will it put you over your allotted time for the week?"

"No, because I took time off to study for the exam."

"Sounds good. All quiet?"

"Yes, Chief. All is quiet. You know, we can handle anything that comes up without you. It's all right to take a day off once in a while."

"I'm not there, am I?"

"No. Where are you, anyhow? Sounds like you're outside."

"I am. I'm house hunting."

"Good for you, setting down roots. About time."

"Ethan," Becca called from the porch where she and Joey stood.

"You're not house hunting alone?"

"That was the realtor," Ethan hedged.

"Is that the only other person there?"

He looked to the sky, trying to figure out how to answer. "No," he finally said.

"Ooh hoo! You're with that lodge manager, aren't you? Wait. You can't be house hunting together. You've only just met."

"We're not hunting for a house together. We're looking at houses—individual houses—at the same time. Made sense to do it together. We can play devil's advocate for each other."

"And play at something else, I hope."

"Riley." Ethan's voice slipped into chief mode.

"All right. I'll stop. Just… forget about work for a moment and enjoy having a beautiful lady beside you. Because if you don't snap her up, someone else will. Bye, Chief."

Ethan stared at his phone. Was Riley still thinking of asking Joey out? Ethan looked at her, leaning on the balustrade, about as close to a white picket fence as you could get even if it wasn't in the yard.

Despite the cool weather, sweat beaded on Ethan's forehead. He'd never been more conflicted than right now. Joey grinned at him, her happiness infectious. Riley was right. Enjoy the moment. He pushed his worries and questions to the back of his mind. Letting out the smile he held inside, he walked to the bottom of the stairs. "Ready to go?" he asked Joey.

"No, but I have to."

"I'm done with my day now," Becca said, her eyes on Ethan.

"That's great. I hope you have a nice, relaxing evening in store," Ethan said, holding out his hand for Joey. When she settled hers in his, his world tipped into place. "Thanks for all the help today, Becca."

"Yes," Joey said, smiling at the realtor. "I'll give this some thought and get back to you as soon as possible."

"You do that." Without another word, Becca went back in the house.

Ethan held Joey's hand until they got to his truck, half afraid she'd run back to the house.

"I feel sorry for Becca," Joey said as she climbed

in.

"She's a nice lady. I wish I could make her feel better, but I don't think I'm the person to do that."

"You could by asking her out." Joey chewed on her lip.

"Not going to happen." Ethan looked out at the deepening darkness. "Where do you want to have dinner? At the lodge?"

"God, no. I want to stay away from work unless I get a call. How about the Grog and Vine?"

"If you promise not to tase me this time."

Joey, her eyes lit with laughter, raised her chin in the air. "I'll only tase you if you behave yourself."

"You mean if I don't behave myself, right?"

"No, actually, I said what I meant." Her eyes darkened and grew serious as she held his gaze.

"Is that another dare from you, Miss Sanderson?"

"Most definitely."

Ethan gulped. The woman wasn't kidding. His body reacted lightning-quick to the suggestive nature of this discussion.

"Dinner," he said. "We need dinner."

"Yes, we do. And the rest, we'll play by, um, ear, eh?"

He gulped again, his dick bobbing in time to his Adam's apple. In his mind, he saw Joey, spread across his bed, naked. Him, undoing the band and freeing her long, blonde hair, running his fingers through it.

No. That was not going to happen. Ethan was more than capable of reining in his libido and he did so now, though it wasn't easy.

Inside the Grog and Vine, Joey took off her coat and Ethan guided her to a booth with a hand at her back. A hand that felt heat even through the royal blue sweater she wore. How can one petite woman generate so much heat?

Joey slid into the U-shaped booth and patted the seat beside her.

Ethan, with a mind for his sanity, took the seat across the booth, causing Joey to laugh.

"Chicken."

"Where you are concerned, yes."

Gene stopped at their table and took their drink and food orders. Joey ordered red wine. Ethan chose to stick with coffee.

"Afraid a beer will tear down those defenses, Chief?" Joey said, grinning.

Because Joey wore her emotions on her sleeve, Ethan felt she deserved some honesty. He reached across the table and took her hand in his, threading their fingers together. "I'm in real danger of losing my focus around you."

"Would that be so bad?"

He rubbed his thumb along her hand. "Yes."

"Why?"

While considering how to answer, Ethan looked around the quiet interior of the pub. Not many people there on a Monday night. The perfect environment for baring one's soul. Peaceful, with lots of liquor to drown sorrows. "I don't talk about it. Ever. But yes, there are reasons. Strong ones. I get that you want to understand why I can't—won't—date you. I'm sorry, but it's not going to happen."

Joey chewed on her lower lip for a moment, then covered their entwined fingers with her other hand. "No one should talk about wounds from their past until they're ready, Ethan. I understand that more than most."

Ethan cocked his head, wondering if she realized how telling that comment was.

"So why don't we just relax and talk about things we're comfortable with and see where things go," she added, pulling her hands away as Gene brought her wine and his coffee.

She took a sip and his gaze dropped to her lips as they pursed on the edge of the wine glass. Lips he'd love to have— Damn it. No. Ethan clenched and unclenched a hand under the table, trying to reset which brain was doing the thinking at the moment.

"What's your take on the houses you saw today?" Joey asked.

Safe ground. Thank God.

"Some good ones, some not so good," he said.

"Yeah, like that one with the awesome view? I don't have the know-how or money for that kind of fixer-upper." Joey swirled her wine and took another sip.

"I might enjoy it, but I don't have the time. The first one, the modern one, was nice."

"If you like that sort of thing. Seemed kind of sterile to me."

"Nothing wrong with sterile."

"I'd have to, I don't know, paint a mural on a wall or something to liven the place up."

Ethan cringed at the thought of wild, Peter-Maxx-style colors splashed across one wall. "I like utilitarian. It works for me. As for you and that last one, I never saw anyone fall head over heels for a house so quickly."

The wide, dreamy smile that brightened everything around them returned. "I fell hard, huh?"

"Oh, yeah. Remind me to never take you car shopping. Those salespeople will see your enthusiasm coming a mile away and take you for every dime you have."

"I can't help it. If I like something, I show it." Her gaze never dropped from his. Desire sparked in her eyes, her cheeks were flushed, her lips slightly parted. Perfect for kissing.

For a long moment, she held his eyes. "Not trying to suggest anything with this, but that last place kind of embodies the best of both of us, doesn't it?"

Yes. He didn't answer out loud. He couldn't. The marriage of styles was uncanny and if Joey hadn't loved it so much, he'd consider putting an offer in himself. Joey's effervescence when touring that house had entranced him. The woman was sunshine in the middle of winter at the ocean and her enthusiasm had only grown with each room.

"Are you going to make an offer?"

"Yes."

"Not even going to think about it?"

"Nope. Going to the bank first thing tomorrow."

"I'm glad. The house suits you." It did, and he truly was happy for her.

"We'll have to keep looking for the right place for you," she said, as Gene arrived and placed their food on the table. A beer-braised cheeseburger with a mound of fries for Ethan and a chicken sandwich on white bread for Joey.

Ethan was struck by the bland food she'd ordered. "Pretty tame food for you, isn't it?"

"Why do you say that?" she asked, taking a bite.

He shrugged, stuffing a fry in his mouth. "You live life to the fullest. I figured you'd eat spicy and add Tabasco for a bigger rush."

Joey chuckled. "Sometimes I do."

"Why not tonight?" Ethan took a bite of the best burger in Willow Bay, savoring the taste and almost missing the intensity of Joey's gaze.

"I'm saving my spice for later," she said.

Ethan choked on the bite he'd just tried to swallow. Joey got up and patted him on the back while he coughed. She handed him his water and he sipped it while the fit subsided. She didn't sit down until he'd stopped coughing altogether.

Taking another a bite of her sandwich, she watched him with the innocence of a witch.

"What am I going to do with you?" Ethan muttered.

"Anything you want."

His pants tightened as thoughts of exactly what he wanted to do raced through his mind.

"We can't, Joey."

"Why not? Look, I get that you feel you can't get involved. I don't exactly understand it, but I get it. What's wrong with sex for sex's sake? You're hot, Ethan. I'm attracted to you and you to me. Why not scratch the itch?"

Slack jawed, he listened to her. Were they in some sort of role-reversal, alternate reality where women propositioned men?

"I don't do casual, Joey. Never have. Never will."

"Have you had a serious relationship lately?"

Lately? Try never. "No."

Joey bit her lip but the grin just wouldn't stay stashed away.

"No, Joey. Not going to happen."

"You know we're right back to all work and no play, right?"

"I'm fine with that."

"Well, I'm not."

"Then we're at a crossroads. Remember how we started today out? With a promise that, at the end of it, I would walk away." His words caused an ache in his chest and he rubbed it. He must be getting heartburn.

Finished with her sandwich, Joey wiped her mouth with her napkin, took a drink of water, and scooted around the U-shaped booth until she and Ethan were hip-to-hip.

He watched her with wary eyes as she turned his

head her way and ran a hand along his cheek. "I like the beard." Her voice, a siren song of whispered words, held him spellbound.

"I don't shave on my days off."

"I like you clean-shaven, but this makes you look like you're ready to rumble. I'm going to kiss you now, Ethan. Been wanting to all day and I can't wait any longer. Try not to think, just relax and enjoy. I know full well you can do that."

Her lips touched his, the briefest contact, then pulled back.

"This is where you say no," she whispered.

No. The word screamed through Ethan's gut, roared into his throat, and died before ever being uttered. He wanted this. He wanted her. Now. Tomorrow be damned. Twisting toward her, he grasped her arms and pulled her in, his lips descending on hers with the energy of a ravenous tiger. She tasted good. God, she tasted so good. Like wine and happiness and all the goddamned words he couldn't come up with at the moment. He wanted to devour her. Pull her spirit into his. To forget everything beneath her hands. To heal.

As with life, Joey gave everything to the kiss. Her hands roamed, her lips crushed Ethan's right back. Her heart pounded against his chest. Heart to heart, as much as they could in the tight booth.

"Ahem."

Both of them whipped their heads up to find Gene standing there.

"You want the rest of that burger to go?" he asked, grinning.

Joey, her lips puffed from being well-kissed, had a yearning in her eyes Ethan couldn't have ignored if he tried. "Yes. And the bill," he said to Gene. "Quick."

"Got what I need right here." Gene handed Ethan

a bill and packaged up his food. "Figured you wouldn't be here much longer, otherwise I'd have to break up the show. It was getting pretty hot."

Ethan's face didn't turn warm. It turned molten. He must be red as a ripe apple. Damn. He fumbled for his wallet and handed over enough bills to cover, plus some. Within seconds, he and Joey were out the door and in his truck, her lips locked on his again. And there was nowhere else Ethan wanted to be.

"Where?" he panted as they kissed.

"My place is work, so not there."

"My place it is." Ethan broke the kiss and started the truck. Joey slid across the console that was flat enough to make the front seat almost a bench and tucked herself up next to him.

"Seat belt," he said, putting the truck in drive. He was about to burst out of his jeans he was so hard. They needed to be at his place now.

"It's only a short distance and I want to be close to you."

"Joey. Seat belt."

"No. Just go, Ethan. I'm ready to explode. I can't wait much longer."

He debated staying put until she complied, but he wasn't sure he could wait her out. Letting his pants decide for him, he tore out of the parking lot and headed for his apartment.

They kissed before they exited the truck, and kissed their way up the stairs to his apartment, tripping twice. Once inside, he backed her up to the door and crushed her lips with his. A hot ache grew in his throat as she gasped into the kiss. They broke apart long enough to shed coats, then Ethan picked Joey up in his arms and carried her into his bedroom.

Next to the bed, they stood there staring at one another. Were they really going to do this? He saw the question mark in her eyes and grinned. She mimicked him, a slow, sexy grin spreading across her face as she reached for the edges of her sweater.

"No. Let me," Ethan said, covering her hands with his.

Joey dropped her hands.

No longer interested in rushing things, Ethan stepped closer, resting his hands on her hips. Slowly, he slid them under her sweater, against her skin.

She shivered.

"Are my hands cold?"

With a deep sigh, she shook her head. "Feels good. Very good."

Oh, yeah. He moved his hands up her back, bringing the sweater with him. Her skin was satin-soft and every inch he bared fueled the fire inside him. Sliding his hands to her sides, he nudged her arms up and slid the sweater up her arms and over her head. He stepped back to fold and set her sweater on the chair before turning back. Joey stood there, hands clutched in front, biting her lower lip. Vulnerable. And sunshine on a cloudy day.

How could one person be so many things?

"You are amazing," he whispered, moving closer.

The smile she flashed mesmerized him. He ran a finger over her lips. "You have the most beautiful smile."

"And you have the gentlest touch."

"I want to touch you. All over."

"Please do, because I plan to do the exact same thing." Joey pulled him down toward her delectable lips.

Ethan eased her back onto the bed as he deepened the kiss. His tongue touched her lips and she opened to him, tangled with him, even as her hands tugged at his shirt. He stepped back and Joey moaned.

"Just for a moment." Peeling his shirt off, he folded it loosely and added it to the chair. Next came his jeans. Then hers.

"If you take the time to fold those, too, I'm leaving."

He froze. She looked serious. "You wouldn't."

Joey arched an eyebrow.

For a long moment, he admired her, all legs and lingerie, then tossed her unfolded jeans over his shoulder to land on the floor. He leaped onto the bed, landing beside her. She whooped in surprise and he pulled her into his arms, sliding onto his back so she was on top. She straddled him, squirming. Ethan gasped and Joey laughed softly. "I love affecting you. I love being affected by you."

"Come here, vixen," he said, tugging her down. Their lips met again and the fun became serious, the need became all-consuming. His hands roved her body, her hands clutched his head as they kissed. He devoured her velvet warmth, pulled her hunger into him, letting it soothe his soul.

Once he'd flicked the clasp on her bra, she sat up, letting it fall off her arms until she flung it behind her.

"So beautiful," he whispered, awed at the vision in front of him. He cupped her breasts, perfect in his hands, and she stretched, eyes toward the ceiling, leaning into his touch. When her gaze lowered to his again, the fire there built his own even higher.

Ethan flipped her beneath him and kissed her with an abandon unfamiliar to him, burying his face in her neck, kissing a trail of fire to her breast, and capturing a taut nipple in his mouth. She was a siren, calling to him, begging him with her arched back, for more.

He wanted, needed to touch her, to brand her. Ethan kissed his way down her stomach to the edge of panties that left little to the imagination. She groaned when he stood up, the groan turning into a sigh when he pulled the lace from her and tossed it over his shoulder. He slipped between her legs and she opened to him.

Her purrs thrummed through him as he explored her. She was everything he wanted, her taste perfect to his palate. When she exploded—for him, only for him—he savored her scream and her soft sounds as she came down from the high.

"My God, Ethan. What you do to me. I need you. Inside me. Please."

"As my lady commands," he said, reaching for a condom.

Joey took the pack from him and pushed him back onto the bed. Opening the condom with her teeth, she rolled it onto his cock with slow, agonizing precision.

"Woman, if you don't hurry up— "

She threw the packet, climbed atop him, and seated herself all in one fluid movement.

"Shit." He couldn't breathe, couldn't move or he'd explode.

When she ground against him, he stopped her with hands to both her hips. "Give me a second."

A slow smile spread across her face. "Take all the time you need."

Frozen in time, he reveled in how tightly she held him captive. How well they fit together, how complete he felt at that moment.

"Ethan— "

He thrust deeper and she gasped her pleasure, then began to move. Up and down, in and out. Building, blowing his fucking mind. When he thought he couldn't take one more thrust, he flipped her onto her back and plunged into her. Harder, faster, until they sailed over the top of the fucking mountain and sparks flew. His whole body went rigid with a powerful release meant only for her. For them.

"Wow," Joey whispered, relaxing beneath him.

Ethan slid to her side, unable to move beyond that. "Yeah, fucking wow."

Joey chuckled. "You have such a way with words."

"And you have ways to take me places I've never been before."

"I'm not the only one."

Spent and satisfied, he pulled her into his arms and drifted off, unable to keep his eyes open as she snuggled against him. Not much later, he woke, unable to remember a time when he'd fallen asleep so easily. Quietly disengaging from Joey, Ethan went to the bathroom to clean up and decided to take a shower. He needed time to process what had happened between them. Sex with Joey had taken him to new heights. He'd wanted her more than he'd ever wanted anything, and he wanted her again right now. Hot spray couldn't stop the need growing in him.

"Showering without me?" Joey slipped in beside him, a condom between her fingers.

With a happy sigh, Ethan wrapped his arms around her. "Just waiting for you to notice."

The water turned lukewarm as they made love again, Joey against the wall with her legs wrapped around him as he pounded into her. She took everything and he gave it all willingly.

Later, tangled with each other under warm blankets, Ethan listened to Joey's slight snore. He tried to lay still, but reality had sunk in and he shook with the memory of tonight. And tomorrow.

How could he do this? Have a relationship and his vocation? Was it even possible? It scared the hell out of him to even try. God, what was he going to do? Joey deserved more than a sex partner, and Ethan knew they'd blown right past that to full-on lovemaking tonight.

Joey deserved better than him, and he'd just made things between them a thousand times more complicated.

She deserved a whole man, which he wasn't. Ethan closed his eyes, breathing deeply, willing his mind to settle and leave decisions until tomorrow. To just enjoy being there, with her. He knew he wouldn't sleep because he needed to memorize every moment of this night, to brand it into his soul.

Tomorrow would come soon enough.

CHAPTER EIGHT

Light filtered in through Joey's closed eyes. More light than she was used to. She opened them and sat up, not recognizing the window. Then she remembered and sank back into the pillows. What a night! She'd never in her life been so thoroughly loved. Ethan had given her the gift of his need, his desire, the letting-go of his pent-up emotions. It had been the most fantastic night of her life. Wow.

Preening into a full stretch, her arm slid along the sheets to find the other side of the bed empty. Joey frowned and sat up. Where was Ethan? She didn't hear any noise in the apartment.

She lay back down and rolled over, facing the window. That's when she saw the note.

Went in for my shift. Make yourself at home. There's a Keurig in the kitchen for coffee. Call me when you wake up and I'll come take you home. E.

Hmmm. No mention of what last night had meant to him. Granted, she wouldn't expect that from Ethan, but a hint would be nice. Because her world had been rocked. R.O.C.K.E.D. Several times. She stretched again, feeling the amazing ache of being well loved. Her body still thrummed from Ethan's touch.

Joey read the note again. Mushy wasn't Ethan's thing. She got that. However, the fact that he didn't address at all the awesome, stupendous night they'd just spent together could mean second thoughts were rumbling around in his brain. The one on top, because if the other one made the decisions, he'd never have gone to work today. She'd made very sure she gave as good as she got.

Flinging the covers back, she got up and walked to the window. Another rainy day. Not enough to kill Joey's high. Rain just meant tonight would be good for cuddling. She picked up her phone, her eyes widening. Shit. She'd overslept big time and already had three texts from Rose. Shit. Shit. Shit.

After she shot off a text, Joey searched for her clothing, which lay in a neat pile on a chair next to the bed. How like the man. Once dressed, she primped as much as she could in the bathroom, brushing her teeth with a spare one she found in an almost bare medicine cabinet. No secrets there.

Grabbing her purse, she started to call Ethan but changed her mind. While she'd love to be with him for even a few minutes more, time was a luxury she didn't have. So, she called for a rideshare. Before she left, she took her first good look at the main room of his condo. The word spare popped into her mind. A minimalistic couch, mismatched end tables, and the biggest leather recliner she'd ever seen. No rugs, not even a picture on the wall.

Spare. Not the space of a man who felt settled. Maybe, considering he was looking for a house, he was ready for that feeling?

When Joey closed the door behind her, she made sure she heard it lock. Her rideshare pulled up just as she got to the parking lot. Seven minutes later, after the driver dropped her off, she noticed a man standing at the edge of the parking lot watching her. She couldn't see his face clearly because of an umbrella, but he wasn't local. No one who lived there would wear dress shoes, especially on a rainy day. Add in the dark trench coat and the man looked positively spooky. She'd ask John to go talk to the man and make sure everything was all right.

Joey walked through the doors of Pacific Lodge and rushed behind the desk, since she was still in jeans and not in her usual work attire.

Rose stood with her arms crossed over her chest, her eyes bright with laughter.

"Walk of shame?"

Blushing was rare for Joey, but this got her. To her roots. Which made Rose burst out laughing.

What could she do? Joey shook her head, then laughed with Rose. She was in too good a mood to let anything get her down. "Everything good here?"

"All is quiet. I was just worried about you. Called your room, then your cell."

"I'm sorry I worried you. I'm going to slip upstairs and change, then make my rounds."

"Okay, boss. And, um, your light shines bright today. I'm glad you had a good night."

Joey hugged Rose, then slipped up to her room without being seen. An hour later, she'd checked in with all her lead employees and was ensconced in her office.

Able to breathe and think for the first time since she'd looked at her phone, Joey remembered the house and her happy mood went up a couple more notches. That place was perfect for her. She imagined herself furniture shopping. Maybe a pale sea-blue cloth couch with navy leather chairs and a light tan rug.

So different from the dark, cloying colors in the

house where she'd been raised. Joey shuddered and shoved those thoughts out of her mind. Light and airy, that's what she wanted. And white chiffon draped over a light wood, four-poster bed. Chiffon they could pull down to close them off from the world while they loved.

Whoa. That went in a different direction fast. Before she deep dove into reliving the night before, Joey glanced at the clock. The bank was open so she called the loan officer there. She'd talked to Stan before beginning her search and he'd given her a ballpark ceiling for a mortgage that he could guarantee without a full review. This house was a little above that, but she'd do anything, promise anything, to get it.

Fifteen minutes later, she'd given Stan everything he needed to get her approved. Joey turned to work issues, though it wasn't easy with her mind and heart floating so high in the clouds.

Life was good. Very good. And nothing was going to stop her from being happy, ever again.

~ ~ ~

In his office at the station, Ethan stared at the computer screen without seeing it. Last night had transcended anything he'd ever experienced. The high of being everything Joey wanted and needed ranked up there next to finding his sister safe after the fire. Sure, he'd had women in his life, but never like this. Why was that? What was so different about Joey that amped up— everything?

"Hey, Hotlips."

Ethan stifled the groan. He could do nothing about the blush, damn it.

"What the hell do you want?" he growled.

"Just checking to see if those hot lips are raw." Riley leaned over the desk, cocking his head right and left as he eyeballed Ethan's face. He sank into the chair with a cheesy grin Ethan wanted badly to wipe off his face.

Instead, he gave Riley a pointed glare, which probably looked comical with his still blushing skin. "Do you have something work related to discuss?"

"Yep. But first, let's discuss you and Joey making out like rabid teens next to your truck."

"Let's not," Ethan said. No fucking way.

"In public, Ethan. If you don't want to get razzed, don't do things in public. Seriously, man. It's good to see you letting your hair down, so to speak."

Ethan ran a hand over his short hair. "Look, it was just a moment. That's all."

"Yeah. A moment. A very hot, long, spicy moment from what I heard."

"Who the hell told you anyhow?" Becca wouldn't have blabbed.

"A neighbor told Gladys."

"Oh, God."

"Yep. It's all over town that you were smooching the lodge manager. And I have to say, most everyone is thrilled."

"Most?"

Riley, never one to miss an opportunity to play annoying little brother to his mentor, made a wide circle with his hands. "Everyone except the hearts you're breaking."

Hearts? What the hell was he talking about?

"Don't look so bewildered," Riley said. "Don't you know how many women have tried to get you to *see* them?"

"There hasn't been anyone."

"Only because you wouldn't let them in. Do you remember when you first got here, all the home-cooked food showing up in the hands of this woman or that one?"

"Well, yes, but that was a welcome for the whole crew."

"No, Ethan, that was a welcome for you."

He thought about it. There had been a few women stopping by with food. Some, like Bernie, were welcome committee people. But others, coming in the mornings looking like they were ready for dinner and dancing... Others, coming in around the end of a shift with an innocuous question...

Riley sank back in his chair. "Wow, you really were clueless."

"Focused. It's called focused."

"Well, whatever it's called, I'm glad to see you thinking about something other than this job. You need some downtime."

"I get days off."

"And you call in each day you aren't here. Enjoy the time with Joey. Forget about this place, Ethan. Just for a little while."

"I can't, and you know why." Riley was the only person who knew the whole story. He sighed and stood up.

"Yeah, I know. Okay, I've had my say. Want to help me study?"

"Yes. Go on and I'll join you in a moment."

Riley hummed his way down the hall to the conference room. Ethan looked at his computer, having completely lost the will to do any work. Instead, he turned and glanced outside at the rain. Was Joey awake? She hadn't called him. She had to be at work already. She was as devoted to her job as he was to his. Well, maybe not *that* devoted.

The night before, he'd woken and laid there with just enough moonlight to watch her sleep. He'd reached over to smooth hair back from her cheek and she'd turned into his hand and sighed before snuggling deeper into her pillow. An angel with golden hair, bright blue eyes, and a body he craved now more than ever.

Mostly, he'd held himself back from sleeping with women. Not so much an enforced celibacy as a matter of focus. He'd chosen to concentrate completely on work. But something about Joey made him forget everything. He'd raced to work in a panic this morning, afraid something had happened. Nothing had, but something could have.

Yesterday, he'd told her that at the end of the day, he'd walk away. Joey hadn't believed him and, in his heart, Ethan didn't want to believe himself. But this couldn't happen. He couldn't slip, couldn't let go or someone else would get hurt.

He'd tell her after the festival. They'd both be so busy for the next few days, they probably wouldn't see each other anyway.

Decision made, he headed back to the conference room to make certain Riley got a particularly brutal Q&A session.

~~~

"Hey, Joey," the maintenance man called out. She stopped in the midst of pulling brochures out of the garbage. The day had gotten busy, with so many people coming into town for the festival that Joey forgot all about the owner until he'd shown up with his family entourage. Ten people, including two newly minted legal drinkers—twenty-one-year-olds who looked like trouble. Mr. Reynolds had taken one look at the brochures on the table, glared at Joey, then swept everything into the trash.

"Please tell me nothing's broken down," Joey said, dreading the maintenance man's answer.

"Only small stuff and we're on top of it," he said. "I wanted to ask, though, if I could be on call tomorrow instead of here in person. My family wants to go to the festival and I can be here in a flash if there's any trouble."

Relief flooded through her. "Sure. No problem at all. Enjoy." As much as she could, she'd scheduled her employees to all get some time off during festival hours, though she doubted she would get away. She'd looked back in the records. Pacific Lodge had never once been at capacity. It was going to be a long, working weekend for her. If she pulled this off and got through the weekend unscathed— Hell, even if she didn't, she'd probably sleep for a week after it was done.

"Hey, John, whatever happened with trench-coat man?"

"No one was there by the time I got outside. Not even down the road. Are you concerned about something?"

Joey waved her hand in dismissal. "It was probably nothing. Just spooked me for some reason."

"Let me know if you see him again and I'll talk to Sheriff Jackson about it."

"Probably just my own nerves building up to this weekend. Enjoy the festival."

She waved again and glanced at her clock. Four p.m. She hadn't heard from Stan at the bank yet. Pulling her phone out of her pocket as she settled into her office, Joey called him.

"I was going to wait until Monday to call you," Stan said. "You know, with the festival and all."

"I'd like to put an offer in ASAP. This is my dream home."

"Well, um… "

Joey's gut clenched. This didn't sound like good news. "What?"

"The figures don't work out. Your pay plus your down payment doesn't quite make it. The bank's formula denied your request for an increase in the loan amount."

Nope. Not good news. Fighting hard to draw breath, Joey ran unsteady fingers through the sand-filled zen garden on her desk, leaving squiggled lines. Was her dream house going to slip through her fingers like grains of sand? "It's not that much of an increase. It would make, what, a $72 difference in my house payment?"

"More like $98, and you were already at the top of your loan capability."

"I have to get that house, Stan. Isn't there anything I can do? Can't we negotiate the price? We're so close."

"The owners have already come down $10,000. I checked. They are firm on their price. Can you come up with a bigger down payment? That's about the only thing I can think of."

"I don't think so. I'm giving you all but a small emergency fund as it is." Oh, God. She was going to lose the place. "Let me think about it over the weekend, see what I can come up with."

"All right. I'm sorry. I know this means a lot to you."

"It does." With her palm, she pushed against her forehead to keep from crying. "Have a good time at the festival."

"You, too."

As soon as she hung up, the tears fell. Joey let them—for about thirty seconds—then swiped at her eyes. She hadn't clawed her way out of Portland, away from a life designed by parents and a fiancé that had nothing to do with what she wanted, just to lose out when she was so close to fulfilling her dreams.

She'd find a way. She had to. Joey stood. Right now, she needed to get her mind off it. Action, something to do. Anything.

Out front, Rose and the new hire, Robin, had things well under control. Even the bustling lobby was orderly. Nothing was needed. Her brochures were back in the trash, which meant Mr. Reynolds had come through. Joey picked them up and walked around chatting with people, handing out brochures and answering questions.

Still, her heart hurt.

So she put on her galoshes, grabbed her raincoat, and walked the path over the dunes to the beach. The rain had stopped and the always-there wind had lessened, but the waves still looked winter-angry.

Joey knew how that felt. She walked up to the surf, letting the waves wash past her. Digging a toe into the sand that undermined her ability to stand steady, Joey decided life was the same way. Constantly trying to pull her down, keep her off balance.

If she hadn't spent so much of Granny's money trying to figure out where she wanted to live, she'd have more to put down on the house. Could she have settled down before this? No, probably not. For three years, she'd been looking over her shoulder, waiting for them to find her. Only in Willow Bay had she found a sense of safety.

Why couldn't just one thing go right?

She walked up the beach, letting the anguish and anger wash over her. By the time she turned around, she couldn't see the lodge, but most of her frustration had washed away with the outgoing tide. Most, but not all.

As she slowly walked back, her heart hurting, her mind was already trying to work the problem, to find a solution. She had to come up with something. She just had to.

CHAPTER NINE

Friday morning, Gladys sat in her winged chair staring at nothing in particular. Ever since Henry's call, her focus had gone to hell. It had been a week and she still couldn't get the conversation out of her mind. She'd become so disconcerted, she'd forgotten all about keeping an eye on her newest couple. Ethan would be a hard nut to crack, but she felt certain Joey was up for the task. However, without nudges, they might pull their heads back into their shells. Maybe not Joey, but Ethan definitely would.

That damn ad in *The New York Times*. Gladys shook her head. George couldn't have picked a better way to get back at her than outing her identity. She'd spent the last week waiting for an *aha* from the community she'd come to think of as her own. So far, nothing. Maybe no one here read *The Times*. And maybe, the *AP* wouldn't pick it up and it wouldn't hit the rags. Gladys didn't think Hawthorne was a big enough name for that, but there were too many maybes. And all those news outlets had a field day back when George had been arrested.

She took a sip of her tea. Tomorrow, the two-day

Beer and Chowder Festival began. This drama couldn't
have come at a worse time, though the thought made
her cringe. It wasn't George's fault he died when he did.
And he'd been a good man. A bit misguided, but a
good man.

Gladys had hoped to enjoy the festival. Willow Bay
would be at its best and she loved seeing her town
shine. Now, she'd be looking over her shoulder,
wondering when the shoe would clunk her in the head.

For now, she'd try to bury that worry. She went to
her bedroom and slipped into her persona. It was time
to check out Willow Bay and make sure no shenanigans
stopped the festival. Willow Bay needed this. She
needed this.

And it was going to happen.

~~~

Jasmin Powter, soon-to-be Mrs. Luke Taylor, sat at
the kitchen table watching her fiancé make breakfast.
She never tired of looking at him. The man's physique,
honed by all his carpentry work, moved in well-earned
concert, smooth and muscled. Especially in the sweats
and a t-shirt she'd just bought him that was tight in all
the right places and that he was only allowed to wear at
home. She'd made the request after the lovemaking
session they'd had the first time he put the shirt on, and
he'd readily agreed. Jasmin grew warm at the memory.

"What are you smiling at?" Luke said, setting a cup
of coffee in front of her.

"Just thinking about how much I love that shirt."

His eyes burned with remembered fire. "After
breakfast, you're welcome to show me again."

"I'd be happy to." Jasmin leaned into the kiss he
offered, lost for the moment in the lips, the man, the
love that still gave her happy, needy shivers. "Except
we have to be somewhere, remember?"

"Nowhere more important than here. With you."

"We said we'd meet Bernie and Paul at the Beer and Chowder Festival and help them set up. Mom and Dad are probably already there so she can snap the before pictures." Her mother, having survived a debilitating stroke, was now the honorary town photographer, and she took her role seriously.

"Ah, yes," Luke said. "Can't disappoint the parents. But honey, if you keep wearing things like this to breakfast, we'll never leave the house." He fingered the silk nightgown she'd thrown on, the one that barely restrained her nipples.

"What, this old thing?"

After a chuckle and one more melting kiss, Luke went back to the stove to finish their omelets. They'd been living together for about three months and it still felt like a surreal honeymoon. Her life had gone from frantic worry about her parents' health, her finances, and her lack of a job to her parents now thriving, just like her website design business. And she got to spend all her free time with the man of her dreams. Life couldn't be better.

Glancing at the tablet she'd been using to browse the news, one story caught her eye—an obituary written by the guy who'd died, oddly enough.

"Whoa. Luke, you've got to see this."

"What?" He set her omelet in front of her.

"Check out this picture. Looks just like Gladys."

He peered over her shoulder, then got closer. When Jasmin looked up at him, he'd gone white.

"Luke, what's the matter?"

"Nothing. That can't be Gladys. Must, uh, must be some sort of doppelganger." He plopped into his chair and dug into his omelet.

"Well, it's uncanny. This could well be Gladys twenty years ago."

"Can't be," he said through a mouthful of omelet.

He continued to stare at his food and not look up.

Which told Jasmin something was up. Luke was eating like he hadn't eaten in days. "What's going on, Luke?"

"Nothing," he said, wiping his mouth. "Hey, you haven't touched your breakfast."

Sitting back, Jasmin folded her arms over her chest. "And I won't until you tell me what's up."

He took his plate to the sink and rinsed it. "I don't know what you're talking about."

She went to him, wrapping her arms around him and leaning against his well-muscled back. "Luke, we've never kept secrets from each other. What's. Going. On?"

"I'm so sorry, Jazz. I can't tell you."

Luke didn't lie and didn't hold back with Jasmin. They'd worked through some significant bumps to get to this crucial point. And now, he was regressing? The misery on his face was palpable. What had brought this on? The article with the picture that she'd thought was Gladys?

Jasmin knew Luke better than she knew her own soul. If he was keeping a secret, there was a very good reason. And she thought she knew what it was. She turned him around, watching him until he wrapped his arms around her, hugging her tight, his lips in the crook of her neck, right near that spot that drove her wild.

"It's not your secret to tell, is it, Luke?"

The movement of his head was barely perceptible, but there. Not a nod by any definition. She'd guessed right. Luke had been in counseling for several months now for PTSD related to his time in the service overseas. Each time he came home, he told her what he and his support group had talked about. Total honestly, that's what he'd promised her. Even the hard stuff. It was the only way to get through it.

When she'd asked him once about the others in the therapy sessions, about their stories, he'd looked at her with profound sadness and whispered almost those same words: "Not my stories to tell."

The only time Luke would withhold something from her was if it wasn't his story.

He backed away from Jasmin, a wariness in his eyes. She drew him down to kiss him, a deep, searing, trusting kiss. When she pulled away, they were both breathing hard.

"I understand," Jasmin said.

"Thank you for trusting me."

"Always."

What Luke didn't know was that the next time Jasmin saw Gladys, she planned to have a long chat with their supposedly homeless friend. A very long talk.

"We'd better get ready. We're meeting Bernie and Paul in an hour."

"Sure you don't want to blow them off?" The spirit had returned to Luke's eyes as he reached for her.

"No. I want to see everything, before the hoards arrive, and figure out whose chowder I'll be first in line to taste."

"You sure?" He moved toward her, one feral step at a time.

Jasmin squealed and leaped back, turning to race for the stairs. Luke caught her at the top and, after another breathless, love-filled kissing session, stopped and jumped up. "Gotta go change or we'll be late."

"Oooh, you!" Jasmin lay on the floor, panting with need. "I don't think I can move."

Luke held out a hand. "Come on, Princess. Let's go socialize. We'll have lots of time later to sate our needs."

"How can you drive me to the brink of madness, then shift from horny to socialite? How?"

"I'm talented." He pulled her against his chest. "Make no mistake, though. Horny never left. It never does where you're concerned."

A slow smile spread across Jasmin's face. "I'm glad to know I'm not the only one."

CHAPTER TEN

Early Saturday morning, Ethan wandered through the conference center, the large open space so packed it felt damn near claustrophobic. Booths in orderly rows stood proudly full of wares, food, and drink, ready to sell. All with themes, like the Square Peg booth that had life-sized beer steins for people to put their names in.

Win free pizza for a year!

Even Joey's lodge had a booth. Ethan headed that way. The space, elegantly decked out in lodge-like décor, held six vibrating massage chairs.

Free chair massages!

They also offered upper back massages by a masseuse for a low fee, with the proceeds going to the women's shelter. And of course, their chef had set up to hand out samples of his chowder. That was, after all, what this weekend was about.

Ethan had a bad feeling about this whole festival. He crouched down to check an in-floor electrical socket. Everything was up to code. He knew that. The festival didn't open for a couple more hours and he couldn't shake his nightmare visions of crowds and tight spaces. This would be a disaster waiting to happen.

"Why the sour look, Chief?"

He glanced up to find Willow Bay's mayor, Josh Morgan. Ethan stood and brushed his hands off. "I don't like this."

Josh leaned back against a pillar, his face blank. Ethan had to sign off on the safety of the venture before they could open the doors.

"What's not up to code?" Josh asked.

"Nothing, damn it."

"Then what's the problem?"

"I guarantee you the place is going to be over capacity."

"The emergency exits only open from the inside, so there's only one way in. We have volunteers scheduled to do counts at the door. They know the max allowed at any one time."

"The booths are too close together."

"Damn it, Ethan. We used your specs to design this."

"I know, but what if there's a panic? People will get trampled." *What if there's a fire?* Sweat trickled down the side of Ethan's face.

Josh glanced around. More vendors had entered, doing final preparations for the First Annual Willow Bay Beer and Chowder Festival. "Come. Take a walk with me."

Outside, the rain had let up for a bit, but the wind hadn't. They sheltered on the leeward side of the building.

"What's this really about?" Josh asked.

Ethan leaned against the wall and shoved his hands into his pockets. He'd never talked about this, not since leaving L.A. He sure as hell didn't want to talk about it now. "You deserve an answer," he finally said. "I'm just not sure I'm ready to give it to you."

"I was part of the committee that hired you. I'm aware something happened in L.A. You were absolved of all responsibility."

"They may have absolved me, but I never forgave myself. I let myself get distracted and people died."

He waited for the reaction. The one that the people in L.A. had shown every time they saw him after that event. The one he saw when he looked in the mirror each and every day.

Josh didn't react at all. He stared out into the gray morning. "Your captain talked very highly of you."

"The captain is the only reason I got through the inquest. I— To be honest, I wanted to turn myself in, plead guilty."

"That's a heavy load of guilt you're carrying," Josh said. "This is as good a time to unburden yourself as any."

Ethan took a deep, guilt-filled breath and stared out at the rain. "It was a festival, something like this. Tight booths, lots of people. In winter. I knew the place was over capacity. I wasn't the one signing off on the setup but I was second in command and gave the okay when I should have shut it down. Anyhow, I tracked down the organizer to discuss closing. At first, he tried to schmooze me into leaving it open. When that didn't work he tried bribery, and finally, anger and threats."

"So far, I'm not seeing a single reason for you to feel culpable."

"I wasn't keeping watch on the weather. I let him distract me." Ethan nodded at Josh. "You came from L.A., right?"

"Yes."

"Then you know how a freak storm can hit, then disappear." He snapped his fingers. "Just like that."

"Rain, sure."

"And the rare unpredictable tornado."

"Oh, shit."

"Yeah. They said it was only on the ground about ten seconds and only a force one. It was enough to buckle the ceiling. Twenty-six people died, more than one hundred injured."

"Oh," Josh said, placing a hand on Ethan's shoulder. "I read about that. That was you?"

"Yeah." Ethan grimaced. "That was me."

"You know— "

"Spare me the platitudes, Mayor." Ethan had tried them all. Nothing worked to absolve him of his guilt. Especially since it hadn't been the first time he screwed up.

Josh tightened his lips for a moment. Then he planted his feet in front of Ethan, forcing the man to meet his eyes.

"You want it hard, you got it. Here's the deal. You did a good job designing the safest layout for our festival. Now you need to decide if you want to trust your design or not. But I'll be damned if I let Willow Bay suffer because you have some sort of phobia about disasters. You might not be ready to let that go, but unless you see a departure from"—Josh tapped Ethan in the chest— "*your* design, then you *will* sign off on this event. I don't have the time to baby you through your guilt. I have a town to help thrive and I thought you wanted the same thing."

"I do."

"Do you see anything inside that's dangerous or not to code?"

"No." Ethan hated to say it, but he couldn't lie.

"Then sign the damn form, Chief." Josh shoved the clipboard at Ethan and held a pen out in his other hand. "Let Willow Bay have this joy."

Ethan bit the inside of his lip—hard—to keep from spouting off to the man he considered a friend.

Instead, he yanked the clipboard from Josh and threw his signature on it like a piece of cooked spaghetti thrown against a door.

"Thank you," Josh said, taking the clipboard back. He stared at Ethan for a long time, his gaze softening while Ethan's remained stoic.

"I was there for all the meetings, Ethan. You went above and beyond to make this a safe venue and I agreed with all the precautions. You did a great job and it's as safe as it can be. The festival is good for Willow Bay. Try to relax and enjoy yourself this weekend."

"I'm working."

"Yeah, coulda figured that out on my own, I guess." Josh chuckled. "At least try to come by for some chowder. There'll be some awesome options."

Josh held out his hand. Ethan shook it, nodded as the man walked away, then stayed staring out at the rain pounding the parking lot as a thread of doom tightened around his neck. He knew he wouldn't relax until the damn festival was over.

Part of him wanted it to fail so they'd never have another one. However, the pragmatist in him knew the hotels were filled, the restaurants and gift shops busy. The First Annual Beer and Chowder Festival would be a success, and Josh was right. It would help Willow Bay to thrive.

Would Joey be there today? He'd thought of her too much in the past few days. She should stay away. He'd call her, ask her to steer clear of the festival. The possibility that hearing her voice was his real motivation poked at him from the edge of his awareness. He pulled his phone out and tapped her name.

"Hi, Chief."

Just the sound of her voice made him smile, damn it. He'd have to talk to her, tell her they couldn't be together. Break it off clean. After the festival.

"Hey," he said. "How's it going?"

"Oh, you know. The usual craziness."

"What's wrong? You sound a little off."

A long pause, followed by a heavy sigh, preceded her response. "I didn't get the house."

Ethan straightened. "Someone outbid you?"

"No. The mortgage I was approved for isn't enough and I don't qualify for more."

The defeat in her voice stole his breath. Even now, with things between them so new, he wanted to make it better. But he couldn't. Slumping back against the wall, he knew this was a battle he couldn't take on, even if he knew how.

"I'm sorry."

"So am I." Her voice was so small, it gutted Ethan. He heard a voice in the background calling her name. "Hang on." She must have put her hand over the phone because her voice was muffled, then she was back and clear. "I'm sorry. I have to go. It's insane here. Was there a reason you called?"

Not wanting to add to her down mood, Ethan let it go. "Nothing that can't wait. Survive your day."

"Thanks for the call," she said.

He shoved his phone in his pocket, wishing more than anything that Joey could have her dream. She lit up people's lives, made them happy. She deserved that happiness herself. After this weekend— No. He couldn't get involved. For now, he'd have to push Joey from his mind and focus on the festival.

Ethan headed for his car, not caring that rain soaked his uniform. If he made it past this weekend unscathed—if Willow Bay made it—he'd try to sort his head out. For now, it was all eyes peeled for issues.

~~~

On Sunday morning, Joey stood beside the center table in Pacific Lodge's lobby, protecting the large vase of flowers while keeping an eagle eye on the two boys wreaking havoc on the place. The beautiful ceramic vase she'd purchased with her own money from Shiri, a local artist, had wobbled a few times after close encounters with the energetic boys. They'd tried her patience each time they entered the lobby with their grandparents, who also happened to own the lodge and her life at the moment.

"Pow!"

"Bam!"

The two hellions raced around the lobby, bringing other patrons up short. They ran into John's tool cart, upending it and John in one fell swoop. The poor man had only stopped by to fix a light and now, he hit the ground hard, tools clattering around him as he glared at the almost-ten-year-olds. Joey had had quite enough. She stepped away from the table as the boys raced her way, timing her lunge and managing to catch one in each arm.

"Oof." Joey lifted them both off the floor, their legs flailing. Good thing she worked out regularly. These two weren't lightweights.

"Let go of me," the blond boy screamed.

"Yeah, let go," the brown-haired boy chimed in.

People were staring. This whole situation was the antithesis of the quiet, elegant lobby she wanted to portray.

"Not letting go until you calm down and stop destroying my lobby."

"We can do whatever we want. We own this place," Blond Boy said.

Brown Hair screamed at the top of his lungs. You'd think she was driving pins into their skull instead of simply holding them. "You need to calm down," she said.

"What is the meaning of this?"

Joey's back stiffened. She turned—a boy still snugged under each arm—to face her boss. Interestingly enough, both boys had gone still.

"Let them go," Mr. Reynolds said. "Now."

She lowered both boys until their feet touched the ground and then let go, giving them her best "don't mess with me" look. She was astounded when they broke into tears and raced for their grandfather, each grabbing an arm.

"That lady hurt us."

Oh, please. Joey bit her lip to keep the retort from bursting free.

"Yeah, she hurt us."

Keeping his stern gaze focused on Joey, Mr. Reynolds pointed behind him. "Your grandmother is in the dining room having breakfast. Go."

Both kids skittered off with more speed than they'd shown in the lobby so far.

"What is the meaning of this, Miss Sanderson?"

Still trying to catch her breath, Joey straightened her clothes. Her arms felt ready to fall off. "Just trying to keep the lobby from being trashed by your grandsons, *sir*." Joey was done sugar-coating things. If that meant she'd lose her job, well, she'd find another.

"They were just being boys. Nothing untoward would have happened."

"Sir, we pride ourselves on a calming, quiet atmosphere here at Pacific Lodge. Your grandsons were disrupting that, upended our facilities man, and no one,"—she stared her boss right in the eye—"was supervising them."

"Again, they were just being boys, and you had no right to touch them. In this day and age? You could land in jail for something like that. Now, I'm going back to finish my breakfast." He dumped the newly replaced brochures from the table into a trash can and eyed Joey.

"You and I will talk after this weekend about how—or if—we will go forward." He started to walk away, then turned back. "Also, add a babysitting service as one of the penthouse perks."

He walked off, giving her not one single idea on how to do that or how to handle the cost, especially when he was using the penthouse for free at the moment.

"Get a babysitter," she mumbled as she walked over to John. "Don't spend so much money."

"What?" John said.

"Nothing," Joey answered, disgusted with herself for not standing up to her boss more. "Are you all right?"

John rubbed his back. "Nothing my chiropractor can't fix. Ugh. Those kids are devils."

"Most definitely," Joey said.

Together, they picked up the tools. Joey walked around the lobby putting things back in order. It was a miracle nothing got broken. Shaking her head, she saw Gladys settling her cart by the door and went to greet her. To hell with Mr. Reynolds.

"Hi, Gladys. How are you doing today?" Joey took her arm and helped her to a bench near the fireplace.

"Oh, these old bones ache in this cold. Getting old, well, it's not for the weak of heart."

Joey chuckled. Sometimes, even young wasn't easy. "You sit and warm yourself as long as you like. Want some hot cocoa?"

"I'd love that, dearie. Thank you so much."

"I'll be right back with it. And if you need a ride anywhere, you let me know."

"I was going to try to get into the festival, but I'm just not sure I can walk that far today. Achier than usual, I guess."

"I can run you and your beloved cart, Mabel, over

there in about an hour. Will that work? I have a few things to look after here, but by then I'll be overdue for a break."

Gladys patted her cheek. "You are such a sweet girl. That would be just fine, and I appreciate it."

As Joey headed into the restaurant to get cocoa, her boss, his wife, and the brats were just exiting. Right away, his gaze landed on Gladys. Then he turned to Joey.

"Rough weather outside today," Joey said. "I won't be turning anyone away that wants to warm up. If you've got a problem with that, you can fire me."

Mrs. Reynold's eyes bulged. "You can't fire her, Christian. She's good for this place."

Nice of someone to notice.

By the way they were shuffling their feet, the boys were getting restless. No way was Joey going to deal with that again.

"If you'll excuse me, Mrs. Reynolds, Mr. Reynolds, I'm going to get some cocoa for our newest visitor."

Shaking because of the way she'd just stood up to her boss, Joey forced herself to march into the restaurant without looking back. It helped when she overheard a comment by her boss's wife.

"I like that girl."

Her face fell at Mr. Reynold's mumbled, "I don't."

If she ever planned to feel fully settled, Joey needed a good-paying job, and this one paid pretty well considering she'd come with a diploma but not much actual work experience. Because room and board were included for the first six months, she'd been saving most of her paychecks. Except it wasn't enough for her house. So far, she hadn't come up with a single option for buying that perfect home. Maybe it was time to look at condos. She couldn't spend the rest of her life living in a hotel room and she sure as hell wasn't going home.

She hung her head in the dark interior of the restaurant, giving in to a momentary despair. What if she got fired? She couldn't go home. Not back to that rigid lifestyle. All it was missing were the Puritan dresses and hats.

Shaking off the melancholy, she poured some hot cocoa and took it out to Gladys.

"Thank you, dearie."

"You are most welcome. I'll go take care of some stuff and be back here in about forty-five minutes to give you a ride. Will that work?"

"Very well, thank you." Gladys sniffed her cocoa, satisfaction smoothing her wrinkles. "Best cocoa in Willow Bay."

Joey laughed. "Oh, I doubt that. Connie's concoction over at the café beats ours any day."

"Not by much. And I didn't have to walk as far to come here."

Was that a clue? Joey's eyes widened. Gladys had never been forthcoming about where she spent her nights, so to tell Joey that about Pacific Lodge was a big deal. Had she said that because she trusted Joey or because she'd forgotten how close to the vest she usually held her personal information? Joey fervently hoped it was the former. Gladys had become important to the people of Willow Bay. The entire town watched out for her, fed her, and offered housing, the latter of which she always refused.

"I'm glad you didn't have to come too far." Joey kept her expression cheerful, and carefully neutral. She'd figured she could ask around to see if Gladys had revealed anything to anyone else. But for now, she'd leave it be. "I'll be back in a bit," she said.

"I'll be right here," Gladys said, a smile plastered on her face.

~~~

The smile disappeared as soon as Joey walked

away. "Why did I say that?" Gladys mumbled, sipping the cocoa that really did warm her chilly bones. All she needed was for this town to start digging into her life. A life exactly how she wanted it—no one could tell her otherwise.

She thought about that press release her late husband had issued, sure it would cause her trouble. A little over a week had passed since it hit the news back in New York. Thankfully, no one here had mentioned it. Hell, it was an old picture. No one here would recognize her, right?

Maybe it was time for this whole charade to come to an end. Gladys took another sip of her cocoa as a couple exited the elevator, chattering about all the chowder they were about to taste.

"And beer!" the dark-haired man said. "Don't forget the beer."

Laughing, they walked out into the pouring rain without a care in the world.

A long time ago, she'd lived that carefree life. Hadn't thought about anything beyond what made her happy, until she wasn't happy anymore. Content with her life now, she didn't want to rock the boat.

Joey waved and headed out the front door. "I'll bring my SUV around."

Gladys stood, feeling the arthritic aches and pains of age, knowing her body might well make the decision for her. She couldn't do this much longer. She headed for the door, shelving her thoughts for later when she was home alone.

CHAPTER ELEVEN

Ethan hadn't slept since Friday before his shift. He was obsessing but couldn't stop himself. On Sunday, he entered the conference center through a delivery door. The back storage area was quiet. No indication of the chaos happening on the other side of the double doors in front of him. Placing a hand on one of the doors, Ethan sent a prayer skyward, then opened the door to the cacophony of festival noise.

Laughter, children's excited calls, and vendors selling wares. Plus, a sea of people. No way this crowd was below the max Ethan had set. Folks dodged each other as they wandered the aisle in front of him. Long lines had formed at Connie's booth to try her award-winning chowder.

Too many. If anything happened, he'd never get them all out in time. Panic hitched Ethan's breathing and he shut the door, shut out the noise and fear, gasping as he leaned against it. He couldn't do this. Couldn't let it happen. Not again.

You are not a wimp. You can handle this. It's a festival. They go on all the time. Ethan tried to talk himself calm between long, slow breaths.

Tap. Tap.

A knock at the door made Ethan jump. He opened it a smidge. Joey stood there, a tremulous smile on her face. An angel in a turbulent sea.

"Saw you open the door, then close it. You okay?"

No. I'm not. But he couldn't get the words out. Ethan scrubbed his face with both hands as his angel slid inside and closed the utility door behind her.

"Sit," she said, pointing to a chair.

Ethan sat. He didn't have the power to refuse.

"Head between your knees."

"I don't need— "

"Head between your knees, Chief."

He leaned down.

"Take a deep, slow breath."

He breathed in and out.

"Another."

As he followed her orders, the panic receded. Something cold wrapped around his neck.

"It's just a wet cloth. Cold water, helping you orient to reality." She stood behind him, her hands kneading his shoulders, his back, easing the tension. "I know a thing or two about panic attacks. You're okay, Ethan. You'll be fine and fit in a minute or two. Just breathe and hang in there."

Ethan gave himself up to her ministrations, taking slow, measured breaths until his heart rate returned to normal and he didn't have to think about breathing any longer. The panic faded.

"Better now, right?" Joey came around in front of him, cupping his cheeks in her hands.

"Yeah."

"Welcome back." She smiled and it lit up the room. Gentle blue eyes crinkled with happiness.

Before the last, lingering sense of confusion left him, Ethan pulled her to him, running his fingers over her soft lips before meeting them with his own. All the angst faded as burning need took over. More. He needed more. He needed her. He deepened the kiss as her hands wound into his hair. For long moments, they played, until reason returned and Ethan slowed the devouring kiss until it became a tender sharing.

When they parted, Joey stepped back and brushed her bruised lips. "Um, didn't really expect that."

"Me, either." Ethan placed a hand over his heart, feeling the usual tha-thump. "You calm men down with a kiss often? Because you're really good at it."

Joey grinned. "Good to have you back, Chief. And you kissed me, remember?"

He had, though he didn't want to delve too deeply into the why. Probably because he'd been vulnerable. That had to be it. Right? With that resolved, Ethan smiled until her next question.

"So, what was that about? Do you have agoraphobia?"

Ethan raked a hand through his hair, his sense of calm fading. No one knew the full story of his life. He was drawn to Joey, sure. She'd calmed his panic and he was grateful. But could he bare his soul to this woman? Kiss the life out of her, yes, but get all emotive and deep? He wasn't ready for that and probably never would be.

"No, I don't."

"Umm, kind of seems like you do."

"I'm fine in crowds," he said, stiffening.

Joey rolled her eyes.

"You're not going to let this go, are you?"

"What do you think?" Joey answered, with that damn angelic smile on her face.

"Look," Ethan stood. Time to get back into chief-mode and regain control of this conversation. "I had a moment and I'm grateful for your help. Trust me. I'm fine with crowds."

She crossed her arms over her chest. "Except when… "

He mirrored her action. "Except when I'm responsible for their safety." What the hell? Had he said that out loud?

To his relief, she didn't make light of this admission. Instead, she unfolded her arms and grabbed his gently. "Thank you for telling me that. I can tell it wasn't easy to say."

Ethan stared into her eyes, big pools of understanding. He wanted to fall into them but he needed to maintain tight control. When he didn't, when he got distracted, bad things happened.

"I need to get out there, wander around, be a presence," he said.

"Me, too. I shouldn't have left the lodge, but I couldn't resist the chance for some chowder."

"Let me buy you lunch. You know, as a thank you." That sounded lame even to him.

"That would be very nice of you, Chief. I accept your invitation."

The chaos in the main hall didn't seem as bad this time. People milled about, but the crowd had thinned. Ethan and Joey made their way to Connie's booth and stood in line for some chowder. Once they had their bowls in hand, they leaned against the wall to eat since all the tables were full.

"Oh, this is sooo good," Joey said, spooning chowder into her mouth. "Connie's a wizard."

Ethan barely heard the words. He leaned a shoulder against the wall to watch Joey eat. The woman loved just about everything she did and knew how to get the maximum pleasure out of anything. She certainly did in bed, and his dick paid attention to the thought. When Joey licked her lips to catch a drop she missed, the brain in his head shut down and the one in his pants took over.

Brushing a crumb from the side of her lips, his hand lingered there. Her wide and expressive blue eyes darkened with serious intent as she stared up at him.

A kid raced by, screaming, and broke the spell. Ethan dropped his hand and stepped away from Joey. Away from the temptation to throw her over his shoulders and head for his place.

Joey leaned against the wall beside him, pulling her lower lip into her mouth as if it needed caressing.

"You know," she said, her voice low and sultry and meant only for his ears. "We really should scratch this itch again one of these days."

His dick jumped again and he willed it to behave. He shouldn't spend time around her. His focus might take a hit. Might? What an understatement. He forgot everything when he was with Joey. So why did he hear himself asking her out to dinner?

Her eyes sparkling, Joey laughed, a lilting, happy sound that drew a smile from Ethan against his wishes. "I'd love to. When?"

"Tomorrow night?"

"About half our guests are checking out tomorrow, so that could work."

"Seven p.m.? I can pick you up."

She nodded, her smile wide. Tossing her empty chowder bowl in a nearby garbage can, Joey stood on tiptoe and pecked Ethan's cheek. "Back to work for me." She grew serious for a moment. "I'm glad you're feeling better. See you tomorrow night."

Without waiting for his response, Joey pushed off the wall and walked off. Ethan could swear there was a touch more sashay to those hips his gaze couldn't leave. He watched until she disappeared, then noticed Gladys sitting there, a wide grin on her face. She gave Ethan a thumb's up and he groaned. Having heard of the woman's penchant for matching people up, he could only pray he wasn't her next victim. Maybe he should go talk with her, remind her he could take care of his own love life.

"If you're thinking of pulling Gladys off her matchmaking plans, don't bother." Josh joined him.

"I don't know what you're talking about," Ethan hedged.

"Yeah, sure. Here's the thing with Gladys. If she's got you in her sights, just give up gracefully. She's not going to let go."

"It's not her decision."

Josh chuckled. "Try telling her that."

Everyone in Willow Bay knew that Josh, having pined after Dana for the first six months she'd been there, had been forced to do something about it by Gladys' machinations. In Josh's case, it had been the right choice. Married for about eight months now, he and Dana were crazy in love and happy.

What was it like, being that happy? A deep longing tugged at Ethan's heart. Would he ever have that?

"How are you doing?" Josh asked.

It grated on Ethan's nerves for anyone to know his weaknesses, but Josh had a right. "Good now. Umm, thanks for the slap in the face yesterday."

"Don't go spreading it around that I slap people or I'll never get re-elected." Josh stroked his chin. "Hmm. On second thought, maybe that's a good idea."

"From the things I hear, you're going to be mayor until you're Old Ben's age."

"Oh, God, I hope not," Josh said. He chuckled before giving Ethan an appraising look. "So, you and Joey, huh?"

"No. And not going to talk about it."

"I understand." Josh's grin said he wouldn't hold

off forever, though. "Good crowd, eh?"

"Yes. Not too many, though at first it seemed so."

"We had a crush at the beginning, but we didn't go over your set numbers."

"Thanks. I appreciate that."

They both watched the crowd for a while, then Josh put out his hand to shake Ethan's. "I've got to get back to my mingling. The job of a mayor is never done."

Not a job Ethan would want to do. He was grateful Josh Morgan was so good at it. "Have fun."

"And you have fun at dinner tomorrow night."

Josh walked off with a wave, so didn't see the frown of frustration on Ethan's face. Did everyone in Willow Bay know everyone's business? He needed to cut this off at the source. Ethan strode over to Gladys and pointed at chair next to her. "Mind if I sit down?"

Gladys's eyes sparkled like an older version of Joey's. "Please do. How lovely to see you, Chief Walker."

Like she hadn't just seen him standing there with Joey, then with Josh. The woman was cagey. And the refinement of the greeting perplexed him, coming as it did from the mouth of someone wearing multiple layers of ratty clothing and whose hair hadn't been brushed in weeks. There was more to this woman than what the outside showed. He'd bet almost anything on that. But it was a mystery for another time.

"How're you doing?" he asked.

"Oh, I'm right as rain, I am. Ha. Rain. We're getting a lot of it again this winter, aren't we?"

"We are."

"Not good for these old bones."

"Do you need some assistance?" Ethan leaned toward her. "Some services that would make your life a little easier?"

"Oh, posh. Nothing like that for me. I'm not done yet and, God willing, I have a few more years before I have to think about things like that."

"Gladys, we need to talk."

She squinted at him for a moment, then looked beyond him. "Oh, look, there's Jasmin and Luke."

Arm in arm, the handyman and his fiancé had eyes more for each other than for the rows of food and wares. Again, that unfamiliar ache filled Ethan's heart. What would that be like, to have someone with eyes only for you? To have a partner, someone to share your burdens.

The flash of fire came out of nowhere. Complete. Devouring.

"Ethan, are you okay?"

Gladys. Gladys was speaking. Ethan blinked himself out of the flashback. They were happening less and less often, though the fade wasn't fast enough for his sense of peace. And now, he couldn't tell which traumatic incident had created them.

He shook his head. "Sorry, Gladys, you were saying?"

"I said, you and Miss Joey looked pretty cozy earlier."

"That's what I need to talk to you about." No way would he let Willow Bay's resident matchmaker settle her sights on him. He didn't need a partner. Partners were distracting.

"Uh oh." Gladys cut him off again.

"What?" Ethan didn't see anything amiss.

"Not sure why, but I think I'm in trouble. Jasmin has that look on her face."

Sure enough, he turned to see Jasmin bearing down on them with stoic determination written all over her face. Yikes.

"Well, that's my cue." Ethan stood. "Have a

wonderful day, Gladys. But we *will* talk later, you and
I." He tapped his hat in hello to Jasmin and slipped
quickly away from the two storm clouds about to merge
into a squall. Women. Something was always pissing
them off.

Except Joey. She seemed perennially happy. Then
he thought about the bonfire and how angry she'd
gotten that night and he chuckled under his breath.
Well, happy until she wasn't.

Ethan wandered the aisles, telling himself he
needed to make sure everyone was safe. Sticking around
there had nothing to do with seeing whether a certain
blonde had gone back to work. Nothing at all.

~~~

"You made Luke keep a secret from me," Jasmin
accused, pulling a chair close to Gladys and sitting
down, for which the older woman was grateful. No one
else needed to hear this conversation.

"Shoot. He told you." Annoyed, Gladys dug her
spoon into some now-cold chowder, moving the
leftover mush around the bowl.

"Not until I made him uncomfortable about
withholding information. And that took some work."

How should she handle this? Gladys could spar
with the best of them, but she didn't want to do that
there. Willow Bay wasn't New York City, so she opted
for a touch of honesty. "Honey, you have to keep my
secret. I'm not ready to out myself."

"Gladys, this whole town has adopted you with no
clue about who you really are."

A genuine smile spread across Gladys's face. She
loved Willow Bay and its people.

"I saw your husband's obituary," Jasmin went on.
"Your picture. You had a life before Willow Bay that
no one knows about."

"That's my business."

"Not when this town has taken you under their wing. People worry about you! For no reason! You can't keep lying to everyone," Jasmin said.

"I'm not lying."

Jasmin waited for a couple to pass by before continuing. "We all think you sleep in the bushes somewhere."

"I have never said I was homeless."

"You didn't correct any of us when we mentioned it."

"Not my fault if you came to the wrong conclusion."

"It is if you hurt this town."

Gladys straightened, no longer the hunched over street person Willow Bay usually saw.

"I would never hurt Willow Bay. I love this town."

"Then why are you doing this? Why not come clean?"

"That, my dear, is a long story."

Jasmin settled back in the chair. "I've got time. Luke is at Paul and Bernie's booth."

"Not here. Not with all these people around."

"Then where? When?"

Gladys looked down the row to see Ethan chatting with Luke, Paul, and Josh. "Oh, that one," she whispered. "He's going to take a while."

"What?" Jasmin asked.

"Never mind." Gladys turned back to Jasmin. "As for my story, you'll just have to wait."

The younger woman's eyes became slits.

"I get that you have a right to hear it," Gladys added, "but I'm not done with what I need to do."

When Jasmin seemed ready to protest, Gladys resorted to the only weapon left in her arsenal, her boardroom queen stare, always a great way to wither the opposition. It worked. Jasmin remained quiet for a full minute.

"When will you be done?" she finally asked.

"Soon. I think."

"Fine. I'll give you some time. But not too long." Jasmin leaned in. "I don't much like secrets." She got up and, with a last stern look for Gladys, walked off to join her husband. He pulled her to his side, whispering in her ear, his eyes full of concern. Gladys could only imagine what Jasmin said in reply. Luke glanced at Gladys over his fiancée's head, shaking his own in disappointment.

Gladys shoved the chowder bowl away. Everything was closing in on her. The charade that had served her so well seemed poised to crumble. She wasn't one bit happy.

But there wasn't a damn thing she could do about it.

CHAPTER TWELVE

Joey checked in with the lodge and found all was quiet. They'd even had one guest leave early due to a family emergency, so she figured it was safe to walk around the festival for a while longer. Browsing the beach-themed knick-knacks at one of the booths, she picked up a distressed wooden sign in faded blue whose white letters proclaimed that a life that began and ended at the beach was a life well lived. It would look great in her dream house.

A fleeting gloom swept through her. She'd found no solution that would make that house hers, so she set the sign back on the table. Better save her money. Heading down another aisle, Joey noticed that the longest line snaked away from the Square Peg booth.

"Ready to wash down that chowder with a beer?" Bernie said as Joey walked up.

"No." A man in line scowled at her.

"Don't worry," she said, holding her hands up, palms out. "Not cutting." She turned back to Bernie. "You need any help?"

"Yes! I'd love some. Things got quiet so I let everyone go wander, then this happened to the line.

Grab an apron. If you'll take orders, I'll fill them."

Slipping an apron over her head, Joey asked the scowler what he wanted. For the next hour, she and Bernie worked in concert, taking and filling orders until finally, another lull occurred. Bernie sank onto a stool.

"How are you feeling?" Joey asked.

Bernie rubbed her distended belly. "Like I'm carrying a bowling ball in my gut."

"When's the baby due?"

"Doc says next month. It can't come soon enough."

"I hear it can get uncomfortable."

"This little lady is going to be a handful if how active she is now is any indication."

Paul came up behind his wife, encircling her with his arms and covering her belly-holding hands with his. "We'll be ready for anything, right?"

"Right." Bernie lifted her head up for his kiss.

"Try to rest while you can. You won't be getting much after she's born."

With Paul's return, Joey hung up her apron and said her goodbyes. Bernie's husband was so supportive. He didn't try to mold her to his image but accepted her as she was, even her flaming red hair. It hadn't been that way for Joey. The one man her parents had chosen for her to date, then decided she would marry without even asking her, had required her to dye her hair mousy brown.

That blonde stands out too much. You want to blend, not showcase yourself. I'm the one who needs to shine. That's how money is made. That's what he'd said to her.

When she'd refused, the punishment had been particularly brutal. So, she'd run. She'd been on her own, and alone, ever since. Sometimes, like now, it got to her. Wouldn't it be nice to have someone to lean on? To share meals with? To cuddle up to at night? To trust that he'd love her for who she was, and not mold her into some perfect likeness.

That kind of life wasn't in the cards for her. Not yet, at least. She had more to do before she could think of finding someone to share her life with. Which was why she was crazy to be going after Ethan Walker. He'd made it pretty clear he wasn't the type of man who wanted those things. But something about him drew her in, made her want to play, to be reckless.

And there he was, at the end of the row, looking relaxed and happy. Superficially, at least. Joey knew better. Even from there, she could see the tightness of his face, the shadows below his eyes. Ethan probably hadn't slept since the festival opened.

More than anything, Joey wanted to make sure he'd be okay. He was the penny she shouldn't turn over, but damn, she wanted to. Taking a step in his direction, she ran smack dab into an elderly gentleman.

"Oof," he said, wobbling on his cane.

Joey steadied him with a hand on his arm. "I'm so sorry. I wasn't looking where I was going." She'd been focused on Ethan, who now watched her intently. "Are you all right?"

"Right as rain," the man said, straightening. "And running into a beautiful woman is never a problem. Besides, this cane is more for looks than stability." He waved it in the air.

The man, tall and regal despite his age, had a full head of white hair, bright blue eyes, and an engaging smile.

"I'm Joey Sanderson." She stuck out her hand. "I manage the Pacific Lodge here in town."

"Henry Forrich, at your service. I know that lodge. Tried to get a room there tonight."

"Oh, I'm so sorry, we've been completely booked because of the festival."

"I found that out."

"Did you find a place to stay?"

"No, I'm afraid not. This may turn out to be a very quick trip."

"Wait. We may have had a cancellation. Let me check."

"That would be lovely of you, my dear."

Funny, he talked a lot like Gladys. Must be the age, since they were probably close in years. Joey pulled out her phone. "Give me one minute." She dialed the front desk. "Rose, how are things?"

"Good. Quiet. Everyone must be at the festival."

"I'll be back within the hour to relieve you so you can come enjoy. Is that room still available? The people who left due to a family emergency?"

"Yes, er, no. I mean, it's available, but not cleaned yet."

"That's excellent. Can you get someone to clean it? If not, I'll do it when I get back. I'm here with someone looking for a room for the night. A Henry Fornich. Would you hold it for him?"

"I'd be happy to."

"Thanks, Rose." Hanging up, she gave Mr. Fornich a wide smile. "The lodge is holding a room for you. Check in any time before eleven p.m. when the front desk closes."

"That is most excellent. Thank you very much, Ms. Sanderson."

"Joey, please. We're all basically family here."

"Joey, then."

"Are you here for the festival?" she asked as they meandered down the row.

"Actually, I'm here to see someone but she doesn't know I'm coming."

"Ooh, I sense some intrigue and I love a good mystery. Are you sure the woman is here?"

"At the festival? No. Here in Willow Bay? Mostly definitely."

"I know a lot of people here. Small town and all. What's her name?"

"Gladys Hawthorne."

"I don't know any Hawthorne." Joey glanced toward the food court tables, now fairly close, where their resident street person had been sitting. He couldn't be looking for Gladys. Could he?

Gladys looked up at that moment and smiled at Joey. When she glanced at the man beside Joey, the smile disappeared and Gladys blanched as if she'd seen a ghost.

What the heck?

"Excuse me," Joey said, hurrying to see if Gladys was all right. She never got the chance because the elderly street person, usually all bent over, leaped from her chair, upended a cup, and fled.

By the time Joey reached the table, Gladys had disappeared.

"What was that all about?" Joey said as she stared, astounded, in the direction Gladys had run.

"Was that Gladys I just saw take off like a bat out of hell?" asked Josh Morgan, coming over with his wife Dana from the end of the aisle.

"Yes," Joey said, nodding to Jasmin as she joined them, too.

Josh shook his head. "I didn't think the woman could hoof it that fast."

"Why did she take off?" Dana asked.

"I don't know. She glanced down the aisle toward me, blanched, then ran off."

As one, they all stared at Joey, who held up her hands in surrender.

"I didn't do anything."

"I think I know why she ran." The white-haired

gentleman said from behind Joey. "It wasn't Joey she was looking at. It was me."

~~~

Ethan, having stepped outside for some air, leaned against the building. Today was about done and he had to admit everything had gone well. More than well. He didn't want to jinx things, but so far nothing serious had happened. A couple more hours and he could breathe normally again. And sleep. Ethan shook his head to clear the fatigue, feeling more peace than he had in a long time. Maybe now, with a successful festival almost over, he could let go of the past. Think about the future. Think about Joey. More and more, he wanted that.

Darkness had fallen. He stood under the eaves watching the rain fall. Ethan liked the rain. There was a peacefulness to it. Plus, it was harder for fires to start in this kind of weather. As he looked out into the grayness, Jackson Smith strolled up.

"Hey, Sheriff," Ethan said.

"Hey," Jackson said in his usual laconic way. "Festival's going well."

"It is. Have you been inside?"

"Just when a kid tried to lift a bag of popcorn. Meeting Aimi here in a few."

They stood surrounded by the quiet for a moment, when suddenly, the door beside them flew open and Gladys raced out.

"Gladys?" Ethan said.

The woman didn't pause or look his way, blowing right past him and racing off, quickly swallowed by the gray and rain.

"What the hell?" Ethan glanced inside the door and saw Josh and Dana talking to Joey and an older gentleman. He and Jackson quickly joined them.

"Did you just see Gladys run off?" Ethan asked.

All heads nodded as they turned to him.

"She didn't even grab Mabel," Ethan continued. "She just rain. Faster than I thought possible for a woman of her, umm, years. Any idea why?"

"We were just about to sit down and figure that out, or try to." Josh indicated the table beside him and, after mopping up the spilled tea, they all sat. Except Ethan and Jackson, both of whom grazed the festival with their gaze, always alert.

~~~

Knocked off her game for a moment by Ethan's sudden appearance with the sheriff, Joey took a deep breath and shifted in her seat towards her companion. "Everyone, this is Henry Fornich," she said. "We got to talking and he told me he's come to find one Gladys Hawthorne."

Before anyone could react, Jasmin and Luke walked up arm-in-arm. Luke did not take his eyes off Joey's new friend. Surprise was plain on his face.

"I'm sorry, sir. What was your name again?" Luke asked. Mr. Fornich repeated his name.

"You know something," Joey said, staring at Luke. "I— "

"First things first," Jasmin said, rubbing her husband's hand. "Mr. Fornich, do you believe our Gladys is the one you're looking for?"

"I do. As soon as I saw those impish blue eyes, I knew I'd found her."

"Okay," Jackson said. "So, you've found Gladys Hawthorne. What do you want with her?" His calm demeanor did nothing to hide the underlying protectiveness.

Mr. Fornich raised both hands in the air briefly. "Nothing you wouldn't approve of, I assure you. And please, call me Henry." He smiled. "It makes me happy that Gladys has found people who think so highly of her. I am not here to disturb that. In fact, I hope to make things better. For her and for everyone."

"How?" Joey said, still trying to digest this new side to their resident homeless person. Apparently, they were not privy to the layers hidden beneath the surface of Willow Bay's most beloved inhabitant. Yet. Gladys had been keeping secrets, and as Joey looked around the table at the blank faces, she knew everyone was trying to wrap their heads around this new information, just like her.

"Hawthorne," she said. "Where do I know that name from?"

Jasmin and Luke glanced at each other as Henry's eyes widened.

"It's a fairly common name," Henry said.

"No," Joey said. "I've seen it recently. In the news. What was it?" She tapped her head with her index finger. "I know! An obituary. New York, I think. A man died and his obit was all about his long-lost love— his wife still—yes! She was named Gladys Hawthorne."

Everyone's eyes turned to the elderly gentleman they'd just met. Everyone except Jasmin and Luke. He looked at the floor while Jasmin stared at her hands. They definitely knew something.

"I can tell you know something, Luke," Joey said. "What is it?"

He shook his head. "I'm sorry. I can't. I promised. Besides, even if I knew her past, it's not my story to tell."

Jasmin clutched his hand.

All heads then turned to Henry Fornich. "It's not my story to tell, either," he said.

Jackson stepped closer to the man. "Are you here to cause any harm to our Gladys?"

Henry waved his hands. "Absolutely not. I love her. I've loved her for years. I came here to have a conversation. To tell her once and for all how I feel and hope it's not too late."

Joey relaxed back in her chair. She believed the man. This wasn't some nefarious plot to harm Gladys. This was a love story, and Joey loved happy endings. Grins spread around the table as everyone settled into the news. Jasmin hugged Luke and he kept her tight to his side.

Their affection got Joey thinking again about how nice it would be to have someone to lean on, to share the good and the bad. Maybe she wasn't ready, but she knew now, it was what she wanted. Someone to talk to at the end of the day, to cuddle with in front of the fireplace in the winter, to share the joys and the tender moments. Someone supportive of her dreams and whose goals she could champion. She slumped in her chair, an unusual melancholy weighing her down.

Until a strong hand settled with tender care on her shoulder. She didn't have to look. She knew it was Ethan. The man had a sixth sense, at least when it came to her. To them.

Did they have a chance to become something… more? Something real and forever? The only way to find out was to dive in head first. Joey covered his hand with hers and he squeezed her shoulder in acknowledgement.

"What do we do now?" Ethan asked. "It's obvious Gladys wasn't happy to see you, Mr., uh, Henry. No offense."

"None taken. I knew she wouldn't be. She doesn't much like having her hand forced. And now, I've lost the element of surprise."

Ethan chuckled, still standing behind Joey. In fact, his thumb was moving in delicious circles over the back of her shoulder.

"Gladys," Jackson said, "is quite good at

subterfuge. If I'm right, none of us know where she spends her nights. We've assumed she sleeps in some bushes somewhere, but does she?"

"Maybe Mabel would give us some clues," Ethan said. "The cart is still outside."

"I don't think going through Gladys's things without permission is the right way to go," Joey said.

"You don't have to rifle through Mabel. Luke has a way of reaching out to Gladys," Jasmin said. "Sorry, honey, but it's time."

All eyes turned to Luke. Jasmin tightened her arms around his waist.

"You know where she lives," Jackson said.

Luke remained mute, gnashing his jaw.

Henry stood and stepped closer to him. "I'm not trying to hurt Gladys, Luke. I only want to have a conversation with her. Is there any way you could facilitate that happening?"

Finally, with a nod to Jasmin, he spoke. "I do have a way to get a hold of her. I'm willing to reach out."

The collective sigh that rumbled through the table made everyone smile.

"But— " Luke speared Henry with a stern look— "if she doesn't want to meet with you, I will honor that."

"Fair enough," Henry said, reaching to shake on it.

With that decided, everyone dispersed to get back to festival fun or work. Joey was about to get up when Ethan squeezed her shoulder. He sat beside her and reached for her hand, caressing the back.

"I know we said tomorrow night for dinner. How about we bump that to tonight?"

Yes. That was Joey's gut answer when she stared into his dark, shuttered eyes. "I have a full lodge tonight again. I'm not sure I'll be able to concentrate. And you need some sleep." Although, with the things his hand was doing to hers, the way he was being so gentle, caressing her, Joey found it hard to remember where she worked.

By now, he'd intertwined their hands and his thumb was doing delightful things to her palm.

"I do want us to be able to concentrate." He sighed. "And yes, I could probably use some sleep."

"Are you getting any at all?" Joey asked, running a hand along his cheek. He had dark circles under his eyes.

"I will tonight. Having things go so well has been very good for my mental state."

"The festival is about to close. We've had our chowder. How about I go back to work and you go home and sleep. As much as I want to be with you, Ethan Walker, tomorrow is soon enough." She wanted to keep holding his hand more than anything. Instead, she stood, leaned in, and kissed him.

"You make me forget everything," Ethan whispered.

"I know the feeling. Until tomorrow, Chief. Pick me up at seven?"

Without waiting for his answering nod, Joey extracted her hand, got up, and sashayed her way down the row toward the door.

She was halfway to her car before she realized she forgot to go back for the African kaftan she wanted to buy. After that exit, no way was she going back. She had the vendor's card in her pocket so she'd have to reach out to them after the festival.

Tomorrow night, Operation Ethan would step up a level. It was time to peel back the layers of Chief Walker. And get back in his bed. Oh, she wanted that. His arms around her, his lips driving her crazy. She shivered with an excitement she hadn't felt since first freeing herself from the oppression of her upbringing.

Tomorrow would be all about forgetting the past and looking to the future.

And tomorrow was going to be fun. She'd make damn sure of that.

Hopping in her car, she drove back to the lodge, plans whirling in her head.

CHAPTER THIRTEEN

Sleep had remained elusive for Ethan. Even with the festival done, he'd had trouble falling asleep. Every time he'd closed his eyes, he saw Joey. In his bed, beneath him, her liquid touch taking him to new heights.

Maybe he should take a couple vacation days. He had enough saved up. Hell, he had them all saved up.

He scrubbed his face as he sank into the chair at his desk, taking a sip of strong coffee. One of the best things about this station was the strong coffee. He sniffed the aroma, willing the caffeine to course through his system and give him enough energy to get through the day.

And dinner. He'd played his hand there, asking her out, but he was done fighting how he felt. He wanted to see her. Wanted to be near her. Life felt... settled, around Joey. Like he could forget about everything and just be happy. It was time to see where this would go, so dinner it would be. And maybe, if he was lucky, more. God, he wanted that.

Speaking of dinner, he needed to talk to Riley. Ethan grabbed his coffee cup and went in search of the man. The board said he was in station, but damned if Ethan could find him. Not in the locker room, kitchen, or main living area, and not sacked out in his bunk. He wasn't in the conference room studying, either.

Finally, he found Riley in the chief's office, sitting behind the desk—in Ethan's chair. "Been looking all over for you, bud. And get out of my chair."

"Good morning, Mr. Grumpy. I'll vacate in a moment. Have a seat."

Ethan sat in the uncomfortable plastic chair.

"Doesn't feel so good, being on that side of the desk, does it?" Riley laughed.

"Not particularly, especially when you're in my chair."

"Just trying it out." Riley swiveled in a full circle.

Gritting his teeth, Ethan got back to why he'd been looking for Riley in the first place. "Good. Because I need you to cover the position tonight."

The chair froze, then swiveled around to face Ethan. Riley's eyes bore into Ethan's, damn near making him squirm in his seat. Riley steepled his fingers and rested his chin on them for a moment, then hit the desk with both hands.

Ethan jumped.

"You've got a date with Joey."

How the hell could the man zero in on that so fast? Ethan, choosing not to answer, glared at his friend and coworker.

"Yep. That look says it all." Riley twirled again in the chair, hands in the air, laughing heartily in between singing, "Ethan's got a da-ate."

"All right, damn it. I have a date. It's not earth-shattering news."

"For you, it is. I tease you, Ethan, because we're friends. But I'm happy for you, finding someone you are interested in."

"It's just dinner."

"Not for you. You haven't been to dinner with a woman in... well, hell. I don't know if you've been on a date since you moved here, what, five years ago?"

He hadn't, choosing to keep his focus on the safety of the people in his care. But Riley didn't need to know that, so Ethan stayed stonily silent.

"Go. Have fun. I've got the station."

"Thanks." Ethan stood. "Now, can have my office back?"

Riley laughed. "For a few hours, I guess." With a wave and a cheerful, "I'll be studying if you need me," he vacated the chief's chair and left.

Ethan shook his head, then sat and tried to get his reports done. When he looked up hours later, he realized he was in danger of being late for dinner.

"You still here?" Riley popped in with his gym bag.

"Leaving now," Ethan said, closing out the files on his computer as he eyed the bag. "You can't move in. I want my job back tomorrow."

"Just my laundry. Taking it home tonight to wash."

"Wow. That's a first, isn't it?"

"Ha ha. Get out of here, chief. I've got work to do."

"I've got my phone if you have any issues." Ethan got up and grabbed his coat.

Riley shook his hand. "We'll be fine. And Ethan? Thanks for having faith in me."

"You've been my backup in everything but the title for a long time. I'll be glad when you're testing is done and you get the actual promotion."

"Me too. Only a few more days."

"Then a couple months of waiting for the results."

"Oh, yeah, there is that."

Ethan chuckled and waved, heading upstairs and dropping clothes as he headed for a shower. With no work to occupy his mind, nerves set in. What was he doing, hooking up with a woman like Joey? She loved life and lived it to the fullest. He was barely a shell of the person he'd wanted to become. Time and circumstance had left him duty-bound. Joey was way out of his league. Besides, he had no business getting distracted. That only meant trouble.

Scrubbing his hair as the water beat down, Ethan considered calling the dinner off.

"Don't do it," Riley said in his head. "Be selfish. For once. There are others who can handle the emergencies."

The flashback hit him out of nowhere. Flames leaping out of the second story, the screams...

Oh, God, the screams were the worst. His responsibilities. Gone in a flash. And he wasn't there to help until it was too late.

The flashback burned slowly to a cinder, but the screams echoed for much longer than the vision. Ethan leaned his hands against the tiled wall to steady himself as the guilt washed over him. He should have been there, damn it. He should have.

He straightened and turned off the shower. Throwing a towel around his neck and wrapping another one around his waist, he snagged his phone from his locker. He was no longer in the right frame of mind to deal with Joey's energy tonight. Her smiling face came to mind and instantly, his body relaxed, his mind following a bit more slowly.

She was a drink of sparkling fresh water. Sunshine on a cloudy day. She soothed his soul, though that was a damn selfish reason. He sat on the bench, staring at his phone.

This was dinner. That's all. Just a meal shared by two people trying to sort out whatever the hell they were to each other. He took a deep breath and threw a hatchet into his feelings, cutting them apart so he could examine them better.

Joey was kind. She was bright. Her smile lit up rooms. But more than that, her spirit called to him. She riled him up with her challenges and settled him at the same time.

Throwing the towel from his neck in the hamper, he knew what he wanted.

Decision made, he got dressed and headed downstairs to find Riley still ensconced in the chief's office.

"Don't get too comfortable, buddy."

"Replace you? Never gonna happen. The least I can do, though, is keep you on your toes." Riley eyed him top to bottom. "You look good."

"Gee, thanks, Mom." Ethan had dressed with more care than he wanted to admit. His slacks, the ones he kept pressed and ready for council meetings, were dark charcoal, his shirt, a crisp, white button down. Not willing to go completely formal and risk looking like he'd put some thought into this, Ethan slipped on his black bomber jacket and, with a wave in Riley's direction, headed for his truck.

Driving through Willow Bay in the deep winter dark calmed Ethan. The quiet, small town, where few lights shone at night, had become his home. His peace. A chance at redemption.

Except right now. His hands were sweating and he almost turned around twice on the way to the lodge, letting old standby thoughts invade. This was a mistake. He couldn't afford the distraction. All of the usual reasons to not get involved with someone flitted through Ethan's brain but he just could not make that U-turn. He pulled into the almost-empty lodge parking lot.

Willow Bay was a ghost town again, but the festival

had been a winter boon for the community. And it was
finally over. He could breathe. Or he could if it weren't
for the lodge manager.

Inside the lobby, he looked around. Joey had never
said where to meet. When he didn't find her in the
lobby, he headed for the restaurant. Halfway there, he
saw her, hair up in a messy bun and still in sweats. She
was reaching on tip toes to affix a large sign about
coming events. Ethan wanted to cover that backside
with his front, to wrap his arms around her and pull her
tight against a need harder and harder to ignore.

Except he'd overdressed. She hadn't seen him yet,
so maybe he could leave, go change, and come back.
She turned then, and lit the whole place up with her
smile, which quickly disappeared when she eyed him
head to toe. She grimaced.

"I'm so sorry," she said, joining him. "We had a
few things break down and I haven't had a moment to
change. Come on up to my room and keep me
company while I get dressed."

Joey stripping out of those sweats.

Joey in virginal white underwear.

Joey naked beneath him.

Ethan gulped. "How about I wait for you in the
restaurant?"

She laughed and it rolled over Ethan like a warm
shower. She leaned in, her breath tickling his ear. "Why,
Chief Walker, are you having dirty thoughts?"

Warmth flooded his face and Joey laughed again.
"Just so you know, we're on the same page there yet
again." She stepped back, regret on her face. "You're
probably right. It won't take me long to change, and I
reserved us a table." She pecked him on the cheek. "I'll
be back in a flash."

As she sprinted for the elevators, Ethan folded his
hands in front of him to cover his raging hard-on. If

this was any indication of how the night would go, he'd be taking a very long, very cold shower at the end of it.

The hostess seated him at a secluded booth in a corner. Great. Was everything about tonight meant to look like a seduction?

"Can I get you something to drink?" she asked.

"Coffee and water." Ethan frowned. He had no idea what Joey liked. Wine? "On second thought, I'll just wait and order— "

"When Joey gets here. I get it. However, I do happen to know our manager likes the lodge's seriously dark local IPA."

Was everyone in Willow Bay trying to set them up? Ethan shook his head but ordered for both of them.

Their drinks arrived just as Joey entered the restaurant. Ethan had to work hard to keep his jaw from dropping to the floor. Dressed conservatively in a body-hugging black turtleneck dress, she couldn't have looked sexier had she been naked.

She turned to talk to the hostess and Ethan's mouth went dry. There was no fucking back to the dress. Just a clasp at the neck, sleeves, and nothing else until the base of her spine. Which meant she didn't have a bra on. And, oh, did that give him ideas. He wanted to take her up to her room and slowly peel that dress off her shoulders and—

"Now that I'm more presentable, may I say that you clean up very, very nice, Chief."

He scooted out of the booth trying to look cool but failing miserably. He never should have sat in the center. Standing, Ethan reached for one of Joey's hands. "You are stunning."

Joey's smile lit up their corner of the world and Ethan was lost. There was nowhere else he wanted to be but right here in the company of this vivacious, beautiful woman. No one he wanted to spend time with but her. No one he wanted to take to his bed. Only her.

Once he'd helped her into the booth, he scooted in beside her, unwilling to let go of her hand.

"You ordered my favorite brew." Surprise and happiness lit up Joey's face. The woman was radiant.

"I had a little help deciding."

She laughed. "Which probably means I spend a little too much time in this bar."

"No, it means you train your staff in good customer service."

When she spread her hand in his palm, Ethan stared at the long, feminine fingers, nails covered in a pale, neutral polish.

"I figured you for bold polish."

Joey looked at her nails. "I like to enjoy life. I don't necessarily like to stand out in a crowd."

"But you always will."

"Thank you." She leaned back to gaze at Ethan. "That's a lovely compliment." She feathered her fingers along the calluses on his hand and it was like she'd pulled a rope that went straight to his dick, yanking it to attention. Damn. If he didn't get his mind out of the bedroom Ethan would never accomplish his goal, which was to figure out if they had anything in common. Though even that scared the shit out of him.

"What are you thinking about so deeply?" Joey asked.

"I was just wondering what, if anything, we might have in common."

She cocked her head and Ethan found it endearing. It didn't matter what Joey did, she was adorable and sexy all at the same time.

"So, you think we have to have things in common to hang out together?"

"Makes sense. Otherwise, wouldn't we just be fighting all the time?"

Leaning in, Joey ran a nail along the stubble of Ethan's chin, doing strange things to his heart. He hadn't shaved and had convinced himself that it had nothing to do with her liking a shadow on his jaw.

"Ah," Joey said, "but the part *after* the fight is so much fun."

Here they were, right back in the bedroom. "Sex isn't all there is to life, you know." Ethan heard the insincerity in his words.

So did Joey, based on her laugh. "Honey, you've been undressing me since I showed you the back of this dress."

"Not true. Since you first walked in." Before, if he was honest with himself. Long before.

Again, that laugh. Ethan wanted to just sink into it and get lost forever—to forget about everything. All the responsibility, all the pain. All of it.

"Uh oh."

"What?"

"That fierce frown of yours is edging its way in. You're thinking too hard and we're going to have to do something about that."

Without waiting for a response, she slanted toward him. Just before their lips touched, he caught a moment's hesitation, a vulnerability in Joey's eyes that made him want to protect her and keep her safe from whatever had caused that doubt.

Then she closed the distance and Ethan forgot about everything except Joey and the magic of her lips. Soft, playful, she nipped at him. When he went deeper, she eased pressure. "Whoa, there, chief. We've got all night."

"The hell we do." He wrapped a hand around her neck and pulled her in closer, tighter. It still wasn't enough.

"Ahem."

Ethan whirled, heart pounding, to see the waitress grinning widely as she held her pad. "Would either of you like to order dinner?"

"Maybe we'll skip— "

"Yes," Ethan said, trying not to let her breathy answer make him even harder. "We're ready to order. I'll have the steak, medium, and lobster with baked potato. No sour cream, please."

Joey's eyes were glazed over. Ethan felt like the worst kind of heel. He squeezed her knee under the table. "Joey? What do you want to eat?"

She reached for her beer, took a long pull, then looked at the waitress. "I'll have a cup of chowder and a small chop salad, Gail. And another one of these." She waggled her bottle of beer.

"Very good. I'll get this put in and bring your beer."

"Thanks," Joey said, then turned to glare at Ethan after the woman walked away.

Uh oh.

~~~

Her heart racing, Joey tried hard to calm down. This man had the most extraordinary effect on her senses. One kiss and she lost all control and inhibition. Wow. She glanced at him from under lowered lashes. Cool as a cucumber. Joey frowned.

"Are you toying with me?"

Ethan set his coffee cup down with a thud. "Why the hell would you ask that?"

"Because one minute your sparkler hot, and the next it's like you've doused yourself with ice-cold water. I don't get you, and I sure as hell don't play those kinds of games."

When Ethan took a deep breath, it pushed his magnificent chest out further, straining the buttons on his shirt. Joey forced her eyes to not dip down, to keep eye contact.

"I rarely date," he finally said.

"Define rarely. Like, when's the last time you took a woman out, other than me?" Ethan was such a handsome man and he obviously cared about people. If he shut himself away from relationships, a lot of women must be crying. A part of Joey was thrilled that Ethan had chosen her to break his self-imposed solitude.

"Before I came to Willow Bay," he said.

"Wait. You've been here for a few years. You haven't dated once in that time?"

He shook his head.

"That's a crying shame, Chief."

"It's worked for me."

"You should be out meeting people. Enjoying life."

"I meet people."

She canted her head. "I mean people you can become friends with. Maybe someone you can be more than friends with."

Ethan's nostrils flared. "Up to now, I've been good with my life as it is. Serious isn't an easy thing for me to do."

That was an understatement. Joey choked back a laugh at the pained expression on Ethan's face. The man sure disliked touchy-feely talks. But now was not the time to be amused. He seemed so grave, and she needed to respect that. Because reading between the lines of his last statement meant—he considered seeing her serious.

"You think we could be serious?" A thrill raced through Joey. She wanted this. The serious thing scared the heck out of her and would take some time and thought. But time with Ethan? Hell, yes. She was in.

He grimaced as if she'd insulted him. "Don't you?"

"Honestly, I don't know."

"Which brings us back to your original question, which I now ask you. Are you toying with me? Is this a game?"

Oh, yeah. He went there. And Joey wasn't ready to think about where this was going, much less answer him. Ethan lived life by his own dictates and expected others to follow. She'd lived her life that way once, with others expecting her to follow their lead without question. She had vowed never again. Yet she wanted to see Ethan. Wanted to get to know him. Wanted to smack him in the heart and see what kind of man fell out of the pinata. But decisions about where they were going scared her almost as much as him.

"Ethan, we've barely had a chance to get to know each other. I think that's more important right now than deciding the next fifty years of our lives."

"But if this is just a game, some challenge you've given yourself, then we can stop right here. I don't play games."

A little taken aback, Joey wrapped her hands around Ethan's, which had a vice grip on his coffee mug. "How about this? I promise I'm serious about getting to know you better. Is that enough for now?"

For a long time, Ethan stared at their hands. Joey kept quiet, giving him time to think things over. When he pulled his hands from beneath hers, disappointment raced through her. He wasn't even going to give them a chance.

Instead of leaving, though, he covered her hands, which were still around his cup, and looked at her without a single twinkle or expression on his face. "Just so you know, I prefer to be on top."

If Joey had been taking a drink, she would have spit it out. "Why, Chief Walker, did you just crack a joke?"

He leaned in. "Oh, that's no joke."

Joey couldn't read Ethan. Couldn't tell if he was serious or not, and that was a first for her. She'd become very adept at reading expressions, learning when serious shifted into dangerous territory. The fact that Ethan's face was devoid of giveaways should alarm her. Instead, she let the laughter inside bubble out until Ethan cracked that hint of a smile she knew was in there somewhere.

After a long, exhilarating release of emotion, full-on laughter from her and a rolling chuckle from Ethan, Joey used her napkin to dab at her tearing eyes. "Just when I think I've got you pegged, you go and throw me for another loop. Ethan, we're going to have lots of fun together."

His fingers threaded through hers, warming her with the most delicious sensations. "I think… I'm willing to try."

The admission was huge. Joey could tell by the somber look on Ethan's face. A look that, as she smiled, turned to a smoldering fire. Their lips met and, just like each time she'd kissed him, her world exploded in a whirlwind of sound and color and emotion.

Except it wasn't all internal. Ethan yanked back as claxons sounded outside. His eyes widened as he jumped from the booth, phone in hand.

"What is that?"

He punched a number, put the phone to his ear, and whispered an urgent "tsunami warning" in her direction.

"Talk," he said into his phone, then listened. "On my way." Ethan shoved his phone in his pocket and grabbed Joey by the upper arm, heading for the lobby where her employees milled around like they didn't know what to make of the noise.

"Might be a prank, might not. Get everyone to the

top floor." He speared Joey with a look. "I'll call when I can."

She nodded and let him go, then turned to her employees. "You heard the chief. Everyone grab a tablet, pull up the emergency map, and take a floor. Knock on every door, then open them, telling folks to go immediately to the Topside bar.

"What if the room's empty?"

"Check to be sure it's empty. Now go."

Joey grabbed her own tablet, picked the fullest floor and headed for the stairs, praying this was not a real event. And that Ethan and his firefighters would be safe.

CHAPTER FOURTEEN

Ethan flew down the street in his car, spending equal amounts of time running through the tsunami emergency procedures in his head and berating himself for not being at the ready. If this was real—

No. Don't think ahead. Work the problem and next steps.

He squealed to a stop in the firehouse parking lot, flew out his door and inside. All his guys were in full gear and readying the engines to head out. Riley stood there with the manual in his hand, barking orders.

"Glad you could make it, boss," he said, grimacing.

Ethan didn't need to look at the handbook to know what to do. "Everyone to their trucks. Start circulating and get people to evacuate." His phone rang.

"Chief Walker." In less than thirty seconds he'd slammed it back in his pocket. "Jackson and the outlying sheriffs are converging to keep the evacuation as orderly as possible. Now go. Get out there."

Everyone flew out to the trucks except Riley, who ran a hand through his hair. "Is this real?"

"Don't know. Take the command vehicle and help. I'm going to call the mayor and the tsunami warning center, see if the DART monitors indicate there's a tidal wave inbound. I'll radio as soon as I know."

Riley shoved the binder into Ethan's hands and raced for the command truck, peeling out behind the other vehicles.

Next, Ethan called Josh. It went straight to voicemail so Ethan speed-dialed the tsunami center.

"David Overness here."

"Ethan Walker, fire chief in Willow Bay. Is this real?"

"We can see an alarm got went off. Nothing on the DART buoys, but we're checking further. Hang on."

The firehouse door flew open and Josh strode in, ear to phone. *Anything?* he mouthed to Ethan.

Ethan shook his head.

Josh pointed to his phone. *FEMA.* "I'm with the fire chief. Yes, he's implemented tsunami protocols."

When Josh looked at him with a questioning look, Ethan nodded.

"Okay, I'll get back to you as soon as we know what's going on." Josh lowered the phone and scrubbed his day's shadow.

"What the hell is going on, Chief?"

"You know as much as I do, I think. I'm on hold with the tsunami center." Ethan put his cell on speaker so he could wait and talk.

"Dana okay?"

"Our house is on the bluff and has three stories so I figured she's safest there."

"Good idea."

"Joey?"

"Top floor of the lodge with the guests." Ethan would consider the fact that people already linked them together later.

"The bar. Wish I was there."

Me, too. Though Ethan didn't drink much. *No. Kill*

those thoughts. This was no time to get distracted. Another problem to solve later, though part of him never left Joey. Was she in the bar by now? High enough? Safe? Damn it. This was why he didn't do relationships. He couldn't be in two places at once. He couldn't protect Willow Bay and be at Joey's side to keep her safe.

The front door of the firehouse opened and both Ethan and Josh whirled. Jackson walked in, with Rob, the other sheriff, and two handcuffed teens in their grip. At the same time, David from the tsunami center came back on.

"It's a false alarm," Jackson and David said at the same time.

"You sure?" Ethan said to his phone.

"Yep." Again, they answered at the same time. Jackson zipped his lip and pointed to the phone.

"How sure?" Ethan asked David, who was still on speaker.

"No buoy alerts up or down the coast. Plus, it looks like your system has one isolated tower that's disconnected from the rest of them. Looks like a hack. I'm betting you've been pranked."

"We have," Jackson said, pushing one of the teens into a nearby chair. Rob shoved the other kid into the chair next to him.

"Okay, then. My work here is done," David said. "Have fun cleaning up the mess. Glad you're all safe." Ethan's phone went silent.

"Well, that's it. We've got corroboration that it's a hoax. I'll tell my people to put the word out," Ethan said.

"And I've already passed the information along to law enforcement," Jackson added.

Josh typed away on his phone. "Sending out the town-wide text now to stand down and stay or go home."

Once all that was done, four pairs of eyes turned on the teens. One blond, one dark-haired, both disheveled and looking at the floor.

Ethan walked over and tipped the dark-haired boy's head up. "I know you. You're Connie and Charlie's son." Connie owned the C&C restaurant where Ethan regularly ate breakfast.

The boy—fourteen if Ethan remembered right—started to shake. Tears filled his eyes. "Don't call my mom. Please, God, I'll do anything. We didn't want to hurt anyone, just shake up the town a bit."

"Yeah." The blond boy nodded, his hair flying with the vehemence of his action. "Just harmless fun."

Jackson, imposing enough in a normal stance, stood straight and tall in front of the two boys. "You scared the hell out of an entire town."

"People could have gotten hurt." Ethan stepped up beside Jackson. "At the very least, you've just caused the town of Willow Bay to hesitate the next time the sirens go off. Hesitation can kill."

"And now," said Josh, stepping beside them to complete the wall of stern men, "you'll tell us exactly how you did this."

Good idea. They needed to make sure this never happened again.

"You bet they'll tell you," Connie said, stomping through the door with Charlie right on her heels. "And then they'll be grounded for the rest of their lives, along with whatever restitution Willow Bay may order. Good evening, Mayor, Sheriff, Chief."

The anger in her voice carried through Connie's greeting and all three men took a step back as one unit. "Evening, Connie. Charlie," Josh said.

Charlie raised his hand in greeting, staying mute like the smart man he was. Connie, on the other hand, did not hold back or mince her words. She read her son and his friend the riot act. Ethan was impressed with how she made them cower. He waited until Connie took a breath to interject his question.

"How did you hack the tsunami system?"

"It wasn't hard," Connie's son said. "We found out that if power is cut to an individual siren, it only takes a small amount of code to set it off." He glanced at his friend. "Pretty hackable, just like most government sites."

Connie loomed over them both. "You mean the money I've been spending to make sure you have what you need to get into that Digipen school is being used to hack government sites? Well, I guess I'll be saving money, because that's done."

Her son gulped. "Ah, Mom, this was just a prank. No biggie."

Her face grew redder, if that was even possible. Ethan decided it was time to step in. "Maybe we should shelve the rest of this conversation until the town, and all of us, have gotten some sleep?"

"Oh, there will be no sleeping tonight," Connie said. "But you're right. This conversation can be finished at home. Are the boys under arrest, Sheriff?"

Both boys blanched.

"They should be, but if you'll vouch for them, I'll send them home on their own recognizance."

She glared at the boys. "I no longer know if I can vouch for them. But I will for tonight. I'll talk to Zach's parents and we'll all be in your office tomorrow to hear what you want to do. Extensive community service, maybe? Personally, I think they should wash every car in town."

If the boys could go whiter, they did.

"For sure they'll be picking up trash on the beach," Jackson said. "Rain or shine. And I'll be out there with them to make sure the work gets done."

"So will I," Connie said. "Trust me, we'll have the cleanest beaches on the coast when they are done. Come on." She pointed toward the door and both boys jumped up and rushed out like their asses were on fire.

"Thank you, Sheriff. You're being pretty nice about this," Connie said.

"You have the boys well under control."

"I thought I did."

"I can't say what the state or tsunami people will want to do," Jackson said. "If they choose to press charges, I won't be able to stop them. I'll put in a good word for how well you've taken them in hand, though."

Ethan smiled. That was an understatement.

Connie and Charlie followed the boys out the door and all three men let out a long breath. "I swear, I stood two inches taller when she started talking," Josh said.

"Made me stand at attention, too." Ethan ran a hand through his hair, wishing the adrenaline coursing through his body would slow the fuck down. "Not activity conducive to a good night's sleep."

"No," Josh said. "One positive thing. It tested our emergency procedures."

"Yes," Jackson said, nodding. "And I think we passed with flying colors."

"So other than putting the entire town into panic mode," Josh added, "no harm done?"

No harm? Maybe not to the town, but Ethan could feel the panic bubbling up, his legs getting weaker. He shoved his shaking hands into his pockets. He needed to sit down. "Want to come into my office and decompress?"

Jackson shook his head. "I need to make sure everyone's standing down and things are back to normal. I picked a helluva night to be on duty."

"You'd have been here, duty roster or not," Josh

said.

"Yeah." Jackson laughed. "Maybe tomorrow we can meet and go over everything? See what needs to be tweaked?"

"Sounds good. We can meet here in my office if you like. Around noon?" Ethan offered.

"Works for me," Josh said. "Now, I need to get home and calm down my pregnant wife."

Josh and Jackson walked out together and Ethan let out a shaky breath. He headed into his office to sink into his chair before his legs gave out. With his elbows planted on his desk, he scrubbed his face, then stared at his shaking hands.

This could have been bad. Before taking the job and moving here, Ethan had done his due diligence. Tsunamis were fast and dangerous. Hell, over two thousand people had lost their lives in the Palu, Indonesia quake and tsunami of 2018. If that happened here, it would damn near wipe out the population of Willow Bay. People he'd become friends with, some he considered damn near family.

He could not let that happen. Tonight, he'd been needed and hadn't been there. He'd let distractions pull him away. Well, one distraction. Joey Sanderson. That couldn't happen. Ethan had to remain vigilant and ready for anything.

His phone buzzed and he dug it out of his pocket. *Speak of the devil.*

Ethan needed a drink to have this conversation. He wouldn't have one, though. Tonight had been too close for comfort. He sent a quick false alarm text to her and set his phone down. He couldn't talk to her tonight. He needed to think. To sleep. Tomorrow, he'd see things in a different light. He'd have to. Because tomorrow, he'd be killing any chance of a relationship and reaffirming his role in life. Protector.

This was his only path to redemption. The only way to keep the past at bay and help the people of Willow Bay thrive. He wasn't meant to be happy. Not him. Never him. He was meant to keep people safe.

And he would do that.

No matter what.

~~~

While waiting for news about the tsunami, Joey served drinks and unrattled the nerves of the stunned folks who filed in from their rooms. She answered questions as best she could and helped her guests find a way to process the emergency when they only wanted to get back to their privacy. Most were understanding and even appreciative that the hotel had acted so quickly to secure their safety. Some were irate that their nighttime escapades, be it sleep or something else, had been interrupted. Then there were the few who tried to turn it to their advantage and get free drinks and meals.

Joey had authorized free cocoa for all, but only one alcoholic drink each. Tom, her bartender, was devout in sticking to that rule, especially with the boss glaring at him with each drink he gave out.

Two particularly belligerent men wanted more, and not just from the bar. When one of them pinched her ass, Joey didn't bat an eyelash. She slapped him, shoving him back in his seat.

"Never touch a woman without permission, you asshole. While there is a tsunami warning, you are welcome to rest here in the bar and have some hot cocoa. You will not be served alcohol and you will *not* touch any of the women here. Once the danger is past, security will follow you and your drunk friend to your rooms and watch you pack up and leave. You are no longer welcome in my hotel."

"Sorry, babe," the man said, leering at her with glazed eyes. "You don't run things here. The owner is right over there." The man pointed in the general direction of her boss. "And we're with him." Asshole ran his finger along Joey's arm and she barely stifled a shudder. "So, we'll touch who we want and drink what we want. And there's not a damn thing you can do to stop it."

Standing to her full height, Joey glanced at Mr. Reynolds, who watched them intently. "For the moment, I'm still the manager here. What I say goes." She glared at the man. "And that includes ejecting your ass as soon as it's safe. I don't care who you're with."

"Well, then, you're about to lose your job because here he comes."

"What's going on here?" Mr. Reynolds said as he and his wife joined them.

"Your manager is being rude to us," Ass said.

"Yeah." Mr. Drunk raised his head enough to pipe in. "Rude. To us."

Mr. Reynolds turned on Joey. "These are my nephews. Do you mind explaining your attitude toward them?"

"Just responding to their actions, Sir. They are drunk and he assaulted me."

"Oh, come on. They're just being boys."

"Yeah," slurred Mr. Drunk. Ass just smirked.

Joey smothered the desire to slap Ass again and faced her boss, having had enough of his pompous attitude, job be damned. "I will not accept rudeness or inappropriate behavior from any of our guests. If you have a problem with the choices I make to keep my staff and guests safe, you can tell me to leave. But until you do that, I will run this lodge as I see fit. No one, and I repeat, no one will accost me or anyone else in this lodge."

The ghost of a smile appeared on Mrs. Reynold's lips. Joey fought not to look at her.

Her boss started to bluster. Before he could get a word out, all the staff on shift and helping with the emergency surrounded her. Tom, the bartender, put a hand on her shoulder and spoke to Mr. Reynolds. "If you fire Joey, you'll have to fire us all. We won't work here if she's not our manager." Heads nodded all around and tears sprung to Joey's eyes at their loyalty.

Mrs. Reynolds put a hand on her husband's arms, leaning in so only he would hear her, though Joey managed to catch her words. "Your nephews are being asses and deserve whatever they get. Unless you want to handle this emergency all on your own, leave the girl be. She's good at her job. You and I both know who holds the purse strings in this family. If you want to continue to appear like it's you, you'll go back to our table and keep your mouth shut. Your choice."

Mr. Reynolds stepped back, his face red with rage. No, that wasn't right. The way he looked around, checking to see if anyone had heard, showed he was embarrassed. Sniffing, he turned to Joey.

"Now is not the time for this discussion. We're in an emergency. I'll talk to you about this tomorrow." He stalked back to the table and shrank into his seat.

Joey knew what that kind of defeat felt like and she almost felt sorry for the man. She eyed his wife with speculation.

The woman leaned an arm on the tall table and spoke to her nephews-in-law. "If you know what's good for you, you'll apologize to the manager here, and shut up and order some coffee. Because if you open your traps one more time, you'll be walking to whatever new home you can find. It certainly won't be ours."

Both men gulped, nodding their heads and mumbling apologies. Joey, once again, buried her smile deep. When Mrs. Reynolds turned toward her, the employees crowded in tighter behind her.

"Relax," she said. "Joey's job is secure. So are all of yours. Anyone who garners this level of loyalty is someone I want working for me."

With sighs full of relief, they dispersed and got back to the business of keeping the guests comfortable. That left Joey and Mrs. Reynolds.

"My husband likes to be the big man in town."

Sagely, Joey kept her mouth shut.

"It's what makes him happy and I love him, so I don't interfere unless things go too far. I apologize for tonight. My nephews are about to get a rude awakening about what it takes to be a decent human being in this world."

"I'm betting it's a lesson they won't soon forget."

"Not if they know what's good for them."

All this must mean the family money was hers, not her husband's. Did that truly mean Joey could keep her job? If she didn't, she'd have to leave Willow Bay, start over, and find a new place to hide.

Mrs. Reynolds must have read her expression. "Don't worry, Joey. I'm very pleased with the work you've done here, in spite of Christian's efforts to make it difficult."

She patted Joey's arm. Tears sprung to Joey's eyes. "Thank you. That means a lot."

"You just keep doing what you do and I'll make sure my husband knows that I'm backing you, not him. He's a smart man. He'll figure it out. Might just take a while."

With a smile for Joey and one last glare for her nephews, she went back to her husband, who put his arm around her waist and pulled her into his side. Mrs. Reynolds kissed his cheek. Apparently, all was forgiven quickly in that family. Joey shook her head, wondering about the family dynamic. When one of the nephews behind her made gagging noises, she rolled her eyes and pointed to the bathroom. He raced off, his face the prettiest shade of green Joey had ever witnessed. She never wished harm to anyone, but a bit of the green ick might teach that young man a lesson.

Sinking onto a bar stool, Joey poured herself a cup of cocoa from the ever-present carafe.

"You okay, boss?"

"Yes, thanks, Tom. And thank you all for backing me up there."

He leaned in, his voice low. "Christian Reynolds is an ass."

That he was. But Joey couldn't verbally agree with Tom. "Turns out, his missus is pretty nice."

Tom wiped the bar down. "Yeah. Kind of surprising."

Joey's phone went off. An emergency text from the county.

Tsunami warning cancelled. False alarm.

Phones around the room started beeping as notifications came through to the locals on the network. Joey stood up and cleared her throat to get everyone's attention. "The tsunami warning has been cancelled. You can all return to your rooms."

Relieved murmurs rumbled through the room along with a few grumbles. A sandy haired man trying to corral two young children asked, "What happened?"

"I don't know," Joey said. "Maybe some malfunction? The important thing is, there's no danger. We can all go back to our business."

Once people had filed out, Joey sent the workers home and stayed herself to clean and prep the bar for the next night's crowd. Tom stayed with her, so it didn't take long. When she got to her own room, she kicked off her shoes and pulled her hair out of the ponytail she wore during the day. Rubbing her scalp, she sank into the cushioned chair and flopped her feet up on the ottoman.

"What a day."

Bone tired, she seriously considered sleeping right there in the chair. She snuggled into its comfort. That was one of the first things she'd done when she became manager—replaced the dated, uncomfortable chairs in all the rooms with more comfortable, cushy chairs with ottomans.

What a day. The words echoed through her brain. From Gladys's disappearing act to that very strange dinner to a tsunami warning. No wonder she was exhausted.

Ethan. How had he done through all of this? Was he okay? No longer worried about how tired she was, Joey reached for her phone and checked her texts. Nothing beyond his false alarm message. It was close to midnight. Regardless of the hour, she had to know he was all right. She wanted to call, to hear his voice. That was selfish, though. So instead, she texted.

You all right?

Staring at the phone for a minute, maybe two, Joey realized he might be asleep. No. If Ethan was asleep, he'd still have his phone by him. *Be prepared for every emergency.* That was his mantra. He would look at his phone, which meant he'd gotten her text.

Joey went into the bathroom, washed off her makeup, and changed out of her date clothes and into her comfy, warm pajamas. She grabbed her phone and climbed into bed. With no answer still.

Did he not want to talk to her?

CHAPTER FIFTEEN

Joey woke to her phone pinging away. Through bleary, barely open eyes, she saw it was from Rose.

You okay?

An hour past her start time. Joey laid her head back on the pillow, unable to care much due to very little sleep and a raging headache. After a couple minutes, she picked up her phone.

Not feeling great, so slept in. Be down in a while.

She hadn't had time to put her things back in place after vacating her room for a guest. The beige wall looked dreary, just like her attitude. Pulling herself out of bed, she walked into the bathroom and looked in the mirror.

Big mistake. Tangled hair and deep circles under her eyes. Joey scrubbed at dried tear tracks on her cheek. When had she cried? That was something she never did. She'd learned the hard way that things only got worse if you showed a weakness like that.

Even a shower didn't help, though it did soothe muscles taut from tossing and turning and not relaxing very much.

Ethan had apparently taken a stand. She'd texted

him in the middle of the night, explaining that not telling her, at the very least, that he was all right, was rude. Once again, she got no response. So be it. She didn't need his kind of headache anyhow.

On top of that, she was going to have to let her dream house go. Tomorrow was the last day to amend her offer on the house and she hadn't come up with any way to do that.

So today, Joey gave herself the right to be in a crappy mood.

Nothing in her wardrobe was worthy of wearing. Happy, sunny clothes. No way. She dug out some black leggings and pulled on darkest tunic, black with delicate white embroidery around the neckline, sleeves, and hem. Pulling her hair back in a ponytail, she put on mascara and blush, but nothing else. Presentable, barely, she pulled her door shut and went to start her day. A lightbulb blew as she walked down the hall, making it darker than usual.

Figures. She texted John to fix it and got in the elevator.

A quiet lobby greeted her. Joey glanced at her watch, surprised Gladys wasn't there for her standard cocoa rest.

She joined Rose behind the counter.

"You look like death warmed over," Rose said.

"I feel like it."

"Rough night?"

"You heard about the false tsunami warning?"

"Yeah. Glad I wasn't here for that."

"Made for a late night."

"Is that all that's wrong?" Rose asked. The woman saw everything, which was why she'd make a good manager one day. Joey, however, wasn't in the mood to discuss her private life.

"I'm fine. Or I will be after some coffee. Have you

seen Gladys?"

"No. She hasn't come in yet today."

"That's unusual," Joey said, staring at the bench where Gladys usually sat.

"I hope she's okay."

"Me, too," Joey said. "I'm getting some coffee then I'll be in my office if you need me."

A few minutes later, Joey took a couple of ibuprofen and sat at her desk staring out the window at the rain. It really was incessant this time of year. Summers were so beautiful here. And fall storms were awesome to watch rolling in from offshore. Winter, though, just dragged on. Dreary and gray.

Just like her life at the moment. Joey tapped a pen on her desk. This wasn't like her. She could normally shake these glum emotions. Too much had happened too fast. With Ethan, with finding that house, then losing them both. Everything was weighing her down and she needed to get a handle on it. She'd made a conscious decision when she left her parents' house to never let depression rule her life, and she wasn't going to change because of a couple setbacks.

She'd have to let the house and Ethan go. His silence said he'd made his choice, and she wouldn't badger him into changing it. He either wanted to be with her or didn't. So, she'd start over. Not in a new town. Willow Bay had become home. She'd start the search for a place of her own again. And she'd make her own happiness. Again. No one could do it for her.

With her headache receding and her resolve strengthening, Joey pasted a not quite natural—yet— smile on her face and left the office, ready for her daily walk-through and check-ins with her staff.

When she saw the three people standing at the front desk, she stopped short. All the breath left her, and the blood drained from her head to pool in her feet.

Four heads turned in her direction, one of them with concern, the other three with triumph on their faces.

How could they be here?

Joey barely heard Rose excuse herself. She rushed to Joey and put an arm around her.

"You're swaying and white as a sheet. Are you all right?"

She opened her mouth, but nothing came out. Joey couldn't speak, couldn't do anything but stare into the satisfied grin of her ex-fiancé, Robert. With her mind full of crippling fear, her fight-or-flight response took over. She looked around for the closest means of escape. The main doors. Her car. She always kept a Go Bag in the trunk with essentials. But her keys were in her room. Damn. Why hadn't she kept them on her? She used to all the time. Joey had grown complacent in Willow Bay.

Damn. Damn. Damn. She struggled against the fear that froze her to the spot. Fear that had festered because her parents used it to keep her in line, even beyond legal adulthood. They didn't cause her to be afraid, though. Fear was her reaction, not theirs. Maybe the time had come to have it out with them. Joey was tired of looking over her shoulder, waiting for this day.

"I'm fine," she told a concerned Rose.

"I don't think so. You should get checked out."

"Just seeing ghosts. It's all right, Rose. I'll take care of these… guests."

"Do you know them? They just checked in. No reservation."

Sounds about right. They'd always loved the element of surprise. And they got rooms? That meant they planned to stick around, something Joey wasn't about to tolerate.

"Oh, yes. I know them."

"Who are they?"

Joey ignored the question. She rubbed sweaty hands on her tunic and, swallowing the dread that had robbed her speech, she walked up to the trio, who stood out like elephants on a Washington beach. All dressed in long overcoats, the men had dark slacks, black gloves, and well-shined shoes. The woman's fur collar looked real, though that was the least of Joey's worries.

"Hello, Mother. Father. Robert."

~~~

Ethan sat at his desk, unable to concentrate. His phone sat at the edge of his vision like a black hole, trying to suck him in. He should respond to Joey's texts. In fact, he'd picked up his phone several times already to do just that.

And had set it back down with the texts unanswered. It was better this way, right? A clean break, even if it was the coward's way out. His focus must be on the safety of the people in his care. He had no attention to spare for a dalliance with Joey. He squinted as the thought stuck at the front of his brain. What he felt for Joey wasn't a dalliance by any definition. It went way deeper than that, which meant he had to nip it in the bud.

Stay focused.

Keep people safe.

He moved the mouse to light up his computer screen and focused on the report about last night. He typed one line, another, then glanced at his phone.

After a couple more attempts, he gave up. He grabbed his phone and jacket, told Riley he'd be back in a while, and headed for his truck. Joey deserved better than being ghosted. She deserved, at the very least, a conversation.

The closer he got to the lodge, the drier his mouth got. Could he do this? He could barely stay away from her. Could he tell her he couldn't see her anymore?

Ethan had to try. The design of his life would crumble if he didn't. He didn't like talking about his past, but Joey deserved to know.

Pulling in and parking, he stared at the front of the lodge for a while before getting up the courage to get out. Inside, the lobby showed no signs of how full the lodge had been only one day before. Empty except for the woman behind the front desk, it looked pristine.

That woman—who'd been staring at the entrance to the restaurant—turned to him as he approached. "Hi, Chief. Can I help you?"

"Rose, right?"

The woman nodded, her bright red curls bouncing.

"I'm looking for Joey."

"Everyone's looking for Joey today."

What did that mean? The worry on her face was palpable and Ethan's spidey-sense tingled.

"She's in the restaurant, but she's got company."

"Who?"

"Apparently, her parents. And, if I heard right, her fiancé. Oh, geesh, I shouldn't have told you that." Her face flamed with mortification.

Fiancé? Joey had a fiancé? What the hell? The idea hit Ethan like a gut punch, drawing all the air out of his lungs. He would never have believed Joey would string him along, but she'd never mentioned a fiancé. They'd spent very little time hashing out their pasts, his or hers, but the fact that she was already promised to someone hurt. A lot. Ethan glanced toward the doorway, wondering if he should leave.

"I needed to know," he told Rose.

"I didn't get the impression she was happy to see them," Rose said. "In fact, she appeared terrified at first."

"Of someone she plans to marry?"

Rose shrugged, but the worry on her face stuck with Ethan. "You were here when they arrived?"

"Yes. Joey damn near fainted at the sight of them. She went white as a sheet."

What the hell was going on and why would she be terrified? Every protective instinct in Ethan screamed at him to help her. If these people—her parents—frightened Joey, he couldn't leave.

"I'm going in there."

"Good," Rose said. "The mother told her, didn't ask, but *told* her they would meet in her office. It looked like Joey found her backbone at that point because she laughed, said something about hell freezing over, and walked into the restaurant."

Nodding, Ethan headed in, pausing just inside the entrance. The four of them sat at a center table—two stern, elderly people on one side and a tall, dark-haired man sitting next to a stiff-backed Joey. He couldn't see Joey's expression since she had her back to him, but the rigid line of her back spoke volumes.

"You've had your little fling, Josephine. Now it's time to resume your place, move back home, and marry Robert," the elder woman said, her voice cold and unemotional.

Had she just called Joey Josephine? The thought got filed away for another time.

"You're not listening to me, Mother. I won't subject myself to your rules any longer."

Damn, her voice was shaking. She was still scared.

"You see?" the woman turned to her husband. "She's disrespectful and needs to be taught—again—about the importance of doing what's best for the family."

Joey's laugh turned harsh. "Family? What family?"

Having heard enough, Ethan strode to the table.

"Hi, Joey. I was hoping to find you here."

She jumped, bumping straight into Robert. Ethan reached for her, his instinct to pull her away from the scowling man. Before he could, she straightened herself. Looking pointedly at each person at the table, Ethan asked Joey if she was going to introduce him.

With her lips pressed into thin lines, she did. "This is George and Sandra Sanderson. My parents. And their family friend, Robert Winchester."

"Not a friend. A fiancé. Hers."

"You can't keep telling people you're my fiancé," Joey said, biting the words as they left her mouth. "I broke our engagement before I left." She gestured to Ethan. "This is our fire chief, Ethan Walker."

Ethan, seeing the panic barely hidden behind Joey's eyes, buried his relief that she was, in fact, not engaged. He grabbed a nearby chair, flipped it around and sat on it, leaning his arms on the back. Something in him wanted to throw these people out on their asses, but he opted for a peaceable entry into the discussion. "It's nice to meet you, Mr. and Mrs. Sanderson. Robert. What brings you to our lovely little hamlet?"

"Excuse us, Mr., umm, Walker, was it?" Robert said. "This is a private family discussion."

"Doesn't seem like Joey's enjoying this conversation much. I think I'll stick around and make sure you all don't upset her. Joey means a lot to us here in Willow Bay." He reached for her hand but she pulled away from him, spearing him with her eyes.

"I don't think— " Mrs. Sanderson said.

Joey cut her off. "I'm sorry, Ethan. Can I get with you later? This really is a discussion between my parents and me."

"No, Joey. You're obviously upset that they are here." He glared at Robert. "You're not engaged to this man and you are old enough to make your own choices. They can't railroad you into doing what they want."

"I know— "

"So, it seems to me this discussion is over and you all need to leave."

Robert stood, so Ethan stood with him.

"You can't tell us what to do," Robert said.

"No? I can, and I will, protect those under my care. Joey is part of Willow Bay, and she's not happy you are here. That's all I need to know to escort you out of here."

"Ethan— " Joey tried to stand, but Ethan put a hand on her shoulder. He could feel her shaking.

"I've got this, Joey."

"No. You don't. Can I talk to you privately for a moment, Chief?"

He glanced at her, expecting fear but seeing anger. What the hell? They moved off to a corner of the room and Joey poked him in the chest.

"What the hell are you doing?" she said, her voice shaking.

"I'm protecting you."

"I don't need your protection. I can take care of myself."

When he reached for her hand, she ripped it out of his grasp. "Joey, you're frightened of these people," he said. "Rose saw that. I see it. You can't deal with this alone."

Joey poked him in the chest again. "If I can't handle them myself, I'll never be rid of them. You coming in here acting like a testosterone-filled dumbbell isn't helping."

Another poke. His chest was getting sore. "I can help you."

"Like you did last night? When I was worried something had happened to you? You didn't even give me the courtesy of letting me know you were all right. So, no thanks. You made your stand. I'll take care of my own life. Please leave." Her voice, low and monotone, meant business.

Shit. Ethan had been so wrapped up in his own misery, he hadn't taken a moment to consider how much his lack of response to her texts would hurt her. "Joey— "

She pointed to the door. "Leave or I'll call the sheriff."

"On me?" She should be calling Jackson on the trio watching them from the table.

"Please, Ethan. You're making this so much worse than it has to be. Just leave."

He saw the resolve in her eyes and knew he'd been defeated. He'd really fucked up. "I'll leave, but only because you want me to. And only if you promise to call Jackson if they give you any trouble. Any at all."

"Not your choice to make."

Ethan reached for her, but Joey stepped back. The final defeat, and it hurt like hell. Knowing there was no more he could say, Ethan walked out of the restaurant and out of her life when every fiber of his being wanted to race back in there and protect her. Letting her fend for herself was his worst nightmare and the hardest thing he'd ever done. His heart pounded and he scraped a palm over his forehead, wiping away damp sweat.

The lobby looked miles long. Ethan kept his gaze on the doors, putting one foot in front of the other though it felt like he was walking through sludge.

"Chief?" Rose called from behind the counter.

He didn't stop. He got in his car, but he didn't drive off. He sat there watching the rain hit his windshield, seeing his gray future laid out before him. He'd lost Joey. And now he knew the truth. She was the most important thing in the world to him.

What had he done?

CHAPTER SIXTEEN

"Who is that man to you?" Robert asked when Joey sat back down at the table.

"A concerned friend."

Robert sat back down, turning so he faced Joey, who held up her hand. It was time for this farce to stop.

She pointed to each one of them. "You, all three of you, abused me."

"We did not!" her father said, glancing around to make sure no one heard.

No one did except Tom the bartender, who'd slipped in to do some cleaning that wasn't his job. Was this whole town going to try to protect her? Joey had realized she'd never be free of her past until she dealt with it.

"How dare you," her mother said. "We never laid a hand on you."

"There are many types of abuse. How many times did you put me in that tiny attic, door locked from the outside, with no food or water."

"Completely normal. Every child must learn to behave."

"Your punishments were extraordinary and abusive. And then you select a husband for me? This isn't the dark ages. I have a right to pick my own life partner."

"Life partner?" Robert sneered. "Even your terminology has changed."

"Yes, and for the better. I broke off our engagement before I left, Robert. You have no claim on me and you really need to get on with your life. A life I will be no part of, in any way."

"You have no choice. Your parents and I have a contract that was set before you turned eighteen."

"Ah, yes, the contract. The elevation to the next level of society our marriage would give them. Appearances are more important to all of you than my happiness."

"You owe us that much," her mother said. "After all we went through to raise you and turn you into a young lady. The least you can do is marry well to ensure our future and yours."

"Oh, I'll marry well, but it will be someone I select." The look on Ethan's face as he left flashed before her and punched her in the gut. She rubbed her stomach before continuing. "I don't care one whit if the man I choose to love is homeless or lives in a mansion. Now, we could talk until we're blue in the face, but I don't see any of you changing your opinions."

Three stoic faces answered her without words.

"And I will not change my mind. I will never return to that house."

"It's your home."

"Willow Bay is my home."

"You like living in a hotel room?" her mother asked.

"It's bigger than the attic room I lived in for most of my upbringing." Wait. How did they know? "You found out I'm staying here in the lodge?"

Robert answered. "We hired a private investigator to find you." He glanced at Joey's parents. "Another cost we'll have to discuss."

"You see?" her mother said, her face suffused with color that had nothing to do with embarrassment and everything to do with anger. "You see what you are costing us? If you don't come home, you'll have to pay us back, and we have it on good authority that you've about run through your grandmother's trust."

Joey stood. "First, I left you a letter explaining that I was of age and leaving of my own free will. There was no reason for you to go to *any* expense to find me when I clearly stated I did not want to be found." Though she'd known they would search for her, Joey was done looking over her shoulder. No more.

"Second, any expense that got you here today is your responsibility, not mine."

"Young lady— " her father started.

"No." Joey slashed her hand through the air. "You are my parents. You are supposed to love me and nurture me. Never once did I get a hug from either of you, or words of encouragement, or even praise when I complied with your orders. All you saw were the flaws of your own imagination. I am not your daughter. I am nothing but a commodity to you and I realized years ago that would never change." Joey hung her head for a long moment, then looked at each of them in turn. "I don't know what made me try one more time to help you see the truth. I'm done hiding, worrying, being afraid. I'm done with all three of you and this conversation is also done. I'll be refunding you the cost of the rooms and I'd like you to leave. We have nothing more to say to each other and I'd appreciate it if none of you ever contacted me again. If you do, I'll get a protection order."

Robert stood and grabbed her arm. "Wait a minute."

The self-defense techniques that Joey had practiced diligently over the last few years did not desert her. She grabbed his hand, turned it up and away from his body, then bent it until he had no choice but to kneel. She let go and Robert rubbed his wrist, glaring at her.

"Touch me again and I'll call the sheriff now and press charges."

"You wouldn't dare," he said.

Joey whipped her phone out of her pocket. Hand poised, she waited.

"Fine. We'll leave. But you haven't heard the end of this."

"Yes, I have. You have no legal right to force me to go with you, so I'm telling you now. I kept a journal all those years. Wrote all that abuse down. Every single moment. If you ever come back to Willow Bay or anywhere else I might settle looking to make me do your bidding, I'll hand it over to law enforcement. I'll splash the sordid details all over social media. I will ruin you." She speared each of them with a brow-arching stare. Then, with legs barely able to hold herself up, she walked out of the restaurant and didn't stop until she was behind the front desk.

"I'll be in my office, Rose. Those people aren't staying. I'll handle the refund myself. If they haven't left the lodge in the next ten minutes, call Sheriff Jackson."

"Yes, Ma'am," Rose said, saluting. "And nice ass-whooping, if I might add."

"Oh, God, how many heard?"

"Just me and Tom. No one else was around, and we'll keep our mouths shut."

Joey hugged Rose. "Thank you."

Inside her office, Joey sank into her chair before her legs gave out. She'd done it. She'd finally stood up to her parents and told them how much they'd hurt her. Not that it mattered. The validated truth stuck in her heart like a knife. They'd never be proud of her, never see her as a beloved daughter. She was nothing but a means to an end and her decision to leave that environment had been the right one.

She should be elated. Or, at the very least, relieved it was over and that she was free to live her life without looking over her shoulder. Instead, an overwhelming sadness filled her. Knowing the people who brought her into the world—she would never call them her parents again—were incapable of love didn't lessen the deeply rooted belief that she was unlovable. All the positive projecting in the world couldn't quite erase that.

One person could. Or had. Ethan. The emotions he'd stirred in her made her believe maybe, just maybe, someone could love her. She was free now, but for what? There was no one to share her life with. No one to love back, ever. if she wanted to. Ethan, despite his blustering about wanting to protect her, had made his choice.

In the privacy of her office, where no one would see, Joey gave into the tears.

~ ~ ~

Ethan sat in his car stewing. No way Joey should be in there dealing with those shits by herself. When she'd told him to leave, it had crushed him. Damn it. He couldn't be with her, but he wanted her safe and happy. He should be able to fix this for her, yet he sat here paralyzed.

Joey's parents and ex-fiancé walked through the door and stood there for a moment talking angrily. The father grabbed something from the ex's hands and stomped out into the rain. Apparently, he lost the argument about who would get the car.

Tempted to walk up to them and have it out on Joey's behalf, Ethan gripped the wheel tightly. He watched the car pull up, Robert get in the front seat, and Joey's mother open the back door and climb in. All were scowling. Good. They deserved to be out of sorts after what they'd put Joey through.

As soon as the car pulled away, Ethan jumped out of his truck and raced for the door. He strode up to and around the front desk toward Joey's office.

"Hey," Rose started, holding up her hand.

His deadly glare made her pull her hand back. "You better not hurt her or you'll deal with me," Rose said. "You'll deal with all of us."

Not bothering to acknowledge her comment, Ethan turned the handle of Joey's office door and walked inside. He had to know she was all right.

Her chair was turned to the window. Now, she whipped around, her tear-filled eyes wide with apprehension.

"Joey— "

"You don't belong here, Ethan."

He deserved that. It didn't mean he'd leave, but she had a right. He'd treated her like shit and now she looked defeated. Like she'd lost the battle when, in reality, she'd won. Those people had left. It about tore him apart to see her like this.

"What happened after I left?" he asked, sitting down in the comfy armchair across from her desk. Giving her space, but close enough to provide comfort if she'd let him.

She took a long breath, reached for a Kleenex, and wiped the tears away. "Your parents are alive, right?"

He nodded. "I have a brother and a sister, too."

"So, you know love."

"I do, and I'm grateful for it." Truly he was, even if rampant guilt plagued him every time he thought of his family. They'd never shown an ounce of disbelief in his abilities.

"I don't," Joey said, turning to look back out the window. "The people that gave birth to me considered me merchandise, an object to further their own careers and social standing. They signed a contract with Robert before I was of legal age, betrothing me to him. Even after I turned eighteen, I thought that was how things were done. Then someone I met at college set me straight. At that point, I broke things off with Robert, left a letter telling my DNA-donors that I did not accept their plan for me and to not try to find me. Apparently, they chose not to listen."

"I can't even imagine— "

Joey turned back to him. "I left a situation where I grew up unloved. I've worked hard to find my happiness and I won't give that up. So, now you know why I balk at people who order me around or try to fix things *for* me. I need to control my own life."

Ethan nodded. He got it now. He understood why she needed to make her own choices. "Maybe I should explain— "

Folding her hands together, Joey rested her forearms on the desk. "Ethan, you've made it pretty clear by your actions that you don't want to be with me. Or can't. I don't think I'm the right person for you to finally tell your story to. I— I can't help you when I have my own turmoil to deal with. I can't let my feelings for you get any stronger when you can't make the choice to be with me."

"You're important to me." So important. "I'm sorry I can't give you what you want. What we both want."

The sad smile on her face broke Ethan's heart. He

wanted to leap across the desk and pull her into his arms, make all the hurt go away.

"I know."

"I want to help you, Joey. Please let me."

"You can't. You need to stay focused on your job, on keeping people safe. I get it. Please, just go."

"I want to keep you safe, too."

New tears formed in her eyes, which just about did Ethan in. "That's my job. Please, Ethan. Don't make this any harder for me. Just leave."

He did, though it took all his strength to do so. In his truck, he laid his head on the steering wheel, realizing he'd just walked away from the woman he loved. God, this hurt. More than anything. More than the tornado in L.A. More than the fire, when he hadn't been there to pull his sister out. What he felt for Joey was stronger than that guilt. He knew that now. And he'd walked away.

For the second time in less than an hour, Ethan wondered what he'd done. Except he knew. He'd pushed away the only thing in his life that meant anything.

Now, more than ever, all he had was his job. His mission in life.

That was no longer enough.

CHAPTER SEVENTEEN

For the last couple mornings, Riley watched Ethan drag himself into work, looking worse each day. This morning, he watched Ethan get out of his truck and head inside as if he were sludging through mud. By the time he knew people could see him, he'd straightened and walked like everything was normal.

Except it wasn't. Oh, sure, he was dressed with impeccable precision, like always. But he had deep circles under his eyes, and a shadow of stubble on a man who always shaved. And the closed-off look of a man who didn't want to talk about what haunted him.

Riley, though, would no longer tolerate the silent treatment. When Ethan went into his office and tried to close the door, Riley put a hand out to keep it from closing.

Ethan scowled. "I don't want to talk right now."

"Tough." Riley stepped in and closed the door. Ethan, his mouth a thin line, stepped to the window and looked out.

"What's going on with you?" Riley asked.

Squaring his shoulders, Ethan sat at his desk. He slumped into his chair and hit the switch for his computer, signing in. "Don't know what you're talking about."

"I'm talking about you moping around here like a lovesick puppy."

"I don't mope."

Bullshit. "Ethan, you're normally a bit, uh, reserved. The last couple days, you've gone as cold as the polar caps. Something's going on." Riley sank into one of the plastic chairs. "Not to make it all about me, but I need you in the right frame of mind when I take my test tomorrow. Worrying about you isn't helping me study, either."

"I'm fine. No need to worry about me." Ethan's face showed the first emotion Riley had seen in days: pride. "You'll ace the test. You're ready."

"Well thanks. But again, I'd rather be focusing than wondering what's going on with you." Riley could see that Ethan was stuck in his own misery. It would take something big to pull him out of it, so Riley led with his biggest volley, knowing his friend's protective instinct. "What the hell did Joey Sanderson do to you?"

"Nothing."

"Bullshit. You're hurting, and I'm betting she's the cause." Riley stood. "I'm going to go have a little chat with her."

Ethan was around the desk in a flash. He grabbed Riley by the lapels and shoved him back against the wall. "You stay away from Joey."

"If you want me to stay away from her, then you'd better spill. What the hell happened between you two?"

"Damn it, Riley. This is none of your business." Ethan let go of him and paced to the furthest corner of his small office.

Riley straightened his shirt and leaned against the wall, giving Ethan his space. "You're my boss, Ethan. But also my friend. I'm worried about you."

Who knew the truth would get through? Ethan's face crumbled and he slumped to a squat, staring at the floor. "I drove her away," he said quietly after long moments of silence. He looked up at Riley, frowning, his eyes full of misery. Pulling himself up like an old, old man, he went back to his desk and sat down. "Happy now? Is that the answer you needed to hear?"

"Hell, no." Riley put his hands on the desk, leaning toward Ethan. "I want nothing but the best for you, and if Joey is it, then I want you two together."

"Too late." Ethan shook his head.

"It's never too late."

"I screwed up, Ri. She never wants to speak to me again."

"That's a tall order for this small town. If you're miserable and missing her, go get her back."

"She won't have me. I closed the door and she locked it tight."

"Again, I'm calling bullshit." How could he get through to Ethan? "Look, it's like there's an apartment fire and someone, a mother and child, are stuck on the second floor. The ladder truck is down and the stairs have buckled. What would you do?"

"I'd climb the side of the building if I had to. Set up a human ladder to lower them down. Whatever it took to save those people."

"That is the out-of-the-box thinking that makes you so good at this job. Maybe you should try to think outside the box when it comes to Joey." He opened the door.

"What do you mean?"

"I don't know her, Ethan. You do. What would make her take notice and give you another chance? Go big or go home."

Riley could see Ethan's brain churning through possibilities and smiled as he let himself out of the office. Ethan and Joey belonged together. He had done what he could. The rest would be up to them. Damn, he hoped they figured it out.

While Riley wanted to go to Joey and console her, he didn't think she'd take him sticking his nose into her affairs any better than Ethan did. She had friends. For now, all he could do was hope she relied on them. If Ethan let this go much longer, though, screw propriety. He wanted Joey to be okay almost as much as he wanted Ethan happy.

Whistling as he went for another round of studying, Riley hoped he'd done enough.

~ ~ ~

Gladys parked her Mabel next to the front door of Pacific Lodge and shuffled inside to her spot by the fireplace. The weather had eased and rare, early March sunshine hovered over Willow Bay like a halo. Rain or shine, this town was paradise to Gladys. And right now, there was trouble in paradise.

She watched Joey walk out of her office and head for the elevators, head down, shoulders rounded. Having run into that cute fireman Riley yesterday, she knew Ethan wore the same hang-dog look on his face.

What was wrong with people these days that they had to be knocked upside their heads with love to recognize it? And how was she going to fix this? Those two belonged together.

Rose walked over with a genuine smile on her face. "How are you, Gladys?"

"Ticked off at the moment. Those two are too stubborn for their own good."

Rose turned in the direction of Gladys's gaze and saw Joey entering the elevator. "I agree. But what can we do about it?"

"I'm getting a little tired of having to nudge people," Gladys said. "So, Miss Rose, if you ever find yourself in love, you jump in with both feet. Don't make me have to push you in like these two." And Cade and Grace, Luke and Jasmin, Jackson and Aimi, Bernie and Paul, and their illustrious mayor, Josh, and his wife, Dana.

When people accept love their whole lives opens up. A notion tapped at the inside of Gladys's head, reminding her that maybe she should consider taking her own medicine. *Poppycock*. She still had work to do here. She headed for the door.

"Where are you going?" Rose asked. "You haven't had your cocoa."

"Too much to do. Too many heads to knock together." Gladys waved over her shoulder as she headed outside and looked at Mabel. She was in a hurry and it would take her close to an hour to get to the fire station on foot. She went back inside.

"Rose, would you keep an eye on Mabel for me? If we're going to get these two to see past their pride, I need to make haste."

"I will gladly watch Mabel," Rose said. "I'll conspire with you anytime."

"Thank you." Gladys went back outside, patted Mabel, then headed out to the street, where she pulled her phone from her pocket and ordered a rideshare. When a blue Toyota pulled up a few minutes later, she was grateful it wasn't someone she knew. No one was around, so she slipped into the back seat.

"Get me to the fire station pronto, mister."

The blond kid turned around. "Are you okay?"

"This isn't a medical emergency, it's a life and death one. Now hurry." She swatted at the seat in front of her.

The driver sped away and got her to the station faster than Gladys thought possible. She was glad Jackson wasn't around, though she'd have gladly paid the ticket.

"This won't take long. A couple minutes, once I'm in there. If you wait, I'll give you a hundred dollar bill." He gulped and nodded. Without a backward glance, Gladys marched into the fire station and right past Riley at the front desk.

"Gladys, can I help— "

She pushed open the door to Ethan's office and marched right up to his desk. Riley ran up behind her.

"Sorry, boss. Couldn't stop her."

Ethan looked up. Gladys got even angrier when she saw how love sick the man was.

"It's all right, Riley," Ethan said. "Have a seat, Gladys. How can I help you?"

"I don't need a seat. I need you to get your head out of your ass and go apologize to that girl for whatever you did to hurt her."

Eyes wide, Ethan pushed his chair back. "Umm, I don't think this is any of your— "

Gladys marched right around the desk and poked Ethan in the chest. "You listen to me. That girl is the best thing that's ever happened to you. She's the best thing that ever *will* happen to you. You smile when you're with her. You relax." She rolled her eyes. "Well, you relax more than usual. You need her. And if the misery on her face is any indication, she needs you. Now you go make it up to her or you'll have me to deal with."

She stomped out as fast as she'd come in, got back in the car, and asked the boy to take her back to the lodge. Darn kids. Maybe one of these days, they'd listen to her. It would sure save her a lot of head-knocking.

The boy took the hundred from her with a wide smile. "I can get the PS5 I've been saving for now. Thanks, lady."

As she walked toward the lodge, Gladys wondered

what a PS5 was.

"Did you do something to help Joey and Ethan?" Rose asked, meeting her outside.

"Only time will tell. It's hard to break through stubborn. I'm going home now."

Gladys took less time than usual to get back to her house. She stowed Mabel and let herself in the back, still shivering with adrenaline and her lingering anger. Those two better get together. Gladys wasn't sure she had the bones for any more of this gallivanting around town playing matchmaker. And she had her own problems to solve. What was Henry doing in town? The man could unravel her carefully designed persona. She'd told him to stay away. Leave it to Henry to do what he thought was right, not what she needed him to do.

~~~

Riley disappeared as Gladys left, but came back moments later. "That woman's got more energy than a four-alarm fire."

Ethan agreed. Rubbing his chest, he wondered what it was with women poking him. It didn't feel good.

"She made sense, though," Riley said, grinning.

"Get out." Ethan pointed at the door.

He did, but not without some serious chuckling on the way. Ethan wondered if the whole damn world was trying to get up in his business. Had he done something to screw up his karma, or whatever it was called? Because life was kicking him in the ass right now.

Correction. Life wasn't kicking him. Caring friends were trying to get it through his thick head that he was kicking himself. And that it wasn't too late.

Or was it?

Ethan rubbed the beard he'd started, needing something to distract him from his misery when he looked in the mirror. He'd trained his brain to follow logic patterns like a flow chart and he tapped into that now.

Could he be with Joey and focus on the job?

Unknown.

Did he want to find out?

Yes. More than anything. He loved Joey, and he'd picked mission over love.

The next logical question was whether he would grovel to get her back or not.

Yes. Easy answer.

How could he get Joey's attention and prove how sorry he was? Ethan tapped his fingers on the desk, looking outside but not seeing the sunshine. After a long time frozen in thought, he clapped his hands on the desk, then reached for his phone. A few minutes later, he grabbed his hat and coat.

"I'm going out."

"Where?" Riley asked, looking up from a book on fire codes.

"None of your business. I've got my phone if we get a call."

Heading out to his truck, he smiled for the first time in days.

CHAPTER EIGHTEEN

Joey hung up her cell phone and crawled out of bed. Everything had been so quiet in the lodge that she'd snuck up to her room with the hope of getting a nap. That is, until her phone rang. No way she would sleep now.

Her house had been taken off the market. Ethan's inability to love her and now this? With all the things already tearing at her heart, this was the final blow. Joey looked out the window at the town as twilight descended. She'd been happy here until the last few days. She actually thought this might be the home she'd been looking for.

Maybe she should cut her losses and leave. Find something else. A new job, a new boss, a new outlook. Except, she'd met some exceptional people here. People she'd miss, like Gladys. Joey didn't want to move.

With that decision made, the next one was to figure out how to be happy again. She wasn't going to give in. She'd crawled her way to happy once and she could do it again. But how? Right now, the task seemed insurmountable.

She climbed back into bed and pulled the covers up over her head. Maybe she'd try to sleep after all. Maybe a good nap would give her some ideas. Right now, wallowing in misery took every single bit of her energy.

~~~

Gladys, having spoken with Luke, had all but forgotten Joey and Ethan for the moment. She had her own problems to deal with and the sound of a car door shutting outside her home told her that one of them had arrived.

She listened as he climbed the steps and waited until the doorbell chimed before she got up.

"Come in, Henry," she said, opening the door wide.

He stepped inside and took off his coat. His hair, whiter than it had been back in 2009 when she'd left New York, was still full. Naturally tanned, the white hair was a stark contrast to his skin. Time had been good to him. Even his age lines didn't compare to hers.

Hanging his coat on the nearby tree, Gladys motioned him into the drawing room.

"I've made tea."

"Before I even arrived?"

"I assumed you'd be as punctual now as you were back then."

Henry smiled. "You know me well."

"Knew, Henry. Knew."

His voice softened. "You still know me, Gladys. And I you. Not that much has changed."

"Everything has changed."

"Name one thing," he challenged.

"We're older."

"Not too old. Not yet. There's still some living left in both of us."

That gentle tone of his. It had always melted her

heart. Gladys could not, would not, succumb to it. She gripped the sides of her armchair. The man looked as good as ever, making Gladys glad she'd showered and put a dress on. If Henry saw her in her street rags, she'd be mortified. Had he? When she'd seen him at the festival, she'd lit out of there so fast, maybe he hadn't. Loosening her grip, Gladys poured tea, grateful to see her hands barely shook at all.

Once they each had a cup in hand, she asked Henry why he'd come to Willow Bay.

"I came to find you."

"I know that." She couldn't keep the exasperation from her voice. "But why?"

Henry set his cup down and leaned forward, an earnest look on his face. "To finally ask you to marry me."

Gladys gasped and tipped her cup, spilling tea onto her dress. Henry leaped up to help her, taking the cup. When their hands touched, sparks flew up her arm and straight to her heart. Wasn't she too old for this?

She reached for a cloth and wiped as much of the tea off as she could, then folded the damp cloth on her lap a couple of times before she looked at Henry, who sat patiently waiting for her answer.

"Henry— "

"Before you answer, I have a few things to say."

"I'll listen, but only if you let me have my say at the end. There are reasons I left."

"I know, and yes, definitely, you'll get your say." Henry sat back, making Gladys feel a touch more at ease.

"You know how tough 2009 was," he started.

"Of course. I lived through that financial crisis with George."

"And with me."

"The only reason I stayed with him so long was

because you asked me to stay."

"I didn't ask you to stay for George's sake. I asked you for mine. I love you, Gladys. Have since the day I met you."

"You know I loved you, too."

Henry squinted at the past tense.

"But you turned me down when I proposed," Gladys said, not sure she wanted to hear the reason.

"I did, and it was the hardest thing I've ever done."

"Then why did you do it, Henry?"

"Because George loved you, too."

Gladys's heart thumped. "Well of course he loved me. He asked me to marry him." *And you didn't say yes to me.*

"I came here to tell you what I should have told you years ago. Should have said before George proposed to you. I love you, Gladys. I always have. George— " He paused and swiped a hand down his face. "George was my best friend. We were a trio, you and him and me. And when I realized my feelings for you had changed, I decided to talk to George."

"I never heard anything about you two having a conversation."

"That's because it never happened. He proposed to you the very same day I decided to tell him how I felt."

"I didn't answer him that night. I asked for some time. I gave you time to step up."

"I couldn't." Agony filled Henry's face. "That choice has haunted me for all these years."

"Why, Henry? Why couldn't you tell me before I accepted George's hand?"

"Because George was my best friend. He loved you as much as I did. I couldn't do that to him."

Gladys sat back, trying to digest this new information. She'd liked George, even grew to love him, but not the way she'd loved Henry. The fact that he hadn't stepped forward, hadn't told her how he felt, had been a tumor on her heart that had grown, year after year. A growth of bitterness she'd tried to leave behind when she left New York. Henry was the only person from those days Gladys had stayed in touch with, trying to recapture their friendship. He was the one person she regretted leaving. Staying married to George through all their years apart had been safe. No choices, no hashing out old hurts.

Yet now, here they were, doing exactly that, and Gladys didn't know what to do or how to react. Her heart hurt for younger Gladys. She'd pined for Henry for years after her marriage to George. Only leaving New York had given her enough perspective to be friends with him again.

"You never told me why you left," Henry said.

"New York?"

He nodded, taking a sip of his tea.

She poured more for herself. "You know what it was like. The financial crisis. What George did. What I did."

Henry waved a hand dismissively. "You did what you had to do."

"I turned my husband into the authorities, Henry, for taking government money he wasn't entitled to and we didn't need."

"It was the right thing to do. I agreed with you."

"But our social and professional circle didn't agree. George paid the money back and thankfully dodged jail time, but the deed was done. No matter how right it might have been, I was ostracized."

"I knew there were a few grumblings."

"I was disinvited from all social events and even, on a couple occasions, snubbed right on the sidewalks of New York. The people I called friends tossed me out like their garbage."

"I didn't."

Gladys sighed. "No, Henry, you didn't."

"It would have all blown over."

"Maybe. But honestly? I was done anyway. I didn't like George's focus on money. I didn't like our back-stabbing community. I didn't like myself much, either, so I left. As you know, since you're my accountant, I wandered around for a while, finally settling in Willow Bay. Thank you for growing my money so I was able to help some people."

Henry nodded. "So why the street-person persona? I believe that's what the people here think you are?"

"Because I didn't want to be known as the rich lady. I wanted to be liked for me, and I am."

"You definitely are. When I showed up at the festival, it was like the wagons circled to protect you."

"And now, thanks to George, the cat is out of the bag."

"He only wanted you to live your best life."

Gladys sighed. "I know that. But his ideas about my best life were quite different from mine."

"They always were." Henry chuckled. "But you went along with him."

"Until our points of view differed on the important stuff. I stand by my choices," Gladys said.

"And I by mine. Things are different now, though." Henry took a deep breath, set his teacup down, and reached across the table for Gladys's hand. "Do you think we could rewind the clock? Start over, you and me? I still love you, Gladys Hawthorne. I want to be part of your life. I came here to convince you to marry me."

Smart enough to recognize that she'd stayed married to George because it had been safe, Gladys now found herself in unfamiliar territory. Something she'd wanted desperately as a younger woman was within her grasp, but so much time had passed. Did she love Henry? Yes. As much as she'd loved him then.

What held her back?

She thought of all the couples she'd helped to break down the barriers between them. In each instance, stubbornness had blocked their way forward. How could she expect people to see things from a different perspective if she wasn't willing to do so herself?

Gladys looked at Henry, let him see the honesty in her eyes. "I need some time to wrap my head around this. Can you understand that?"

Despair filled his eyes for a moment before he hid it behind a well-used shield. "Of course, I can." He stood. "I'll leave you to your thoughts. I'll honor whatever you choose, but know this. I'm not leaving Willow Bay without your answer. I love you, Gladys. I want to spend what's left of our lives together. I hope you do, too."

They walked together to the door. With her hand on the knob, she turned to Henry, saw the hope in his face and glimpsed the young man she'd fallen for all those years ago. As he walked past her to leave, she put a hand on his arm.

"I think that's enough thinking time." Without waiting for his response, she walked into his arms and pressed her lips to his. He tasted like Earl Grey and home and Gladys's heart picked up the pace. The man could still make her feel like a young woman.

"I love you, Gladys," Henry said, looking down at her with tender eyes. "I'll spend the rest of my life making up for our years apart."

"I love you, too, Henry. And we'll make up for those years together."

Gladys closed the door and they walked arm in

arm into the drawing room to sit on the sofa and begin making up for lost time.

CHAPTER NINETEEN

"Some guy in the lobby is asking for the manager."

Joey, in the middle of her rounds, had the urge to toss her phone in the ice machine. "I won't be back down there for another ten or fifteen minutes. Can you handle it?" Rose could handle just about anything, and Joey was tired. She didn't want to deal with some irritated guy this morning. She wanted to crawl back into bed.

"Sorry. I can't handle this one. You'll have to deal with him in person."

What the hell was going on? "Why?"

"He wouldn't say, except that he'd only talk to you."

Did she have to do everything around here? "Fine. I'll be down as soon as I can." She shoved her phone in her back pocket. Whoever it was could just stew until she finished checking in with her employees.

Ten minutes later, she strode off the elevator and into the lobby to deal with this mystery man. She stopped short when she saw broad shoulders and black hair that she'd sunk her fingers into only a few days earlier. He was facing away from her, rubbing his hands on the side of his jeans.

From the back, he looked good. And she looked like crap. She hadn't even brushed her hair, just tossed it up into a messy bun. Joey looked down at her slacks and ivory shirt. Passable, but business-like. Maybe that was a good look for right now and would shore up her resolve.

He turned then, and Joey saw the dark shadows, the beard, the pain that receded from his eyes when he saw her. Ethan smiled and Joey's heart melted. Damn it all. Why did he have to come here? Why did he ask for her? Why couldn't he just leave her alone in her misery? She envisioned cement blocks surrounding her heart, one by one, to keep out the pain.

The smile she loved faltered and Ethan walked over to her. "Can we talk?"

Just the sound of his voice made one of those hastily stacked blocks tumble away.

"Why? Doesn't feel like there's much to say."

"There is. Can you get away? I'd like to take a short drive. I'd like to show you something."

"I don't think— "

"Everything's quiet here, boss," Rose chimed in from the front desk.

Joey sent her a "stay out of my business" look.

"See? You can spare a few minutes, right?" His renewed smile, tremulous as it widened, pulled her in, just like always.

"It's not far?"

"Less than ten minutes from here. Come on, you'll feel better afterwards."

She bit her bottom lip, then nodded. "I'll get my coat."

With a wide grin now, Ethan nodded.

Joey gave Rose the evil eye as she passed, but the woman stared at her monitor refusing to look up. In too short a time, Joey was back beside Ethan with her coat on.

He took her arm and heat spread through her from his touch, despite the coat.

Always the gentleman, Ethan helped her up into his truck and went around to his side.

"Where are we going?" she asked.

"It's a surprise."

Normally a huge fan of surprises, Joey slumped down into her seat. She didn't want the man she loved but couldn't have trying to make her feel better. She didn't want anything from Ethan but to leave her alone.

Staring out the window, Joey didn't notice where they were going. She didn't notice the second day of winter sunshine, or the fact that they turned down a familiar street. Nothing sank in until Ethan pulled the car to the curb. Then she saw it and turned to Ethan with tears in her eyes.

"How could you bring me here?"

Wide-eyed worry hit Ethan's face like a backdraft. "I thought you loved this place."

"I did. I do. And it got sold, so there's no chance I'll ever own it. Please, Ethan, just take me back."

The worry receded and his grin was back. "Just come with me. All will be explained in a moment."

"Fine. If that's the only way you'll take me back to the lodge, let's get this over with." Joey opened the truck door, jumped out, and stomped to the sidewalk in front of the house.

Ethan joined her and nudged her up the steps onto the porch. She looked at the door knocker—two intertwined dolphins—and a tear slipped free. Everything had started out so well for her here in Willow Bay. Why had it all gone sour? She'd worked hard to keep her attitude positive, but lately, she'd gotten dumped on so badly that it had become almost impossible. Now, she was only trying to survive until her heart healed.

" —ass." Ethan had been talking but she didn't hear anything but the last word. Joey turned away from the house, toward Ethan, focusing.

"What?"

"I said, 'I've been a complete ass.'"

Joey's eyes widened. She opened her mouth to speak, but Ethan placed a finger on her lips.

"Let me finish."

So, Joey closed her mouth and waited, albeit impatiently.

"I've been an ass. I was so focused on my job, on saving everyone possible that I couldn't see that you were saving me. I need to tell you my story sometime. About the incident in Los Angeles, a disaster and loss of life that I didn't stop when I could have. And about my sister. She has burns on thirty percent of her body because of a house fire when I was a teenager. I wasn't there. I snuck out to hang with my friends. I should have been there. It would have been different If I'd have been there. And I know I should be able to lose the guilt because my sister has never blamed me and has moved on with her life. She's happily married with two children and a dog. But I've been stuck. For years, I couldn't get out of my deep well of remorse. You pulled me out, and I'm more than grateful that you opened my eyes."

"Not grateful enough to give us a try."

"You're right. I let my own stubbornness and fear keep me from seeing what was right in front of me."

"And what was that?"

"You. I love you, Joey. Not just because of who you make me become, but because you bring light to everything. You accept everyone on their own terms. Well, maybe you did decide to tweak me a bit."

He loved her. Those were the words she'd been waiting to hear. Cautious joy bubbled up inside her. Joey grinned. "I called it Operation Ethan."

"Why am I not surprised?" Ethan shuffled his feet and plunged both hands into his pockets. "I'm sorry, Joey. I treated you like shit. You deserve so much better than a broken man like me, but I'm asking you to take another chance on us. Let me prove myself."

Another block fell from her heart wall. Ethan wanted another chance. That should be music to Joey's ears but her heart wasn't quite able to dismiss the pain and hurt. "What makes you think things will be better this time?"

"Because my eyes are wide open. I know what I did wrong. You are the most important thing to me, Joey Sanderson. Not my job, not my mission. You. It took me a while to figure that out, but the last few miserable days have helped. I don't want to be without you anymore. And I want to make that pain and sorrow in your eyes disappear."

Ethan pulled a hand out of his pocket and cupped her cheek, running a thumb along the tender skin under her eye. "I hurt you and I'll spend the rest of my life making that up to you if you'll let me."

Hope slipped inside the wall and a few more blocks disappeared.

"And, well, there's one last thing."

Joey gasped, a hand over her mouth as Ethan went down on one knee, a set of keys dangling from the finger he held out. "Will you cohabitate with me, Joey Sanderson? And maybe, eventually, agree to be my wife?"

"Co— " Joey's gaze went back and forth between Ethan's face and the keys. "Ethan, what have you done?"

"The house is in both our names. Half yours, half

mine. Or will be, once all the paperwork is done. The house didn't get sold, uh, I mean, it got sold to me. I bought it. For you. For us."

She looked at the dolphins on the door, then back at Ethan. "You bought the house?"

"I figured a big screw-up deserved a big make-up gift. What do you think?"

He knelt there, waiting, giving her time. Joey didn't need any, though. The remaining blocks burst into dust and her heart opened wide, letting all the love and happiness in her world back in. She knelt in front of Ethan, her hand covering his and the keys. "That is a mighty fine gift, Chief Walker. And I do believe I'll accept your request."

A slow smile spread across Ethan's face as Joey turned serious. "I love you, Ethan. I didn't want to get attached at first, just wanted to have a little fun. But you tugged at me, pulled me in. Your abundance of love for the people around you, your desire to keep them safe, your ability to see—mostly—the other side of the coin. I love you, and I would love to cohabitate with you."

"And that marriage thing?" he asked.

"One thing at a time, Chief. One thing at a time." Joey stood and Ethan joined her. "Now let's go look at our dream house."

"First things first," he said, pulling her into his arms, his lips claiming hers. And Joey claimed his right back. Then he unlocked the door and Joey whooped as he picked her up and carried her across the threshold into their new life.

Together. Forever. At last.

EPILOGUE

With her right hand in Ethan's gentle grip, Joey showed off her engagement ring. A month of cohabitating with Ethan had been the best time of her life. They'd moved into the house together, shopped for furniture together. After settling in, they'd shopped for rings together.

"It's beautiful," Dana said, admiring the simple solitaire.

"Gorgeous," Bernie said, joining them.

"Thank you both." Joey looked around at the festive decorations. "Square Peg is ready for a party."

"Best party of the spring," Bernie said.

"I hope you two didn't overdo it," Ethan said, ever protective. Bernie and Dana were both due to deliver anytime. In fact, Bernie was about a week overdue.

"Don't worry." Paul and Josh came up beside their wives. "We made them let us do the work. They were barking orders like drill sergeants."

"And look how beautiful it all looks," Bernie said, kissing Paul as both their hands covered her baby pumpkin.

"Enough mushy stuff. Come on, Ethan. We'll buy

you a celebratory beer."

Ethan tightened his hold on Joey. Before the last month, she'd have balked at that. But now, she knew it wasn't that he wanted to direct her movements. He didn't want to leave her side. And she didn't want to leave his, truth be told. "Go," she said, going up on tiptoe to kiss him. "I'm going to help Dana and Bernie watch out the window for the happy couple."

"I won't be far," he said, claiming another kiss.

"You'd better not be." Smiling, she went over to sit by the window with the women she'd come to admire and respect.

"Can you believe it? Gladys is married!" Dana said.

"When I found out she lived in that big mansion, I laughed like crazy. Can't let Gladys have the last laugh, hence this surprise party," Bernie said.

"She's done a lot for Willow Bay, though, and we never knew," Dana said.

"The women's shelter is thriving because of her donations," said Aimi, who'd just come through the door to join them. Her husband, Jackson, kissed the top of her head as she sat down, then headed for the men at the bar.

Grace walked in with her guy, Cade, and Jasmin came with them.

"Luke is bringing the newlyweds," Jasmin said.

"We were just talking about the profound support Gladys has given Willow Bay," Joey said.

While tucking an errant lock of hair back in her bun, Grace nodded. "She has. And not just the town. If she hadn't pushed me and Cade, I'm not sure we'd be together."

All the women turned to eye the men standing at the bar.

"None of us would," Dana said, her hand on her stomach.

"I don't know," Bernie said. "I like to think true love would find a way no matter what. It just happened a hell of a lot quicker with Gladys's interventions."

They all laughed at that, nodding their heads.

Bernie squirmed.

"You okay?" Joey asked.

"I just can't get comfortable. I'll be very glad when this little girl is born and I can see my toes again."

"Same with me. This boy is kicking up a storm."

Grace gave Bernie the once over. "How uncomfortable are you?"

"Been having these digging Braxton-Hicks contractions all day."

The women looked at the smile on Grace's face, then back at Bernie's shocked face.

"It can't be."

"Yes, it can," Grace said.

"She's in labor?" Dana squealed.

"We won't know for sure without an exam or worsening contractions, but my guess would be yes. That she's in early labor."

"I can't be. I have to be here for the party!" Bernie cried.

"You're in luck," Jasmin said. "Luke just arrived with Gladys and Henry."

"Okay, you're all sworn to secrecy. No telling any of the men, especially Paul, or they'll whisk me away to the hospital before I get to enjoy the party."

As one person, the women all turned back to Dr. Grace, who shrugged. "She should be fine for a couple of hours. If the contractions get any stronger, Bernie, or your water breaks, we take you to the hospital, immediately. Got it?"

"Got it. Now let's go congratulate Willow Bay's newest couple.

The women joined the men, who handed them

champagne and sparkling cider. When the door opened, they broke into "For She's a Jolly Good Person" as a toast.

Joey grinned to see the new couple. Gladys was resplendent in an ivory wool skirt and jacket. Henry looked very handsome in his blue suit. Together, they shined with happiness.

"You guys are too good to us," Gladys said.

"You deserve it," Josh said.

Here-here's resounded and Gladys blushed deeply. Gladys. Blushed. Dana and Bernie looked at each other. "That's a first," Bernie mouthed.

Moving forward, Joey hugged Gladys. "We're so happy for you. You helped us find our true love and now you have yours. It's completely, absolutely perfect."

Henry, who'd been accepting back slaps from the guys, reached for Gladys's hand. "I couldn't agree more."

"Now come on," Gladys said. "Enough congratulating. This food smells divine and my stomach is growling."

"Once again, we're all feeding Gladys. Oh, that reminds me," Josh said. "What did you do with Mabel?"

"She's out back behind the restaurant for now," Bernie said, gasping as she clutched her belly.

"All right," Grace said, standing beside Bernie. "This party's over for you. It's hospital time."

"What?" Paul said.

"She's in labor. Has been for a while."

Paul raced to Bernie's side. "You didn't tell me?"

"I wanted to congratulate Gladys and Henry."

Rolling his eyes, he took Bernie by the arm and led her out to the cheerful good wishes of everyone there. Gladys's eyes glowed with pride. "I brought them together."

"You brought us *all* together," Josh said, hugging her. "And we're all grateful to you."

"Yes, but maybe you could let us figure things out now and focus on your new life," Dana said, snuggling her arm around her husband's waist.

Gladys held up her hands in acceptance.

"I plan to keep her too busy to get involved in everyone's lives," Henry said.

"It'll never happen." Gladys laughed. "You are all my family."

"Well, there's really only one mystery left to solve. If you don't mind my asking," Joey said. "What all do you have in that cart you call Mabel? We've all been wondering."

When Gladys finished chuckling, she regarded them with impish eyes. "Nothing except a framework to make it look like it was full of belongings. That and the few cans I picked up along the road. I don't abide littering."

Everyone laughed, then Luke led the guests of honor to the buffet and everyone lined up behind them.

Joey, tucked into Ethan's side at the back of the line, watched the camaraderie. "Willow Bay is a special place."

Ethan hugged her tight. "It certainly is."

"I'm so glad I found this town, it's people, and most especially, you."

He kissed the top of her head. "Me, too."

After Ethan finally told her his stories, he'd had a long conversation with his sister and the guilt began to ease. He laughed readily now and Riley, in particular, had thanked Joey for making his boss much easier to work for.

"I have a question to ask you," Ethan said with a gleam in his eye.

Joey looked down at the ring she still hadn't gotten used to. "What's that?"

"Is your name really Josephine?" The gleam brightened and he grinned so widely she almost didn't hear him, she was so taken with his happiness.

She felt heat from her blush to the roots of her hair. "God, where did you hear that?"

"Back in the restaurant."

The day she'd finally rid herself of the fear and angst of her upbringing.

Curling into Ethan, Joey tapped his chest with a finger. "If you ever call me that name, I'll make you pay for it."

Ethan laughed with an abandon that drew a smile from Joey, no matter the subject at hand.

He hugged her to him. "Don't worry. That name will never pass my lips again. Maybe you'd like to legally change it when we get married?" His smile dimmed. "Unless you want to keep your name? Because I'm okay with that."

"You are so adorable when you're covering bases. I fully intend to become Mrs. Walker when we tie the knot. It's a new life, a new beginning and I want to acknowledge that. Changing my first name legally to Joey is a good idea, too."

She turned in Ethan's arms so her back rested against his chest. Together, they watched the happiness around them. Riley leaned against a wall talking to Rose and Becca both. Joey could see interest in both their eyes and expected that Riley would be having some interesting times in the near future.

"Has Riley heard about his test?"

"This morning." Ethan grinned. "Top five percent. He'll be my replacement someday."

"I'm happy for him."

"You're happy for everyone."

Joey laughed. "I am. But most of all, I'm happy for us."

"Me, too, darling. Me, too."

~~~

Thank you for reading **Operation Ethan**, the sixth story in the *Willow Bay* series. If you enjoyed this book, please consider leaving a review wherever you prefer, and know that it would be greatly appreciated.

For new release information and news about Laurie Ryan, please join her **newsletter**.

NOTE/ACKNOWLEDGEMENTS

Operation Ethan is the last planned book in the world of Willow Bay. There may be more, here and there. I certainly have other characters, like Riley, rumbling around in my brain. For now, there's a new series on the horizon. More on that later.

As a writer, we become so embedded in these series. The worlds, the characters, all of it. And there's a certain grieving period when that series comes to an end. Willow Bay is my happy place. I love it there. The first inkling of the story was the entrance scene in Finding Home. From there, other characters became part of the Willow Bay family and I love them all, even grumpy Ethan. ☺

I'm sad to leave this world and I hope to revisit it with the occasional story down the road. But I'm also excited for new beginnings. Sign up for my newsletter to keep up on all the happenings.

As with any writing journey, it takes a village. I wouldn't be where I am today without the invaluable expertise of fellow authors Marie Tuhart, Lavada Dee, and Faye Avalon. And my prose shines because of Libby Doyle at Fairhill Editing. Last, but definitely not least, Cari Friesen at Defiance Books envisions my stories in cover form.

To all of you, a heartfelt thank you. And to my readers… Without you, there would be no story. I am humbled that you read my imaginings. Thank you.

BOOKLIST

Contemporary romance stories by Laurie Ryan

Willow Bay Series
Last Resort
Finding Home
Chances Are
Tender Tide
Reluctant Christmas
Operation Ethan

Tropical Persuasions Series
Stolen Treasures
Pirate's Promise
Dare to Love

Standalone
Rudy's Heart
Lost and Found
Northern Lights
Healing Love
(also part of the Holiday Magic anthology)

Women's Fiction by Laurie Ryan
Show Me

Fantasy by Laurie Ryan
Survival
Enlightenment
Birthright
Awakening
Wolf's Call

BIO

Laurie Ryan writes contemporary romance and fantasy. Growing up a devoted reader, Laurie Ryan immersed herself in the diverse works of authors like Tolkien and Woodiwiss. She is passionate about every aspect of a book: beginning, middle, and end. She can't arrive to a movie five minutes late, has never been able to read the end of a book before the beginning, and is a strong believer in reading the book before seeing the movie.

Laurie lives in the beautiful Pacific Northwest, in the shadow of Mt. Rainier and a short drive to beach-walking next to the Pacific Ocean, with her handsome, he-can-fix-anything husband.

Find Me Here:
Website
Newsletter
Facebook
Twitter
Bingebooks

A SAMPLE OF NORTHERN LIGHTS

A STAND-ALONE NOVEL

By Laurie Ryan

Finding love in the heart of Alaska.

When New York CEO Renzo Gallini shows up with papers saying he owns the waystation Jess lives and breathes for, she laughs in his face. But things get tense when he's got the paperwork to prove it...and her father, who apparently signed her home away, is nowhere to be found.

Alaskan native Jess Jenkins has lived most of her life at Last Chance Camp, a man's world where femininity is relegated to wisps of time behind closed doors. Yet she's proud of what they've built here. Last Chance is all she needs to be happy and no amber-eyed city-boy will convince her otherwise.

Ren left New York on his mother's foolish errand, to turn an Alaskan truck stop into a vacation destination. He finds little of merit in the wide spot in the road until the small community, led by a fiercely loyal tomboy, shows him there's more to Alaska than just ruts in the road. That survival depends not just on good planning, but on each other. And love can be found in places where you least expect it.

CHAPTER ONE

Jess Jenkins dealt with complications on a regular basis. When home was a truck stop in Nowhere, Alaska, they came with the territory. Today, however, those complications seemed bent on finding the breaking point of her patience. It was as if the machinery had gone on strike. First, the coffeemaker sprang a leak, then the commercial dryer conked out. With a busload of tourists due in—she glanced at her watch—less than an hour, she had no time left for fixing broken equipment. And her computer seemed to sense her mood. It wouldn't bring up the latest weather forecast. The satellite must be in cantankerous mode...again.

She smacked the side of the monitor and leaned her elbows on a desk overrun with paperwork and equipment manuals and rubbed her forehead. Just one more problem. That's all it would take for her to scream.

"Uh, boss?"

Jess's straight, dark hair, a gift from her Alaskan mother, swung as she turned to glare at the young man standing in the doorway of her office. Rocky Thompson was her junior by only a couple years. Being lanky and long-limbed, coupled with sandy blond hair cut in some eye-covering modern style, made him appear much younger than twenty-two. He'd been working for them for a couple years now and had quickly become a pseudo-brother to her.

"What?" She recognized the terseness in her voice and made an effort to regroup. "Sorry. Bad day. What's up?"

"Well, uh, I kind of hate to mention this, but..."

An urge to pummel something grew until Jess hid her clenched hands under the desk. "Spit it out, Rocky."

"The plumbing's gone south again."

"Over at the inn?"

"Yep."

He looked as if he would split and run if she so much as twitched. Did she really appear that menacing? Forcing herself to relax, Jess tried to smile at the absurdity of her day. The change in her attitude worked on Rocky. He relaxed against the door jam, shoving his hands into the pockets of jeans with more holes than the current trends allowed as acceptable. Jess reached for her to-do list and wrote down *order jeans-Rocky*, rolling her eyes. He wouldn't think to buy them on his own.

"Did you shut the water off?" she asked.

"Yep."

"Has John taken a look at it?" Now that they'd let the seasonal help go, John and Mary Martin, along with Rocky, helped maintain the place, although John was getting up in years, as his wife reminded everyone on a regular basis.

Rocky nodded. "Said it was beyond him and needed the boss's talents, since you designed the system."

"Okay. I'll be over there in a bit. Is everything else done? Are the rooms ready?"

"Close. Another load out of the dryer and the last of the beds will be made up."

Jess sent a quick prayer skyward that her jury-rigged fix would keep the dryer working. They were so close to the end of the adventuring-tourist season. If they could just make it through a few more days, she'd have time to fix things properly over the long, dark winter.

"Okay," she answered Rocky. "Thanks. Tell John I'll check on the plumbing, then you can go see if Mary needs help with food prep."

The salute he tossed her way as he left made her smile. Offering Rocky a job and bringing him to Last Chance Camp had been a good idea. A spontaneous one, but he'd proven himself a hard worker again and again, and was an integral part of their Last Chance family.

A family missing it's patriarch. Jess glanced over at the photo close to being shoved off her desk by paperwork. She steadied it, and her fingers lingered on the image of her father. A tourist had emailed it to her last year. Owen Jenkins stood on the restaurant's porch, greeting a new batch of guests. That was the part of owning the camp he loved...socializing. It showed in the wide smile and sea-blue eyes that sparkled with pleasure.

Where are you, Dad? He had picked the worst

possible time to go on one of his walkabouts. This place, both their livelihood and their home, needed him. Jess pushed off the desk and headed in search of her plumbing supplies.

She needed him.

Jess sighed, trying to slough off of the sixth sense that told her ill winds were about to blow in. If they were, there was nothing she could do about it until it happened. She settled her tool belt around her waist and glanced at her nails, rubbing the cuticles. They were in dire need of a manicure, which, as usual, would have to wait.

She paused on her way across the gravel lot to frown as a sleek black SUV with tinted windows drove into the camp. No rigs were due in today other than the tour bus. Last Chance was pretty much the only way station between Fairbanks and the oil fields, and no one drove here without a plan. Not this time of year. She looked up at a sky that had the smell of snow. The first of the season would be here soon, and she still had a lot to do before it hit. With another glance at the parking area, Jess headed for the inn. If the folks in that SUV had driven up here on a whim, they didn't have much sense, and she had no time to knock it into them.

~~~

"My mother must be out of her mind." Standing outside his car, Renzo Gallini turned a full three-hundred-and-sixty degrees. "What the devil could she possibly see in a place like this?"

Last Chance Camp, the newest property his mother seemed bent on acquiring, lay spread out around him. A few buildings plunked down in the

middle of nowhere, surrounded by the color of dull
with a splash of yellow.

He turned again, a critical eye scanning the wide
stretch of gravel that served as both an informal
parking lot and building access. One structure stood out
on the opposite side. As near as he could tell, it was a
building. It looked like five or six generic white cargo
containers had been laid end-to-end, with a porch
added to the front for effect. A sign hung from the
railing that indicated it was an inn of some sort.

Someone marched across the compound wearing a
tool belt. The jeans, work boots, flannel shirt, and ball
cap all said male. Hips that swayed in a distinctly un-
masculine way said something quite different, and Ren
paused a moment to appreciate the movement.
Whoever the woman was, she walked with an assurance
and grace that, even from this distance, stirred a long-
suppressed need inside him.

She disappeared inside the inn and Ren wondered
for a moment what she looked like. Shaking his head,
he re-focused on his mother's foolish errand. He had
firsthand knowledge of the aggravation involved when
business got mixed up with pleasure. Hence the
lengthy, self-imposed celibacy.

Turning away, Ren leaned a hand on his rented
GMC Yukon, then brushed his hand off. Over two
hundred miles of dirt and grit covered the SUV. His
mother insisted this backwater camp was salvageable.
Since he was in charge of acquisitions for the family
business, she'd tasked him with personally checking it
out.

He should have flown. He'd intended to, if only to

gain some distance from the women in his life. Between his mother's pointed remarks about wanting grandchildren and Kathryn, his company's human resource director and sometimes date, indicating her willingness to fulfill his mother's desire, Ren spent most of his time dodging the decision they were both bent on pushing him into. So Ren had hopped a plane from New York with more speed than normal. In Fairbanks, where he'd intended to charter a plane to get to Last Chance Camp. Instead, he'd given into an unusual restlessness and headed north by car. Six hours and a whole lot of dirt later, he was well inside the Arctic Circle and wondering what the hell he'd signed up for.

Pulling his leather jacket closed to ward off the cold, Ren glanced around again. This had to be some sort of colossal joke, but he didn't feel much like laughing. Nothing he saw seemed worth salvaging. He cocked his head from side to side, stretching neck muscles tight from too many hours behind the wheel. Tomorrow, he'd call and give Mother his assessment and she'd see the error of her ways. For tonight, he needed a stiff drink and a comfortable bed, something he doubted he could find in a truck stop in the middle of nowhere.

Ren headed for the nearest building, pulling up short as he passed a truck well beyond its prime with what appeared to be a dead caribou casually laid across the hood. He stared at the lifeless eyes and wondered what episode of *The Twilight Zone* his mother had thrust him into. Shaking his head, he climbed the few steps to a porch that, like everything else here, had seen better days, and opened the door.

Inside the restaurant, mouth-watering aromas assailed him, and his stomach did a very un-gentlemanly grumble. Ren sniffed and realized it wasn't just food he smelled. There was coffee. Even if it was drip-brewed, the caffeine would be the jolt his body needed to dispel the nightmare he'd driven into.

A portly woman walked by with a tray of dirty dishes, her salt and pepper braid trailing all the way down her back. She glanced his way, curiosity peeking out from behind warm eyes, but didn't stop.

"Excuse me," Ren said.

Without breaking stride, she spoke over her shoulder. "Grab whatever grub you want, then pay on the way out."

"I'd like a cup—"

He was too late. She'd disappeared into what must be the kitchen. Ren investigated and found the commercial coffeemaker. He picked up an ivory mug that had a network of cracks covering its surface and was gratified to find the inside clean, at least in appearance. The coffee he poured was dark and aromatic. With an appreciative sniff, Ren smiled. He could tell this brew packed a caffeine punch he would appreciate. He sniffed again. Nothing beat the strong scent of good coffee.

Cradling the cup in both hands, he searched out the woman he'd seen earlier. He found her in the kitchen, brandishing a spatula like some sort of weapon.

"Employees only back here. Food's out that way." She waved at the doorway he'd just come through. Ren imagined the gravel in her voice and that brusque manner fit in well with life here.

"I'm looking for the proprietor."

"The...what?" She stared at him.

He sighed. "The owner?"

"I know what a proprietor is, mister." She waved the spatula again. "Don't get smart with me. I just haven't heard that word around these parts in, well—" She shrugged. "Heck, I don't think I've ever heard that word used here."

Starting to lose patience, Ren drew a breath and tried the smile that usually got him what he wanted. Only it didn't disarm the woman. In fact, she raised the spatula even higher.

The absurdity of Ren's day caught up with him, and he chuckled. When the cook's lips quirked up, his chuckle turned into a full-on, long, hard laugh. He damn near had to wipe his eyes dry.

"My apologies, ma'am," he said. "I can only claim that it's been a very long day. I'd dearly love to complete my business and be done with it, but I'm looking for the owner of this camp. Would you know where I can find him?"

She set the spatula down, and he could see the effort she made to keep the grin off her face. "That would be Owen Jenkins."

Ren waited for more information, but none was forthcoming. Apparently, no one here liked to talk. He shook his head. "And I can find him where?"

She shrugged. "He's not in camp at the moment."

As his humor faded, Ren vowed to have a long talk with his mother about wild goose chases. "All right. Who takes charge in his absence?"

The woman stared him down for a long moment.

"That would be Jess."

"Fine. And where might I find him?"

"Since a busload of sky-watchers are about to show up, I'm guessing Jess will be makin' sure everything's ready over at the inn."

"The inn, which is...on the other side of the lot?" Ren could hold eye contact longer than anyone he knew. He refused to flinch first.

Finally, she looked down briefly, then waved the spatula, indicating the door behind him. "Yes."

"Thank you—" Ren let the question intentionally hang until the woman responded.

"Mary."

He grinned. "Thank you, Mary. That wasn't so hard, was it?"

When the spatula in her hand started tapping on the counter, Ren decided retreat was the best option. With a stop to refill his coffee, he headed outside. The blast of cold momentarily stripped the breath from his lungs. Leather clearly was not warm enough for this climate. He pulled the jacket tighter in a futile effort to ward off the chill.

The walk across to the "inn" seemed to take forever. It was probably only a couple hundred yards, but felt like a mile in the mid-October weather. White puffs of breath led the way as he clutched both jacket and mug in an effort to hoard as much warmth as possible.

He tromped up stairs that didn't budge or creak. Once inside, he shut the door against the cold, looked around, and saw little in the way of welcoming. Things looked no better than on the outside. Indoor-outdoor carpet, in a shade he expected was called something akin to beaver-skin brown, looked a little threadbare. Paneling straight out of the seventies covered the walls. There were no tables or chairs, just a small mantle along one side that sported a steno notebook with "Lights/Wake Up" written at the top. Underneath were a few names and what he surmised were room numbers. Good grief. Was this their wake-up call system?

Ren shook his head and set his mug on the mantle, after one last sip. So far, the only thing he'd found of any merit here was the coffee. He needed to find this guy, Jess, say what he'd come to say, and get the hell out of here.

"Damn it all to hell. Budge, you crotchety old bucket of bolts!"

He couldn't quite tell if the voice was male or female, but since it was the only sound he'd heard since entering, Ren followed it down one of the long corridors. Used to upscale hotels with expansive hallways, this one made him feel almost claustrophobic.

At the end, he turned to an open doorway and froze. The first thing he saw were the hips he'd admired earlier. They were encased in jeans molding a backside that teased his imagination more than any had in quite a while. When he saw the wisp of material that could only be a thong, he started to sweat as a long-denied libido struggled for dominance. A will not entirely his own nudged him forward for a better look. If the strap he saw was any indication, the thong was hot pink...and almost hidden underneath lumberjack's clothing.

Would her bra match?

That was the moment the pipe burst, spewing water in every direction. The perfectly shaped ass in front of him backed out of what appeared to be a plumbing room in a hurry, and straight into his arms. He grabbed hold as they were both propelled backward.

"Oof!"

His arms tightened around her midsection as the momentum slammed them into the wall and the breath whooshed out of him. Before he had a chance to regain his equilibrium, the woman was squirming.

"Let go of me!"

Ren released her and she yanked off the flannel shirt, then crawled back into the spray. He couldn't tell what she was doing, but it couldn't be easy, the way she was grunting and groaning.

"Hand me a wrench," she yelled.

He grabbed the wrench from the tool belt sitting on the floor and thrust it into the disembodied hand that snaked out from the spray of water.

After some more indistinguishable sounds, the spray lessened and then, finally, stopped. Ren swiped water off his face as she backed out of the room shaking her head and mumbling. "What a messed up day." She threw the wrench at the tool belt and glanced up.

Cocoa-brown eyes stared at Ren. She looked young, mid-twenties at the most. With skin that hinted at some native Alaskan heritage, a heart-shaped face, and hair the color of gleaming wet obsidian, she gave off wholesome beauty in waves.

When she sank down to sit with her back against the wall, Ren's mouth went dry. Years of honing skills for boardroom negotiations threatened to desert him as his jaw went slack. Her white t-shirt, soaked through, clung to curves that were only outdone by perfect round breasts encased in that hot pink bra he'd been thinking about. Nipples protesting the wet-cold held him spellbound. It took everything he had to yank his forgotten manners out of his back pocket and stop staring.

When he looked up, fire had replaced the warm cocoa in her eyes. She clutched her arms in front of her, and her face took on the contortions of a storm cloud as she gnashed her teeth.

Even her obvious anger couldn't completely quell the spark of need inside him. What the hell was happening that some wisp of a girl could affect him like this? More off-kilter than he'd ever been before, he cleared his throat, trying to dig up some saliva—and some intelligence—so he could speak.

He failed at both.

~~~

Jess Jenkins glared at the stranger in front of her and felt a cold permeate her that had nothing to do with being soaked. She'd seen that hungry look in men's eyes before and all it meant was trouble. She didn't care how handsome the guy was...and he was smokin' hot, with those hypnotic amber eyes, the neatly-styled dark hair, and a day's stubble.

She steeled herself to go beyond the physical, because the expression on his face told her everything she needed to know. Even that last glimpse—confusion, maybe—had to be contrived. She'd lived in this camp her entire life and had seen a lot of comings and goings. Most of the regulars were good folk. It was the transients, some single, some not so much, that tried to push the limits. Those were the ones who would say anything to get what they wanted. This guy was no different. Ever since she'd grown boobs, she'd been hit on. Her frown deepened.

Well, she had no need for any guy ruled by his junk.

Jess struggled to get up using one arm. There was no way she'd pull the one that covered her chest. Where was her flannel? When she saw it, piled in a sodden heap on the floor, she swore. Now what was she going to do? Her trailer was back behind the restaurant and she couldn't cross the camp wet. She'd freeze before she reached it.

Sensing movement, she jerked back from the man who now stood with a leather jacket held out in front of him.

"If you live across the way, you'll never make it to dry clothes."

Jess eyed the jacket. "It's wet."

He shrugged. "It's better than nothing."

Searching for the ulterior motive in his gesture, she couldn't find one. So Jess reached for the jacket. "What about you? How will you get across the way?"

He spread his arms. "I'm open to suggestions."

Jess found herself momentarily speechless as the wet Henley-style shirt clung to pecs that screamed regular workouts. When he smiled, any remaining chill switched to instant heat. Damn. Even the man's teeth were perfect. That smile could melt glaciers, and Jess tightened her arms over her chest. No matter how good looking he was, or how warm her body had begun to feel, she knew nothing about him. She needed to remember that.

His grin took on a bit of a cockeyed lift to it and she realized she'd been caught staring, so she yanked the jacket around her shoulders with one hand, feeling his lingering warmth.

"Have a little care with my coat, beautiful." His voice, low and inviting, warmed her further, damn it.

"I'll try to find you something to wear," she mumbled.

"No need. You can bring my jacket back to me or grab the duffle out of that filthy Yukon. I've got a change of clothes in there."

Good thing. She didn't think anyone who worked here wore a size that would cover those shoulders. He reached for her hand and a tingle slid up her arm and wound its way around her spinal column. He turned her palm up, placed keys in it, then folded her fingers over the keys. Was it her imagination or did it seem like he took his time at the task? She looked up and saw the smoldering smile still on his face. Her own face flamed red in response, and Jess did the only thing she could think of.

She ran.

~~~

For more information about *Northern Lights* or other books by Laurie Ryan, please visit her website.

www.ingramcontent.com/pod-product-compliance
Lightning Source LLC
Chambersburg PA
CBHW072212170626
46813CB00003B/909